# Praise for *Sleeping in th*

MW00639462

"With meticulous attention to detail, Howard paints a vivid portrait of colonial India through the perspectives of an American family and their Indian servant, skillfully blending historical events with familial moments. Through the eyes of her characters, readers are transported to a world where identities are questioned and the true meaning of home is explored. As the narrative builds toward an explosive climax, *Sleeping in the Sun* becomes more than just a story—it is a poignant exploration of the human experience that resonates far beyond the last chapter."

—Veena Rao, author of *Purple Lotus*

"Joanne Howard's *Sleeping in the Sun* is a quiet and deeply moving novel, a story of a nation trying to reclaim itself, while one man and one boy try to discover who they are themselves. Howard shows us all this not by looking at the big picture, but at the individuals caught at the center of their sometimes conflicting, sometimes heartbreaking goals. A beautiful story, beautifully revealed."

—Pete Fromm, author of *Indian Creek Chronicles*

"Large and saga-like in scope, and set in 1930s India, Joanne Howard's *Sleeping in the Sun* delivers a compassionate portrayal of a missionary family as they struggle to navigate the personal and political crosscurrents of enchantment, terror, love, and deceit. What I admire most in her debut novel is the courage with which this writer lifts the masks of disguise from her characters and reveals, as if superimposed on the place itself, that secret, interior world of human emotions."

—Jack Driscoll, author of *20 Stories: New & Selected*

"Howard explores the tribulations and tragic ironies of imperialism in British India. Relationships are not what they appear to be, people have hidden dark sides, and one person's faith is another's sin. After a crime has been committed, it must be determined who did what and why. Yet Howard leaves you wondering who are the good guys and who are the bad guys in a country where religion and culture have been forcibly imposed. A thoughtful read, using historical fiction to shine light on the praxis of decolonization in our current century."

—Jude Berman, author of *The Die* and *The Vow*

"Set against the backdrop of India in the 1930s, *Sleeping in the Sun* tells the story of the Hintons, a family of American missionaries sent to bring Christianity to the city of Midnapore. Told from the point of view of Gene, the Hintons' youngest son, and Arthur, their Indian servant, this sweeping historical novel flawlessly transports readers to another time and place. Political, racial, and interpersonal conflicts ensure you won't be able to put it down. I know I couldn't."

—Susen Edwards, author of *What a Trip* and *Lookin' for Love*

# SLEEPING IN THE SUN

# SLEEPING IN THE SUN

A Novel

Joanne Howard

She Writes Press

Published 2024
Printed in the United States of America
Print ISBN: 978-1-64742-798-6
E-ISBN: 978-1-64742-799-3
Library of Congress Control Number: 2024913220

For information, address:
She Writes Press
1569 Solano Ave #546
Berkeley, CA 94707

Interior Design by Kiran Spees
She Writes Press is a division of SparkPoint Studio, LLC.

*For Dad,*
*the reason I love books.*

# CHAPTER 1

The last morning stars lingered over the Big House when Gene Hinton saw the mourners coming up the road. Under the dormant frangipani trees, still yet to bloom, the procession approached slowly, quietly. As it came closer, Gene rubbed the sleep out of his eyes and folded his arms, hugging himself against the morning breeze in the front yard. He knew the afternoon would be hot—and maybe less humid than yesterday, the Lord willing—but for now, nothing could warm him. He dug his shoes into the dirt and watched the road. The sight of the man in the front, dressed in white robes and with a shaved head, pulled at Gene's heart.

"The eldest son," came a voice from behind. Gene turned to see Arthur, the Hintons' servant, standing on the porch steps. He held his arms behind his back, allowing the front of his crisp, ironed kurta to billow in the breeze. "Kindly, sahib," Arthur said, asking permission to approach. When Gene nodded, Arthur stepped forward and continued. "For Hindus, the eldest son leads the mourning of the father." A pause, and then, "But you won't ever have to worry about that, sahib."

As if on cue, chattering voices and loud footsteps arose from somewhere inside the house. Gene's older brothers were awake. A cold dread filled him down to his shoes. In a few minutes, they'd have to leave to meet Uncle Ellis at the train station. But Gene couldn't stop watching the lane.

He didn't want to think about his father's inevitable death, or of

1

anyone's—twelve-year-old boys didn't have to think of that sort of thing, so he changed the subject.

"Did you know the man?" Gene said. "The one who died?"

The procession passed the gate now. A swathe of saffron was draped over the litter, carried by what looked like a dozen men, all either shouldering its burden or placing a hand on the litter, wherever there was space among the garlands of marigolds that dangled from the edges and danced with every step.

Arthur wobbled his head. "I would see him in the marketplace, when I did the shopping for memsahib."

But Gene could tell from his unsteady lip that the man had meant more to Arthur than that. "Should you maybe go with them? Wherever they're going?"

"The Kangsabati River, to be cremated," Arthur said. He bit his lip and looked at the road for a moment. "No, I am needed by the Padre Sahib. We are leaving soon for the burra sahib, *na*?"

The sound of the car engine firing up startled Gene. Wild monkeys scampered to life in the branches above him, screeching into the dawn. Gene turned to see his father ready at the wheel of the old Chevy. It would take the jalopy a few minutes to warm up. Gene looked back at the lane, but the men had passed them now, leaving only a mottled trail of dust that floated behind them, as if they walked on a cloud.

"To tell you the truth," Gene said, leaning in, "I'm nervous about meeting the judge. Or Uncle Ellis, I suppose I should call him."

Arthur tilted his head and looked at him the way one would study a bug.

"I mean, I know my brothers all like him. I don't remember the last time I met him. I must have been too young. But from what everyone tells me about him, I feel like I should be . . . I don't know . . ." He trailed off as he scuffed his dusty shoe in the dirt and frowned at his wrinkled trousers. "Better *groomed*, at least."

Gene realized the absurdity of his words, reminding himself of the dead man that just passed by not a minute ago. He met Arthur's eyes and nearly jumped at the dark look on his face. Arthur bent close, his eyes serious.

"There are larger things to worry about with the burra sahib," he said.

Gene didn't know what to say. He was about to ask Arthur what he meant when they were interrupted.

"Come on, Gene! Smallest in the middle!"

He looked to see John, Will, and Lee pouring through the front doors, a collective storm of barely contained teenage energy that felt absurd in the quiet morning. They whooped and hollered for no reason that Gene could tell, until he remembered. They had been looking forward to this day all week. Arthur retreated to the car to check that all was set to go, slipping away into the background of the family's lives again.

"Scooch!" Will said, shoving Gene into the car.

"I'm going," Gene said, bumping his head on the roof as Will's shoulder blade jabbed into his chest.

"Come on, make room!" John said, squishing a leg into Gene's lap.

Then more pressure, this time on his other side, as Lee squeezed in. "Sorry," Lee said. Lee was only two years older than Gene, but he felt enormous.

Gene couldn't move while his brothers arranged themselves for the long ride, their limbs sticking out of the open sides of the car.

"That's better," John said.

"Humph," Gene grumbled.

Mrs. Hinton got in on the passenger side. Her cheeks were flushed, her clothes smelling of rose water. "Oh, I look awful," she said, squinting into her compact mirror. She brushed the faded blonde hairs out of her face. "He'll think I haven't been taking care of myself."

"You look fine," said Mr. Hinton. He straightened his topi—a large pith helmet to keep out the sun—and switched the headlights on, illuminating the sparse lawn and vine-choked trees in the yard.

"It's just times like this I wish we could afford another servant, one who could do my hair. Boys! Make room for Arthur to stand."

Arthur stepped onto the running board and held on to the side of the roof. Even though there was just enough room in the front for one more person, it was reserved for Judge Ellis on the way back, and it didn't occur to anyone that it might be safer and more comfortable for Arthur to sit there for at least half the ride. "Ready, sahib," Arthur said. Gene thought he might suffocate before the sun rose.

They turned out of the drive and down the lane and passed the procession along the side of the road. As Mr. Hinton slowed the car, the men kept their heads down and continued walking on their steady and gentle march to the river.

▪▪▪

They took a right turn off Grand Trunk Road, and suddenly the station was right in front of them. The rich red brick blended in with the city and yet stood out at the same time—too organized, too neat, too British. As the car made its stop-and-go progress down the road, Gene felt his stomach churn. Without thinking, he raked his fingers through his hair, patted it down, then straightened his collar.

"Boys, try to look decent now," Mrs. Hinton called over her shoulder. "Pith helmets on. And sit up straight!" She held her compact in one hand as she pinched color into her cheek.

"He won't be seeing us in the car, Mother," said John. Mrs. Hinton snapped the mirror shut and turned around, glaring. The boys shifted to more presentable positions.

Only a few vendors were set up in their stalls this early, but the energy around the station always felt the same, always the buzz of anticipation for those who were leaving and those coming home.

Mr. Hinton slowed the car.

"Oh, get closer," said Mrs. Hinton. "I don't want to make him walk so far."

Mr. Hinton somehow managed to wedge the car in between two stalls, its destitute appearance blending in with the humble surroundings. They didn't worry about leaving it there but instead headed for the station without a look back, dodging hawkers and waste in the street. Much earlier than they had planned to arrive, they sought out the friendly chai *wallah* and waited by his cart. The old man's face lit up at the sight of them, salaaming with incantations of "Padre Sahib! Padre Sahib!" Mr. Hinton salaamed back and inquired in Bengali about his health, as the man poured the tea, the freshest of the day.

Gene took his cup and looked around the station. People running late dodged and zipped past everyone, minding the train whistles. Guards slapped their canes to wake the sleepers scattered on the pavement. Gene was used to rushing around, too, always running late for the train to and from school. But today he had time. He saw the girl, no older than himself, rock her baby back and forth in one arm while holding the other aloft as she pleaded with the people who passed by. A cow stood in the archway, flicking away flies with its ears and long eyelashes, chewing something it had no doubt found on the street.

Gene listened to the din of the market echoing off the brick. Clattering tiffin boxes knocked against travelers' thighs while a tide of shouts flowed through the arches from outside. All around, Gene saw haggard faces, but he couldn't help smiling every time he came to Howrah Station. The noise, for all its abrasion and ugliness, was one of his favorite things about being home from school. All the sounds of Bengal forced their way into his ears, and he didn't dare cover them for fear of missing something, anything. In a place like this, so close to the crowded, hot Calcutta, there was no such thing as a breath of fresh air. But the sound breathed life through every being. It pumped through Gene, invigorating him like oxygen, and swam around him until he could almost see it, as rich and packed as the bazaar, as finely detailed as a tapestry, as deep as indigo dye. He closed his eyes and the noise magnified, and he knew that it was something that would never cease.

"Padre Sahib!" A voice struck through his reverie. "Look, Baba, it's the Hintons!"

It was Ved Hari, an Anglo-Indian friend in Will's class at boarding school. Ved waved and made his way with his parents through the crowd toward the tea stall.

"Mr. Hari, how d'you do?" Mr. Hinton said, extending a hand to Ved's father.

"Very good. Do let me buy you another cup, padre. Meeting relatives too?"

"Yes, Judge Ellis is stopping here on his way from Bombay. He's just been on holiday to South Africa, if you can believe it. And no, that's all right, I've had plenty."

"What a beautiful sari, Mrs. Hari," Mrs. Hinton said. "And Ved, you're looking smart! Someone special visiting?"

Mrs. Hari smiled modestly and looked to her husband.

"No one like Mr. Ellis anyway," Mr. Hari said. "Is he a high court judge now?"

Mrs. Hinton beamed. "Soon, I imagine. But he's still stationed in Simla."

"Oh? Trouble up there, I heard."

"Don't worry, he's been on holiday. Far away from all *that*."

Will elbowed Ved. "Training hard for the Games, Ved?"

"Sure I am. Only a month away. And someone's got to unseat the Hinton relay team this year. You know, I think it's unfair you're all on the same team."

"Take it up with the judge," said John.

"I'm just saying you're all so fast. Well, except—"

"Veddie, we're missionary boys," said Lee. "We do everything together."

"Besides," said Will, "Gene's so slow, it evens out."

"It doesn't matter. It's just a farce put on by the British anyway," Gene mumbled, but then caught the glare from his oldest brother. He sank back behind Lee.

"Well. Dad cares," John said. "Says it's good press for the mission. We get a chance to see some donors we don't normally mix with. That, and anyone new to Calcutta is always curious to know who those strapping American boys are who are always winning."

"We're working on Gene," said Lee. "He'll be the next Jesse Owens soon enough."

Will scoffed.

"Who?" said Ved.

"American," said Will, brightening. "They say he'll be the star in Berlin. Set three world records last year! Haven't you been listening to the radio?"

"I don't listen to American radio," Ved said. "Except when we're away at school. Then it's all anyone does. Remember last year? All the girls from John's year skipped German to listen to the Academy Awards."

"Well, we'll bring ours when we go back, and we can listen to the Olympics," said Will.

"I just hope India shows strong in field hockey," said Ved.

The Haris exchanged more pleasantries with Mr. and Mrs. Hinton, then quickly made off for their platform. As they disappeared into the crowd, John shook his head and muttered, "We're not losing to an Anglo team, that's for sure."

# CHAPTER 2

The Hintons navigated through the station to Platform 1 and located the first-class section. Mountains of trunks already stood outside the train cars. Arthur waded into the pile and emerged carrying two massive suitcases marked with G. H. E. in gold.

"Arthur, you remember his luggage?" Gene asked.

"Certainly, sahib."

"That's him!" John shouted, looking somewhere in the direction of the train. But Gene couldn't see over the people.

"Oh, he's got a carpetbag. Arthur, go and help him," Mrs. Hinton said.

Arthur set the suitcases down with a thud and hurried through the crowd. When he popped out again, a pristine bag swayed in his hand and a massive, imperious man shadowed him.

Somehow the judge's khaki shirt held its starchiness, even in the humidity and cramped quarters of the train, as if too terrified to dare wrinkle. The gold buckle of his belt, straining to enclose his circumference, looked as though it might pop open at any moment. He held his topi in his left hand, revealing silver-tipped hair combed impeccably to the side. He looked older than Gene had imagined, the plain, white ascot around his neck hanging just low enough to expose his sagging jowls. His round spectacles magnified his eyes, as though he might be capable of seeing twice as much as the average person. Gene pushed himself forward so that he could be seen by this man.

The judge cracked his neck in the way of one who has been on a long train journey. His gaze passed over each of them. He pulled a handkerchief out of his pocket and covered his nose, inhaling deeply. In a rough voice that seemed to come from his entire being, he said, "First class can keep them out but not their smell."

Everyone laughed, John the loudest. Gene pretended to, watching Arthur set down the bag on the platform and rub his knuckles.

"Nothing ever does." Mrs. Hinton hugged the judge tightly. He kissed her cheek and laid a hand on her waist, then let go, extending it toward Mr. Hinton. Mr. Hinton hesitated before taking it, a flat smile appearing a half second later.

"Hinton, how are you?" the judge said in his British accent. "Good, good. Grand. Looking swell. Boys. John! Eighteen already?" He gave a handshake to each of them, Gene last. As the judge's hand slipped away, Gene was astonished to find a piece of paper in his palm. He looked at it quickly, before anyone else could see. It was a folded twenty-rupee note. He looked up, meaning to thank the judge, but he had already moved on. Gene stuffed the note into his pocket and noticed with pride and a little guilt that his brothers remained empty-handed.

Though the judge seemed to be saying hello to each of them, his eyes were looking away, scanning the platform. As he put a hand to his hip, the hem of his jacket rose just enough to reveal a holstered pistol, the handle a gleaming ivory. He snapped his topi on and looked over his shoulder. "Where are my things?"

"We've already got them for you, Uncle Ellis!" John said, giving one of the trunks a knock.

"Ah? Right then." The judge put both fists on his hips and rotated this way and that, and the crowded platform began to clear around him.

Six dark-skinned men in regiment dress remained, at a distance but at attention, large guns resting on their shoulders. Black bandoliers decorated with gold trim hung across their chests, and shined buttons ran in neat rows down their jackets. They wore turbans, which were uncommon in Bengal. The humidity and the heaviness of cotton made one's head continuously sweat—and indeed, Gene could already see damp outlines on the fabric. Despite their unflinching faces, they looked terribly uncomfortable.

"Ellis, are these men with you?" Mrs. Hinton said.

"Just a precaution. Afghans, you see, not Indians. I've learned they're a safer bet. More reliable at least. Heard there's been trouble here lately."

"Well, we aren't a little hill station," she said. "People are bolder. This is Bengal—they don't mind telling you what they think. Don't forget, it's different out here."

"Believe me, I won't."

"But we mustn't let it spoil your visit," Mrs. Hinton said, and patted his back.

"It's no way to live, but Simla insists they go where I go. I've arranged a car for today."

"But there's room in our—" Mrs. Hinton began.

"Then let's get along," Mr. Hinton interrupted. "You still remember the way?"

"Of course. Now let's get as far away from here as possible."

Lee reached toward the carpet bag at Arthur's feet, but John leaped forward and snatched it away.

"I'll take your bag for you, Uncle Ellis," he said, beaming at the judge, but his uncle had already turned to go.

As the family followed in the judge's wake, Gene took one last look at the platform. Arthur struggled with the trunks until a porter stepped in to help. He looked remarkably like their servant, same stringy limbs and kind eyes. Gene felt in his pockets for a tip, but the twenty-rupee note would be far too much. So he skipped ahead toward the car, leaving the two men to struggle behind.

■■■

The judge's glossy, black car made it to the house first and looked out of place when the Hintons pulled their jalopy up behind it. The ride home had been just as bumpy and cramped as the ride to the station, and the boys sprang from the car the minute it jolted to a stop. Gene rubbed his shoulders and took a few steps as his brothers bounded up to the front door. All around, the guards inspected the yard, familiarizing themselves with the geography of the place.

The Big House owed much of its name to the wide verandah wrapping around it. Without it, the house was quite small, though its whitewashed cement walls were a far cry from the mud huts in the village. First built by British officers, the house had been maintained by a succession of tenants, but its splendor was steadily diminishing. All that remained of its old luxury was an overgrown tennis court on the north side in the shade. The court kept a year-round coating of sticky juice from the surrounding mango trees, and the clean boundary lines painted by the British soldiers were interrupted by tree roots breaking through the pavement in their inexorable reclaiming of the land.

The doors and windows of the house remained open for much of the year, as they were now, although the curtains helped to keep flies out, fluttering in the breeze like waving handkerchiefs. As far as the family was concerned, the greatest difference between indoors and outdoors was not whether there were walls around you but if there was a roof overhead. And as far as any animal was concerned, the house was home to it as well. Gene liked the miniature geckos that Arthur called *tiktikies*, which were no larger than Gene's thumb. Though they occasionally found their way into boots and rice bowls, Gene always let them stay in the house because of their knack for hunting insects, especially mosquitos. And as a bonus, he liked their pleasing faces. It was not uncommon for Gene to find one meekly smiling down at him through the mosquito netting in the morning.

And the house remained open to other humans as well. Now it was Uncle Ellis, of course, but Gene knew his brothers disliked the surprise of finding a native other than Arthur inside their home; however, it was what the Hintons were in India for. It usually happened like this: Gene would come in for supper to see extra places set at the table. Sometimes it would be for two, a mother and child, or even a whole family. And they all would sit there at the table together. Gene never minded, except for the fact that the visitors usually didn't speak or even look at them. Their eyes shifted around the room, marveling not at all shyly at the house.

But instead of marveling, these Afghan guards scrutinized the cobwebs under the eaves, the patchwork lawn, the weathered front steps. Gene got the sense that he himself was being judged, and it was then that he realized they were used to Simla, the hot-season retreat of the Raj, the summer homes of important officials and their muslin-clad families. What must this battered, backwater missionary home look like to them?

The judge leaned against the side of his car. He struck a match and held it to his pipe, shielding it from the nonexistent breeze.

"Just not in the house, please," Mr. Hinton said.

The judge exhaled the smoke in two forceful streams from his nostrils. He lifted his chin. "They've finally lent you an automobile," he said. "Well, I should hope you don't drive it very often. Looks about to give out."

"Not lent," Mr. Hinton said. "Donated from the mission."

"Hm. No giving it back then." With his left hand, he flicked the extinguished match into the dirt. "I could see about getting you a better one."

Mr. Hinton did not respond but turned his head to the side, avoiding the smoke.

Mrs. Hinton stepped in. "Thank you, Ellis. But we're quite grateful for what we have. We've come a long way since you saved us from that little hut in Contai." She took his arm and let him lead her up the front steps. Pausing, she said, "Now, I've got a large supper to whip up tonight. You'd all better stay out of my way."

"Still haven't changed," said the judge. He smiled as he looked at her. "Perhaps I'll get some shooting practice in. Dare say I'm getting rusty."

"Nonsense. You should wash up; that journey must've been ghastly," Mrs. Hinton said. "Arthur, ready a bath for Mr. Ellis."

From the driveway, Arthur struggled to untie the trunks from the top of the car. The jute rope had begun to wind its way around his body somehow, and it was all he could do to find a free hand to wave in acknowledgment. "Yes, memsahib."

# CHAPTER 3

After he drew the bath but before it was time to start on supper, Arthur found himself with a rare moment of idleness. The only place he wanted to be was far away from the Big House, which he could already feel growing sour from the distinct odor of British sweat soaking through khakis. The Hintons were too distracted by their own excitement over the judge's arrival to notice Arthur slip away. He often borrowed the Padre Sahib's rusted bicycle for errands and now found it leaning against the latrine. He shooed a few ants off the saddle, then pedaled down the lane. If anyone said anything, he could always say he was foraging for bay leaves or other such herbs for cooking.

The sky was sickly overcast, like the shell of an egg. Still, Arthur reveled in the wind as he sped around corners, eager to get away. It wasn't a feeling he had often—in fact, he quite liked the sprawling Hinton residence, overgrown and neglected as it might be. But today, he imagined nothing better than the feeling of bicycle tires spinning over dirt, the sun at his back, and the gentle downward slope as he pedaled for the river.

The route to the ghats along the Kangsabati River wound south past the police line, a leafy compound where officers and their families lived, and the new cinema hall, which didn't look new at all. As he wheeled past wizened men squatting in conversation and barefoot children chasing each other through alleys, he felt his apprehension at the judge's arrival dissipate until he could almost believe the man didn't exist at all. But then he would catch sight of a comically bulbous pith helmet, the rigid khaki uniform, the shiny buttons, and the ruddy faces of those who are not meant for the sun—the British police officers. And he would have his guard up again, their glares a little too long, a little too pointed, as if they suspected everyone. He often found himself imagining what it would be like if, one day, they all of a sudden left and never returned.

Eventually, he came to a quiet dead end where an ancient banyan tree grew and under it waited a green bicycle lashed against a post. Arthur smiled—he had hoped his friend Neer would be here, and sure enough, Arthur recognized the man with the newly shaved head crouching by the water.

"Only mad dogs and Englishmen go out in the noonday sun," Arthur called down to him.

"And sons who have lost their fathers, apparently," Neer answered, not rising from his position.

Arthur swung off the bike and walked to his friend. "I'm sorry I didn't come this morning. You know I was—"

"Yeah, busy-busy," Neer wobbled his head and squinted out across the water, then finally looked at Arthur, who was glad to see that his eyes were dry. "I wish I could have missed it myself, but you know. The eldest son must take all the responsibility. But what was the point? My father was gone a long time ago, the last years were just . . ."

Arthur knew. It seemed like every time he ran into Neer at the market, the man was buying herbs and tinctures for his father's pain. Neer's wife could have done it, but Arthur respected Neer for going himself, for doing this last deed for his father at the end.

Neer exhaled. "Anyway, I had to get away. My sisters have been wailing since dawn."

"Sitting by a muddy river is better, *na*?" Arthur joked, then immediately regretted it—Neer's father's ashes were somewhere in this very muddy river, and it felt like a disrespectful thing to say.

Perhaps Neer hadn't heard him or else wasn't in the mood to banter, for he just bowed his head and pushed a toe into the mud, sinking it with gradual but deliberate force until the water seeped up from the earth and clouded around his skin. Out past the lily pads that hugged the banks, the river punts glided along the oily water. Arthur watched a piece of garbage float in its wake. He picked a branch from the ground and tossed it a few meters away. To his surprise, out of the brush came a stray dog after it, her tail wagging, a bounce in her stride. With the twig in her teeth, she rambled back to Arthur and dropped it at his feet, then sat back on her haunches and waited. Stunned, Arthur thought she must play this game often with the street children, but he was in no mood. He turned from her, and eventually he heard her footsteps scratch over the rocky bank, up and away, probably off to the road, where a more suitable playmate could be found.

"Silly, isn't it?" Neer spoke after a time. "This place is so sacred just because Gandhiji stopped here to dip his toes in it ten years ago. He probably doesn't even remember where Midnapore is."

"Nobody does," Arthur replied. "Me, I don't know anywhere *but* Midnapore. These Hinton boys go all over, the Himalayas for boarding school, Europe for holiday; I walk to the other side of the river and think I've traveled the world."

"Ever think about leaving?"

"Where would I go?"

Neer seemed to think about it. "Maybe you just need to meet a woman who will give you a reason to think bigger."

Arthur laughed. "What's with you? Talking about my marital status is an odd way to grieve your father."

"Sorry, sorry. I just can't imagine the last few years without Vaikha. It's not such a bad thing, to have a wife."

"I don't need a wife. I know how to cook and do the shopping."

"You think that is all a wife is good for?"

Arthur didn't answer but let the buzzing horseflies fill the silence. It was not lost on him how generous it was of Neer, on the day his own father died, to think of Arthur and his solitary life. Maybe he should listen.

"But it's too late," Arthur muttered. "I've already given up on finding a match."

"You're younger than me," Neer answered. "Your hair is still more black than it is gray."

"And I am too busy, with my duties to the—"

"That *pardeshi* family? Oh, come on. When will you stop being their pet?"

"I'm not their pet—they give me a job, and I do it, and they pay me."

Neer looked at him hard, making Arthur uncomfortable. Why did he always have to defend his work with the Hintons to everybody?

"If they give you food and water but would kick you out on the street just as soon as they get the notion to, tell me—how is that not like a dog?"

Arthur swallowed. He ran a palm over the back of his neck, wiping off the sweat, gathering himself. "Because they wouldn't kick me out. Not unless I gave them a reason to."

His friend seemed to sense that they were at an impasse. Neer softened, sighed, and broke his gaze away. The far banks of the river were dappled with white birds, all ebbing and flowing with the breeze. It was indeed a peaceful place, and Arthur could see why Neer had come here to get away.

"Well. All I am saying is they can take care of themselves by now. So you can sneak away for an hour or two to meet some girl. They hardly miss you right now, *na*?"

"An hour or two?" Arthur bent to pick up a stone from the rocky bank. He held the weight of it, and with his thumb, he worried the grit from its crevices. "Is that all it takes to make a marriage?"

Neer pushed up from his thighs, finally standing fully in front of Arthur. "Well, maybe it doesn't need to be a marriage. The wedding, all that, maybe it's too much for you. But you know, times are changing. Maybe you can just talk to a woman, and then see where it goes."

Arthur frowned at his friend. "You mean . . . courting?"

Neer wobbled his head. "I think it's called that. I don't know, Vaikha and I were arranged."

"Ah, why am I even listening to you. You don't know what you're talking about. No girls do courting. No *mother* would let their girls do that."

"That's what I'm saying, this country is changing! Come on. I have a cousin in Kharagpur. See? Something in common. You can buy her some chai and tell her all about how you grew up there. Her parents sell sweets in the bazaar. Will you just try? I lost my father today—will you give me this at least?"

"I don't know why you care so much," Arthur said.

Neer's responding grin meant he could tell Arthur was giving in. "I want to find some happiness in this day. Even if it isn't for me."

At that moment, a yelp echoed from up the road, followed by shouting from a harsh British voice. Arthur whirled around and caught sight of one of the British officers he had passed earlier now taking a swing at the stray dog with his lathi. The mutt lunged away with her tail tucked, then paused once out of reach to look over her shoulder at the officer as if bewildered at the outburst. The officer wasn't done. He removed his pith helmet—as if it would make him run faster—and started after the dog, who was caught off guard enough to allow the officer to get in a kick at her ribs.

The dog took off running again, and before Arthur knew it, she was on top of him, eyes wild and ears flattened. She had knocked Arthur over in her agitation, and despite the commotion, he couldn't help thinking that he hadn't another clean shirt for serving supper. He'd have to keep his back to the wall to hide the mud.

"Keep your filthy dog to yourself!" the officer shouted down at them.

Neer scowled as he helped Arthur to his feet. "Should we tell every dog in India to leave him alone too?"

Arthur laughed and gave the stray a pat on the head. She rolled onto her back and looked up at him with watery eyes and perked ears, and as he rubbed her belly, there was something about the way her brows twitched that made him think she had known all along the kind of mischief she was getting into with the officer. Arthur was about to push her away again when she put a paw on his bare foot— gently, with no weight on it—and licked his dusty shin.

"This is the most attention any girl has given me in years," Arthur said, and though he meant it as a joke, it made him feel alarmingly sad. Perhaps he should listen to Neer. "All right, I'll meet your cousin. If she would like to meet me, anyway."

"That's it!" Neer slapped a hand on his knee and grinned. "I'll tell her and send you a chit when it's all set." He walked up to Arthur and ruffled the fur on the stray, then smoothed it over again. "Thanks, girl, for talking my friend into some sense. Now, I've got to get back. Although I wonder if the aunties have even noticed I've been gone . . ."

Arthur watched his friend trot to his bicycle, where it waited under the banyan tree, then push off down the lane. He felt for Neer; the battle of his father's illness had been longer than anyone could possibly take, and yet Neer had shouldered it as if it were weightless, simply a part of him, like an old coat he'd had forever. But Arthur knew—nobody came alone to the river if all was right.

Something soft and sticky touched his fingertips. He looked down to see the stray still by his side, busy licking the sweat from his skin.

"Stop it!" he hissed, eager now to get back to the Big House and on with his duties. "You think you are the first stray who's ever begged at me? I have no more to give than you do!" But the dog backed off only half-heartedly, licking her snout as if she could still taste his sweat on her tongue. Her wagging tail gave Arthur a pit in his stomach— he couldn't bring himself to turn her away again just yet. "All right, come on," he sighed, beckoning her back. But as she approached, Arthur noticed a limp in her gait. The panting smile and wagging tail betrayed no pain, but the limp didn't lie—the officer had gotten in a good blow.

To his surprise, Arthur felt a pang at the realization—he was just beginning to consider letting her follow him home. He imagined sneaking her past the Big House and into his hut, where she could keep him company, or else let her loose in the woods nearby to help chase away the monkeys. But he wouldn't make her run all the way home, and besides, it was a silly idea. She was probably riddled with fleas.

"Sorry, girl," he said, giving her one last pat. "Maybe I'll see you here again, *na*?" He looked over her face and body and tried to remember the tawny marking shaped like a leaf over her eye, how her pricked ears were mismatched colors—one brown, one white—and the limp that he hoped would be gone should he see her again. It was pleasant to think so, anyway.

He threw a stick into the murky water and watched her jump after it, then quickly ran up the embankment before she noticed he was gone. He swung on the Padre Sahib's bike, praying he hadn't been gone long enough for the Hintons to notice yet, and pedaled swiftly for home. Neer's words echoed in his mind: *"When will you stop being their pet?"* Was he right? Was Arthur a dog to them?

He passed the British officer from before, who watched from the shade of a nearby building, panting from the heat. *Only mad dogs and Englishmen*, Arthur thought. *But then, it's not so bad to be like a dog, loyal and trusting, so long as you have the teeth to fight back when you need to.*

# CHAPTER 4

**A**rthur hadn't forgotten the last time the burra sahib had visited. The other boarders had run away, driven out by the judge's antics. He had taken the mission's shared car out for a joyride and returned it in even worse condition than it had already been in, after a harrowing hour with the judge at the wheel, the boys in the back seat, and Arthur holding on to the roof for dear life. But all had been forgiven by the Hintons when the burra sahib left a stack of rupees on his nightstand the morning he left. They ate like rajahs that week.

But he couldn't think about it right now; it was dinnertime and he had a job to do. He had set the table before anyone was even down yet so that no one would see his soiled shirt. Now, with everyone seated and engrossed in conversation, if he just kept his back to the wall, they wouldn't notice.

He moved the bamboo fans of the punkah above the dining table to and fro, trying to match the rhythm with his breathing. It had been a long time since they last had a guest worthy enough for a fanned dinner. But the wooden handle took to his hand like an old friend. He pulled it down to his navel in a fluid, gentle motion and felt the gust on his face. He released it then, guiding it up toward his heart. Down and up, down and up, in time with the crooked grandfather clock in the corner.

Ever since the judge had stepped off the train, Arthur had avoided him. He'd run the trunks up to the guest room while the judge was still downstairs. He'd made sure the room had everything the judge might need—water for washing, mosquito netting, kerosene in the lamps—to minimize the chance of having to go up again later.

Now that everyone was gorging themselves on food and the judge's every word, Arthur was free to look all he wanted at the man. He wasn't really their uncle, only a longtime family friend. Although in certain lighting Arthur swore he could see a resemblance between the burra sahib and John, the judge was absolutely different from the Hintons in nearly every other way. His sophisticated British mannerisms were practically royal compared to those of the missionary family, and Arthur couldn't think for the life of him why he'd stay at the house with them. Usually he preferred to stay at the Grand in Calcutta and have them come to him for tea.

The judge had aged considerably. There was something unmistakable about him, something different, as if he were not the same person as before, but Arthur couldn't yet determine why. One thing was certainly there that wasn't before—the pistol at his hip as he sat down for dinner.

"Still haven't found a cook?" the judge said.

"The mission can't afford to give us one," said Mrs. Hinton.

"But they can afford a car? And a fan boy?" The judge raised his glass in Arthur's direction. Arthur felt as though he were being toasted. His back straightened.

"He's more than a fan boy; he does practically everything besides the driving."

"Has he a name?"

"Of course he does," said Mr. Hinton. "His name is Arthur. He's the same we've always had; you've met him before."

Arthur nodded and smiled a little too broadly. He felt a breeze on his gums and closed his mouth. Of course the judge did not remember him. The family seemed to not know anything else to say about Arthur. Still pulling the handle of the fan, he watched the dishes pass through hands. He felt his stomach gurgle.

"What's the news from Bombay?" Mr. Hinton asked.

"Nobody wants to hear about Bombay," Mrs. Hinton said. "You've got to tell us about South Africa." She leaned forward and set down her fork.

"Yes, Uncle Ellis, did you see a giraffe?" said Will. "I heard they're as tall as the trees. Or a rhinoceros?"

"Yes, yes, yes." The judge waved his handkerchief in front of his face, swatting the questions away. "I saw it all. And a lion pride too. I cursed myself that I didn't have my hunting rifle. Don't think I'll ever get so lucky again. Of course I wasn't expecting to see a lion on my way to the club, but I got lost and took a roundabout way, and there the thing was. All I could do was back away and hope it was too afraid of me to attack. And it just watched, lying there. Stupid thing."

"It?" said Will. "Was it not a whole pride?"

"No, just one lion, just one lion. Pass the fig butter."

"Looks like we're all out," Lee said.

"Arthur!" Mrs. Hinton said.

Arthur let go of the handle and took the empty dish. Brown streaks smudged the silver that he had spent all morning polishing. He bowed and backed out of the room as if he were in the presence of royalty, then made for the back door, careful to keep his footsteps silent.

The jar sat on the highest shelf in the cookhouse. He pulled it down and scooped out what he thought would be enough. Holding the open jar to his eye like a telescope, he decided he better just empty the whole thing. There still remained a few streaks inside, so he wiped a single finger on his dhoti, the fabric that hid under his tunic. He hooked his finger around the inside of the glass and pulled it out covered in goo. He popped it in his mouth and swirled his tongue around, the sweet flavor giving way to earthy nuttiness. God bless Mrs. Hinton. The memsahib did know how to cook. She had even gone to the bazaar herself to pick out the figs this time, not trusting

Arthur to do it right. Last night she had stayed late in the cookhouse, the scent of boiling figs wafting from the door. Arthur had looked in to make sure she didn't need any help, only to find her sweating over the stove, wrestling a large wooden spoon around in the pot. "Ellis's favorite," she had said. And then he understood, backing away. And now here it was, half gone. He picked up the replenished dish and hurried back to the house.

"What difference does it make if it's there or not?" one of the boys was saying, as Arthur placed the dish back on the table like an offering, then retreated to the fan. "Besides, Uncle Ellis approves."

"Course I do. I dare say every good family should have a racing track in their front yard." The judge reached for the fig butter and began spreading it on his bread, turning toward Mrs. Hinton. "Didn't you know I'm the one who started them off the first time? I believe I used my howdah pistol as the starting gun. It was so long ago. Gene wasn't even born yet, were you Gene? Ha! Imagine that. Racing's been in the family longer than you have. And it's right that you finally get a proper course now. I remember you all could barely stand up again after leaping off the fence posts. You've got blocks now. That's good. And just think—they're not running around the house and up and down the porch anymore. They're out of your way, don't you see?"

"I already said it could stay," Mrs. Hinton said.

"But even after the meet, don't you think, Uncle Ellis?"

"Of course. There's going to be another one next year and the year after that, isn't there? Well, not for you, John, once you go back home to America. If you can even call it *home*—but don't worry, the Americans will give you a run for your rupees there."

"It's a good thing I'm an American, then," said John.

"Yes, we're all so proud of him," Mrs. Hinton said. "But it's not for a long while. John's going to wait a year. He won't go without Will, and Will's almost finished with school."

"What's the matter? Can't brave the sea yourself?"

"It's not the sea, it's the States I'm worried about," John said. "That's how they say it there, isn't it?"

"Call it what you want, but it's the future. We can't stay on, Ellis." Mrs. Hinton laid a hand on the judge's thick arm.

He looked for a moment at the delicate hand, then raised his stony face. "It's about time you all got out of here. Even for missionary folk, it's getting too dangerous. I'd come along with you if I could." He patted Mrs. Hinton's hand and reached for more fig butter. A dot of fig juice flung from the knife and splattered on the linen tablecloth. "Keep going, Arthur. It's still blazing hot in India, you can be sure of that. There's no stopping now."

Arthur pulled the wooden handle again, and everyone seemed to liquify under the breeze of the punkah.

"That's better. Ohhh, my. Nothing in the world could be as hot as this." The judge took a bite of his bread. "So," he said, chewing. "You're done with the whole boarding house nonsense."

"What makes you think that?" said Mrs. Hinton.

"Why, there's no one around! And I thought you'd come to your senses at least by now. No matter how long you've been in this coun-try"—he leaned forward as though to lower his voice, but it still came out booming as ever—"there's no trusting them, especially in your own home."

*Slap!* More fig butter. Arthur frowned at the excess. What a ridic-ulous pile of goop for a man whose shirt buttons were already burst-ing. He looked around the table at Mr. Hinton. The Padre Sahib did not seem to notice but instead was peppering his own meal.

"We're proud of the work that we do for the mission, whether it's here in our house or in the village." Mr. Hinton set the pepper shaker down on the table with an authoritative thud.

The judge glanced at Mrs. Hinton, who nodded once. "Well. That's grand. You know I've always supported you. Always. Very admirable thing. Why don't you tell me all about the latest at the mission, then."

The judge looked like he wanted to hear about anything but. Yet the padre began in his solemn voice relaying the goings on at the village, the latest sermon, the slew of repairs to the buildings that they meant to help with in the coming months. The judge's eyes glazed over. The padre must have noticed. But he went on, preaching about God to a nonbeliever.

Arthur scratched at his stomach, wishing to remove it and thus his hunger. He'd never noticed so much waste go on in this house. Had they always been like this? Remembering his duties, he began pulling the handle with renewed vigor.

"That's it, Arthur!" one of the boys said. "Now it feels like heaven in here."

Arthur lowered his head. But when he peeked up again, his heart nearly stopped. The judge raised the piece of bread to his mouth, but this time with practically a knuckle's height of fig butter on it. When he set it back down, a giant bite had been taken out, brown dripping all around.

Arthur wanted to look away but couldn't. He felt the grimace on his face and knew it wasn't proper to be anything but neutral, but he couldn't help it. The fig butter oozed out onto the plate like a wound, and he felt his appetite fade. Whatever they were talking about around the table, he couldn't hear or didn't care. Why did it bother him so? If any of them were to look in his direction, they would have every right to slap the disgust off his face, it was so improper of him. But no one noticed, and it was only as the family rose and tossed the handkerchiefs on the tabletop and pushed their chairs out that he bowed his head.

The setting sun glistened on the empty crystal glasses as Arthur stepped forward to clear the table. He usually liked to whistle as he tidied up, but today it didn't occur to him to do so. He knew which was the judge's plate, but his eyes avoided it. Pretending it wasn't there, he first collected all the linen napkins, examined them for stains, and separated them into two piles, one for washing and the other for those that could be used again. Next he stacked the glasses, took them into the cookhouse, and stacked the plates, being careful not to touch the food. Inside the serving dishes, a few spoonfuls and scrapes of food clung to the porcelain sides. He walked them out to his hut to eat later.

On the way back to the dining room, he thought about what Neer had said that afternoon. Was he like a dog to them, eating their scraps? But they weren't normally like this. Mrs. Hinton sometimes set out an extra plate for him, not always, but sometimes, and Arthur considered that very thoughtful. They were just acting pompous now because the judge was here. That was it—they didn't want the judge to think they were friendly to their servant, lest that make them seem equal.

All had been cleared except the one plate. He shook his head. It was such a waste. The Hintons were so careful with their food, Mrs. Hinton especially, the way she watched over his market shopping and never missed a rupee. So why were they even friends with a man who never knew what it was like to ration food? On impulse, he swiped his index finger directly in the center of the glob and popped it in his mouth. Too sweet. But he didn't want to throw it out, and he didn't think all that sugar would be much help to the garden. So he walked the plate toward the shed, taking a lantern on his way. He would feed the rest to Minnie.

■■■

Upstairs on the sleeping porch, Gene shook his blanket out over the railing; a few ants scattered into the shadows below, but no snakes, praise God. He'd never found one in his bed, but he'd heard enough stories.

"I'm telling you all," Lee said from his bed, "if you tuck your mosquito netting around your mattress, it will help keep—"

"I wish Uncle Ellis had told us more about Africa," Will said over him, slapping his pillow against the railing.

Lee cleared his throat. "I don't believe he actually went."

John sat up in his bed. "What do you mean? Of course he went."

"He's put on an awful amount of weight," Lee continued. "I can't imagine putting on pounds in a place like that."

"You might be right," said Will. "It's been years since we saw him last, but he was always fit. And he didn't bring us any gifts? That's not like him. He'd at least bring Mother something."

"Leave him alone," said John. "He'll be right as rain tomorrow morning. It's his first night back in India, for God's sake."

They grew quiet at the mention of the *G* word, and individually they clasped their hands together and shut their eyes. Gene murmured his thanks—thanks that the car didn't break down on their way home, thanks that he felt full tonight—then climbed into bed. As he rolled onto his side, he could still see Lee at the far end of the sleeping porch, praying out toward the jungle.

"Too hot to sleep," Will said. "One of these days, I'll pay Arthur to just stand here all night and fan me. What d'you think he'd do it for? Chop of mutton?"

But Arthur wasn't there to wave palm fronds over them all night, so they quieted down and tried to find sleep in the intolerable heat.

From under the porch eaves, Gene caught a glimpse of the orange glow dying over the treetops. The air settled like a blanket. The rafters made a popping sound, and Gene pictured a monkey leaping up onto the roof.

A rare breeze brought the scent of jasmine up through the porch. Gene took a long inhale and shut his eyes, imagining he was in a zamindari palace. He settled into the dream, erecting the gilded walls and latticework partitions made of sandalwood, leather-upholstered benches lining the halls, stairwells spiraling off in any direction, and minarets at every corner.

He pictured it situated in the nest of some mountains, as in Mussoorie, where their boarding school was. That, he could envision well, the way the snow still clung to the peaks in summer. He'd never seen anything so steadfast as snow in summer. It made him think it was possible for things to last forever.

A zamindari didn't feel quite right. A visitor, perhaps. A surveyor. An explorer measuring the elevation, who unexpectedly got taken in by the generous rajah. And that's where he could smell the jasmine, perfumed on the ruler's robes and on his ringed hands. He imagined himself as the only Westerner there, and all the men and women alike found his American accent charming. He never thought of himself as charming, but in a place like that, he didn't have to be himself. Perhaps there was a garden, where he would sit under the trees with women gathered all around just to hear him speak. He'd tell them tales so thrilling it didn't matter if they were true. And they'd all laugh and marvel at him and bring him platters of sweets for supper.

Running his tongue around his mouth, all but tasting the sugary *mithai*, he realized he'd forgotten to brush his teeth. He opened his eyes and considered whether it was worth it to get up again. The lamp was by John's bed; he would have to walk the length of the sleeping porch in the dark to get to it, and walking barefoot in the dark was something white people didn't do in India—or so he had been taught all his life.

Gene sat up in bed and peered down at the floorboards. He could just barely make out the shadows from the furniture—or were they snakes and millipedes waiting?

The sleeping porch was silent except for the gentle rhythms of his brothers' breathing. John was already snoring.

A primal scream from the forest set off a frenzy in the surrounding canopy as birds and bats fled from their homes. Gene ran to the railing, not even thinking about his bare feet, and searched the shadows below. A door banged shut, and he caught a glimpse of someone fleeing like mad, a lantern swinging in his hand. All of Gene's brothers had awoken now and leaped out of their beds.

"Gosh! What was that?" someone said, but Gene was too focused on the ground to answer. As his eyes flicked from one patch of darkness to the other, looking for what on earth had set Arthur off like that, his brothers collapsed on the porch in fits of laughter.

"What! What is it?" Gene cried. He craned his neck and stumbled around the furniture to the other side.

"Look at him!" came a gasp out of the laughter. That was Will.

"And look at her go!" said John.

Gene caught sight of the little monkey shadow that followed Arthur, chasing him around the backyard like a demon. She was silent; she wasn't even shrieking at all in that terrifying way monkeys did, although Arthur was doing enough of that for the both of them. Gene couldn't help but allow a few giggles to escape. And in fact, the more he watched the haphazard, gangly outline of a man flying all up and down in the darkness, the more his laughter bubbled forth until at last he was guffawing full-bellied with his brothers. But then, through tears, Gene saw the little shadow leap up and land on Arthur's back, stopping him in his tracks.

The sleeping porch went silent. No one laughed anymore as Arthur flailed around, reaching for the monkey. He didn't even scream, although Gene thought he could hear labored grunts that made Minnie seem far stronger than she should have been.

"Aw, call her off, John," said Lee.

"She's not hurting him," he replied.

"She is!" Gene cried.

John put two fingers in his mouth and whistled a clear, firm note that pulled upward at the end. The monkey hopped off Arthur and slunk toward the porch, hearing her master's signal.

"Put her back in the shed, would you, Arthur?"

"Yes, sahib," came the weary response from below.

"What's all that racket?" The roaring voice of the judge carried through the house.

"Nothing! Just Arthur!" called John.

"Well, tell him to stop screaming blue murder like that! Doesn't he have any respect?"

The boys settled back into bed—all except Gene, who, still at the railing, watched the monkey's slouching silhouette reach the shed and wait. A few steps behind, the glow of the lantern followed timidly until Arthur's skinny arm reached for the door and flung it open. Gene could just see them now as they both disappeared into the shed. It wasn't until Arthur emerged again that Gene tiptoed back to his bed. As he pulled the sheet up to his chin, he could hear John already snoring. How could it be so easy to fall back asleep? And why was it that Gene couldn't remember the last time John had fed Minnie himself rather than making someone else do it? She was his pet after all, and surely he knew what a menace she was to everyone else. And then a thought occurred to him: for all the times John had forced Gene to do some small thing for him, Arthur must have done it a thousand times more. He shut his eyes, resolved to be kinder to Arthur.

■■■

The next day, Uncle Ellis requested breakfast in his room. There were some grumbles of disappointment around the table from Gene's brothers, but they decided he was taking time to settle in and needed to rest. Surely he would come out by afternoon tea.

Yet the clock ticked on as the boys read in the shade of the sleeping porch, waiting out the hot hours before the sun slipped below the trees again. Gene knew his brothers hoped to catch the judge at some point in the day so they could ask him all about his adventures of the past few years. But by the time Gene heard the slam of the car door outside, it was too late. The boys rushed to the railing just as the car engine started up, Uncle Ellis in the backseat, a soldier at the wheel.

"Huh," said Will. "Afghans can drive."

The rest of the week was more of the same, with the judge's daily departure from the house getting earlier and earlier. He continued to take breakfast in his room; he began to stay out past supper as well. But no one wanted to confront the judge; he wasn't the sort of person who inspired dissent. And any time Gene tried to ask his mother why the judge was avoiding them, she sighed, as though she wanted to know, too, but didn't answer. If she wasn't bold enough to talk to Uncle Ellis, Gene certainly wasn't. So each night, no one dared say a word about the empty chair and untouched place setting at the head of the table.

One evening, when Uncle Ellis had still not returned for the night, Gene knocked on the study door. There was a grunt from the other side of the door. He pushed it open and took a step into the room, then took it back and leaned against the doorway. "Where does Uncle Ellis go every day?" he whispered.

For a moment, he thought his father hadn't heard. He kept writing, head bent over the desk. Gene stepped forward, and, as he opened his mouth to repeat himself, his father looked up. "It's not our business, son."

Still, there was a twinge of hurt in his voice. Gene wanted to shout, *Yes! It is our business and you are hosting him and he is being a terrible guest and it is rude to not even sit down to supper with us let alone spend an afternoon together when it had been so long since last we met.* His father's pen stopped, and now the room was truly silent.

Gene moved toward the desk, his hands behind his back. He kept his eyes down, the threadbare rug muffling his steps. Then he stopped; there on the floor, next to the desk, was his father's Bible. It was facedown, and its pages were bent against the ground as if it had been tossed there, the gold letters on the cover barely reflecting the light of the lamp. Gene stooped and picked it up. Before placing it back on the desk, he smoothed his thumbs over the creased pages.

"Gene." Mr. Hinton took the book and leaned back in his chair, finding a page he had seemed to memorize. He pushed his glasses up his nose. "'Be still in the presence of the Lord, and wait patiently for Him to act.'" He looked over his glasses at Gene, but there was nothing in his eyes to give away what it meant, what any of this meant. Gene couldn't make sense of patience and stillness when so much time had passed, so many hollow days gone by waiting for someone who was never there.

■■■

A whole week had passed since the judge arrived when Gene woke before his brothers, thinking he had heard yelling, but he couldn't be sure it hadn't come from his dreams. It was the soft hour before the house came alive, the mist blanketing the roof before the sun stripped it back. Gene blinked the sleep away and scanned the rafters. Heavy dew clung to the railing around the sleeping porch and the undersides of the gutters. The drain dripped a sluggish rhythm. But somewhere outside, he could hear metered footsteps on the gravel. At the same moment he remembered the guards, there came a sharp command in another language and the shuffling of feet as the soldiers repositioned themselves. He looked over to the yard and saw a man, a stranger, shirtless and barefoot. His eyes were cast down, his chin practically resting on his chest. Around him, the guards kept their stone-faced positions. Then, his father's voice came from somewhere inside. He couldn't make out the words, but the man looked up and nodded grimly. Gene pushed the mosquito net aside and went downstairs. He found Mr. Hinton in the entryway, lacing his boots. Boots, Gene noticed, not sandals.

"Morning, Dad."

"Morning."

"Who's that man?"

"He came from the village. His brother is dying, and he wants me to give the last rites."

"Last rites?"

"Catholic. But there's no time to send for a Catholic priest. Catholic, Baptist—it's all the same to them. And we're the closest Christians they've got."

"Catholic? No kidding. Can I come?"

"No. Poor fellow's ill, and I can't have you catching anything." Mr. Hinton shouldered past him and went outside, waving to the man. "*Jaldi aao*, come on."

The two men walked quickly down the road. Gene left the door open and searched for his shoes. He grabbed them from the pile and struggled with the laces. But even as he pulled one on, he saw that his father and the man were already out of sight. The house was still, the sitting room clean; no one had disturbed anything. Except, he could just make out the intricate outline of a spider web in the archway. He kicked off the shoe and stepped out the door, closing it behind him.

He heard the rustling of pots and pans in the cookhouse, and, before Gene even stepped off the verandah, Arthur popped his head out the cookhouse door. His eyebrows raised in surprise at the sight of Gene.

"Padre Sahib has already left, sir."

"I know, Arthur. I was just—"

"And the burra sahib, sir."

Gene stopped. "What do you mean? Not with Dad."

"No, he is gone to the club. The car left early this morning."

Gene looked down the road, as if it weren't too late to catch a glimpse of the car speeding away. But all that was left were tire tracks in the dirt. He sighed and looked back to Arthur, but he had already gone back into the cookhouse.

Gene trudged back up the verandah steps when he remembered

the previous night—how they had all laughed at Arthur as he sprinted round the yard, and how Gene had felt guilty afterward. He cleared his throat. "Can I help, Arthur?"

The rummaging sounds in the kitchen stopped. Arthur leaned out the doorway. "With what, sahib?"

"You know, breakfast. I'm not doing anything today," Gene said, his voice trailing off.

Arthur wobbled his head, thinking how to answer. "Not needed today, sir," he said, as if there were a possibility to help another time.

Gene nodded and climbed the stairs, the steps creaking under his weight. As he reached the top, he found himself out of breath. But he wasn't exhausted—only tired at the thought of another unfilled day spread before him.

He went through the empty bedroom and out to the sleeping porch, where the mosquito nets were still tucked into the beds. He crossed his arms and gave the doorjamb a stout kick. "He's gone," he said. Three disheveled heads appeared above the blankets.

"Gone where?" said Will.

"Down to the club. Left this morning in the car." Gene shook the dirt off his feet and swung up onto his bed.

A groan came from John's corner. "Let's just admit it. There's something up," he said, rubbing his eyes. "The only thing he'd ever get up early for is Mother's cooking. But the club? Who does he even know there anyway? He didn't come all this way just to spend a whole week at the club. Is it even open this early?"

"It's not," said Lee quietly, not that any of them had ever set foot inside the British Club.

Will threw his covers back and moved toward the railing. Below, the jungle was already wide awake. The murmuring of frogs seemed to come from every tree, and here and there the branches shivered as though startled by the monkeys and birds that came and went.

"It would have been a swell day to show him the track," Will said.

"Do you remember how he said he'd bike to the maidan with us? And climb the watchtower of the Old Gope?" John said, gazing at the rafters. "He used to talk about *doing* things."

"Maybe he's just tired from his Africa trip," Gene ventured.

"I don't think so," said Lee.

"Honestly, sis," said Will, "an entire voyage back from Africa is plenty of time to rest up."

"Don't call me that," said Gene.

"Do you think he's hurt himself?" said John. "The little we've seen of him, he's always been in a chair."

"He's getting old . . . ," Lee said.

His brothers turned silent, and Gene knew it was the truth. The judge *was* old.

"If he's getting old, then it's because he's stopped doing all those things," said Will. "If we make him, he'll get out of this rut. This isn't Ellis. He's not meant to live the rest of his life inside some club full of dandy Brits. Let's get him back."

"Yes, he owes us at least one game of cricket," said John.

"But we don't even play cricket . . ."

"Oh, stuff it, Gene," said John.

"What's the big deal?" Gene said. "He's not the first grown-up to stop having fun. Look at Dad. He used to go on bike rides with us, too, and take us hunting more. But we can do stuff ourselves—we don't need Dad or Uncle Ellis."

"Oh, don't be a fool," John said. "You just don't remember. Uncle Ellis . . . he's just . . . he's better at everything than anyone you know."

"And he knows stuff," added Will. "Things not even our teachers tell us. All about the land and how far it is to this city, how to go from Cal to Goa without ever leaving first class, what part of the Himalayas has the finest tea. If you think it's Darjeeling, he'll tell you you're wrong. You'd think he was born in India, like us, the way he knows every river, road, and mountain."

"Hmm." Gene wondered what that must be like, to know every corner of this country by heart. You could step out the door and know where you were going without ever consulting a map. The Hintons hadn't been around the country much—the mission kept them in Midnapore—but Gene knew enough to realize it would take lifetimes in India to know everything about it. "So how long has he been in India?"

"Before Mom and Dad got here," said Lee. "That's all he tells us. Who knows—maybe he *was* born here."

"No," said Will. "Nobody born in India hates it as much as he does. You have to know someplace else first to hate it like that."

"Then why would he know so much about a place he hates?" said Gene.

"Maybe that's how he got to hating it," said Lee. "He knows the worst of it."

"Well if he's such a hateful old man now, I'd rather leave him alone," said Gene.

"He's already leaving us alone just fine," John said. He lay twisted among the sheets, his head smashed into the pillow, his dark hair already damp with fresh sweat. His foot had found its way to the edge of the bed and hung halfway off the mattress. John's toenails hadn't been clipped for weeks, it looked, and in their yellowed edges, Gene recognized the hold the judge had over his brothers. If they couldn't get Ellis back on his feet, his brothers would fall to the same fate. One by one they'd drop off. Soon, they would begin to stay in bed all day, with limbs all turned to mush. John was already well on his way.

Gene imagined a day without his brothers. There'd be no more name-calling, no more "sis." No more squishing into the car or into clothes after they'd been handed down three times. He'd be full after every meal; he'd get the biggest helping—two helpings even! And everyone would notice him, look at him, speak to *him*. He wouldn't be fourth in line for anything anymore. He would be first. Well, there would be no line actually.

He could have the house and the yard all to himself. With his brothers gone, he might have some peace and quiet for a change. But Gene didn't want his brothers gone, or depressed, or hermitic the way the judge was acting. He just wanted them to be . . . a little less. But maybe it wasn't a question of less. It had to do with something *more*.

With his eyes on the floorboards, he said, "What makes Ellis so special to us all that we'll lie in bed sulking if he doesn't show his face? The sun still rises, doesn't it?" His brothers stared at him. Suddenly he was acutely aware that they were all between him and the door. He started to ease a few steps back toward his side of the sleeping porch. "Listen," he continued in a softer voice, "it's not too late. All I'm saying is, if he can get out of bed for the club, he can get out of bed to do something with us. You all remember him, but I don't. I want to see this man who's explored so much of the world he's already sick of it."

John propped himself up on his elbows and frowned at him through the netting. But before John opened his mouth, Lee said, "Gene's right. We should get Uncle Ellis back. And if it comes to it, we'll just have to drag him out of bed and tell him the car's not working and the club is closed." He walked over to Gene and clapped him on the back.

Will sighed. "It's better than another day lounging up here."

They all looked to John, whose scowl had softened a little. "It'll be hard," he said. "Uncle Ellis isn't easy to convince, you know. Once he's stuck his boots in the muck, he's not one to move." He brushed the netting aside and stood up from his bed, making a show of it with his chest out, chin up. "But we've got nothing to lose."

# CHAPTER 5

The moths dappled the walls in suspended sleep when Arthur heard the footsteps coming down the lane the next morning. He was off his charpoy and at the door of his hut before the messenger boy, barefoot and panting, appeared in front of the Big House. Arthur glanced apprehensively at the guards. Out behind the cashew trees, they had set up a makeshift shooting range of old ghee tins balanced on a rickety wooden bar. The slap of their rifles followed by the metal clang of the tins had kept a steady rhythm all morning, and now they were taking a tea break. They seemed unthreatened by this bedraggled and malnourished youth, but even so, Arthur waived them off—he didn't know what their orders were, but he hoped they didn't involve shooting any visitors on sight.

"*Shuprobhat*," Arthur greeted the boy.

The boy responded by holding out a yellowed slip of paper folded in half. "Chit for you," he said.

"You mean for the Padre Sahib," Arthur clarified as he took the letter.

"No, for you, babu," the boy said with a smirk.

"Don't mock me," Arthur said with a jerk of his head to show it was much too early in the day to be taking a tease from this errand boy. Arthur had heard the Indian men who worked for the British officers referred to as babus, and he hated to learn that people in town thought of him that way too. "I don't work for the judge—" he began to explain, but the boy had already moved his attention to the Afghan soldiers and their eye-catching uniforms. So Arthur unfolded the note and recognized Neer's handwriting.

*I spoke with Soni about you. She agreed to meet. Parents insist I chaperone. Gate Bazaar after morning market tomorrow, yes?*

And below that on another line, Neer had written:

*Not to worry about sulka.*

The *sulka*? Just the other day, Neer had been adamant that this didn't have to lead to marriage, to not even say the word *marriage*. Now he was talking about the bride price? For Arthur at his age and due to his parents, paying the bride price was the only way left for him if he ever were to marry. And it was shameful—that was why he had put marriage out of his mind long ago.

"Boy," he called. "Wait here."

Arthur hurried inside the house and scrounged for a scrap of paper and pencil to write a reply. Then he rushed outside again. When he handed the note to the boy, he immediately opened it up.

"Don't read it!" Arthur snapped and smacked the boy on his sunken chest.

"The babu can read *and* write! Fancy," the boy said, laughing, and Arthur could see the boy's dusty fingerprints all over the paper.

"Of course I can. How else am I to read memsahib's grocery lists? They taught me, and maybe someone would teach you one day if they were ever foolish enough to think you capable of more than just running letters around."

"It pays well for me, actually. Speaking of which—" The boy straightened up and held his palm out.

Arthur sighed and fished in the folds of his dhoti for two paise. He held it out to the messenger, but the boy pulled his hand back.

"Ah-ah! That'll be one anna."

"A whole anna! Get out of here. What, you have a centipede in your head?"

"I'm serious. Extra cost incurred for being chased by a rabid dog all the way here. I couldn't shake her off me, see?" He pointed to the tattered hems of his clothing, but Arthur had no doubt they were like that before. And yet, down the road beyond the gate, he could see a silhouette backlit by the morning sun: a dog, sniffing lazily in the ditch like grazing cattle. Arthur shifted his glance to the soldiers to see if they had noticed. But no—most people did not pay any mind to the town's hundreds of pariah dogs.

Arthur pushed three paise into the boy's hand, who seemed satisfied with the bargain and jaunted away, but not without a mock salute at Arthur as if he were someone of importance. "Good day, babu, keep up the good work, *na*?" he called over his shoulder. But Arthur paid no heed. Instead, he hurried to the garbage heap to find some food scraps to lure the dog.

He couldn't remember the last time he'd searched in the food pile for discarded pieces of sustenance. When he was a boy, long before he'd ever heard of people like the Hintons, his family did it to survive. Such was the life of a farmer in the drought years. And though it was considered unclean to dig through rotten food and soiled scraps, his parents had done worse. Much worse.

When he first came here, he found himself so hungry from all the work the Hintons demanded of him that he would sometimes scrounge for anything left behind. He understood it was disagreeable, but only one other person knew—the *ayah*, who cared for the Hinton boys in their infancy—and also the tomcats that milled about the grounds before the monkeys took over. She, in her sun-bleached cotton sari, and he, covered in sweat from cooking over the heat, catching a glimpse of her bare feet, which never seemed to track dust into the house. The *ayah*—called Mary, the name given to her by the Hintons at her christening—had a habit of sneaking past him in the kitchen and scraping together any extra food. Mangled lime rinds, flavorless whites of melons; even the paper-thin cardamom shells were of value to her. And she would sit and eat the scraps on the back steps while the pale children slept upstairs, cats circling her legs as she cooed to them. One she loved so much, she gave it a name. What was it she said? "Moti! Moti!"

Yes, that was it. Pearl. A pearl in the dark and dust, a treasure. A promise. As he walked back to the dog, he whispered the name. "Moti?" he said as he approached the dog and dropped the food scraps he'd scavenged on the ground beside her. She did not pick up her head, but he decided on the name anyway. It was that or nothing.

It was silly to think, but he could swear Moti had the same tamarind eyes as Mary. There was a softness to them that reminded him of her, but more than that, it was the languid way the dog was ignoring him now as she pilfered through the scraps that took him back to that day, to that life.

He couldn't admit it to himself then, but he had felt something for her. It wasn't so much love as it was scarcity, the two of them alone in the house when the family was away on some missionary business or other. It was in those days that he first felt the tug of matrimony, the sense that his unhurried life should be heading toward something more . . . reproductive. But Mary hadn't ever seemed responsive. And after what the messenger boy had said to him that morning, it occurred to him now that perhaps she, too, had seen him as a babu, nothing more than a servant to the Westerners. But wasn't she the same? He put a hand out to Moti, and she lapped up the day-old crumbs he held. No—Mary wasn't the same. She had escaped this.

The discarded bits of *roti* were like a feast to the bone-thin stray. She vanished them from Arthur's hands in one lick, then whined for more. Her pallid tongue quivered as she panted in the growing heat of the day. He knew that dogs didn't mean to smile, not really, but he preferred to think of her breathless grin as intentional. Smiles meant just for him didn't come often, so he took them from whomever he could. And from the outline of her ribs pressing out through her dusty, white coat, it didn't look like food came her way much, either.

It did occur to Arthur how singularly pathetic it was that he had befriended a pariah dog. They were numerous, bothersome, filthy— he knew that. If people didn't ignore them, most actively avoided them. But he couldn't explain the fact that this dog, through her own ability, had found him here. She hadn't followed him home, so how had she known to chase the messenger boy? Was it chance? His old superstitions clamored in his heart. What fortune could this dog bring him?

At that moment, the wind shifted and the dog sniffed the air for something that had wafted their way, something his human nose was too inadequate to pick up. It could have been the gunpowder from the Afghans and their target practice or the tallow balm that Arthur had seen the judge rub on his heat-swollen legs last night. Or something else entirely. The dog's nose twitched as if of its own accord, inching forward in the direction the scent came, and then she flattened her ears and narrowed her eyes. And then Arthur smelled it, too—something he hadn't smelled in years.

The memory, years ago when Arthur met the burra sahib for the first time, flitted into his mind. The boys were still in their infancy, and memsahib had looked as though Christ himself had showed up on her doorstep when Mr. Hinton had brought the judge home from Howrah Station. Arthur was tasked with carrying his bags up to the guest room and hanging his collared shirts and trousers on the wooden rod they had fashioned as a kind of wardrobe. But when he went to open the trunk, the lid sprang open with dozens and dozens of frogs.

After much shrieking from Arthur and searching about the room for every last one, the judge explained to him as a father tells a child of the world that the frogs were a delicacy from Sikkim, where the judge had just been stationed, and Arthur was to cut off their legs and fry them in ghee as a treat for everyone. Except he hadn't explained to Arthur how to do it. So, Arthur had found a stone and bashed the head of every single frog, which had churned his stomach so much that he decided to fry them whole all at once rather than handle the dead and slimy bodies to delicately skin and sever the legs of each one. The smell of the frogs in the ghee had been unlike anything he'd ever smelled before, sour and musty at the same time, mixed with the heaviness of the ghee. And no one had eaten them, so it had all been for nothing.

Now, years later, it appeared Mrs. Hinton was taking it upon herself to cook them and so please the judge. Arthur smirked at the thought—it was fitting that the way to the burra sahib's heart was through frog legs. Arthur half suspected it wasn't the frog legs themselves the judge liked but the barefaced devotion Mrs. Hinton showed in cooking them. She never once made them for anyone else.

Arthur guessed she must have been too preoccupied with the task to give him any duties, as she usually did each morning in this house of never-ending chores. But as it was, his afternoon was free, and he didn't want to stick around to see how her cooking attempt came out. Musing about the endless ways he could spend a free day, he didn't realize Moti had left him until she was beyond the trees and out on the open lawn, following her nose to the cookhouse.

"Moti!" Arthur shouted, but the word was snatched out of the air by the slap of a rifle shot. For a terrible moment, the air seemed to quiver around her body, frozen in her tracks. Then the dog jerked back around and tucked her tail, ran past Arthur, and disappeared into the brush. She was nothing more than a blur, and Arthur could only guess by the lack of blood that she hadn't been hit. He turned his wild eyes back to the soldiers, who were conducting their practice against the cans as if nothing were wrong. It was possible they hadn't seen the dog at all. He let out a breath. This was good. Moti would be afraid of this place. It was better that she not come around here.

He rounded the trees and was surprised to see that the judge himself stood at the mark with his howdah pistol, intended for big game hunting, gripped in his meaty hand. There came a blast, a wisp of smoke, the ghee tin clattering to the ground.

"Sharp shot, Uncle Ellis!" Will said. The boys stood some distance back from the judge, providing a respectful but captivated audience.

The burra sahib cocked the pistol and took aim again, paused, then lowered it. "John," he called without looking behind him. "Step up."

John approached, not needing to be told a second time. The judge turned to him.

"Your father ever teach you to shoot?"

"No."

"Not even on hunts? What do you use?"

"A bow."

"A bow!"

"But he made it himself," Gene piped up.

"Christ, you don't have to live like that. This is the jungle; you ought to keep a pistol around or at least know how to shoot one. Here. Left-handed, right? Just like me." He took John's hand and curled it around the handle, raising it up and level with the tins. "Stagger your feet and use your arm to line up your sight. That's it. Grip it tightly now."

For a few beats, Arthur thought the boy wouldn't fire the pistol. He held his breath all the same, and then—*blast!* An echoing crack split the wooden bar to pieces, sending the ghee tins flying, clattering horribly to a pile in the dust.

"Christ! Well, you hit something at least." The judge, sounding satisfied, took the pistol from John and locked the safety in place.

John grinned. "I meant to do that."

"Well, now the afternoon's shot. Ha!" The judge holstered the pistol and clapped the dust off his hands, then straightened his jacket. "Just as well. Can't stand this heat; I think I'll stay inside."

"It's hardly hot," Will said. "And we wanted to show you the ponds today. Up for a hike?"

The judge didn't look interested but raised a brow. "How long's it going to take?"

"An hour," Will said.

"That's all?"

"Yes, and we can go now, before it gets hot," Lee said. "Come on, Uncle Ellis, it's nice this time of day."

Arthur shook his head and kept walking until he was on the far side of his little hut, out of sight and in the shade. He took a *bidi* out of his pocket and found the matchbox he kept hidden behind the stones in the wall. He lit it, took one drag, and leaned back, closing his eyes and melting into the cool stones.

Smoking was his one constant sin. Mr. Hinton said the Lord condemned it. Arthur wondered if that was really what the Bible said, but still, he didn't let anyone know.

He tried to make sense of the history, of where the judge fit in the family. He knew they weren't related, and the boys only called him *uncle* because they didn't have any other people in this country to call family. Over the years, he'd pieced together enough tidbits from Mrs. Hinton's praising and reminiscing to figure out that they'd known the burra sahib ever since they'd arrived in India, in that first little town where the Hooghly met the Bay of Bengal, before any of the boys had been born and before they'd even had their first convert. But he'd always wondered how the judge had ever found them in the first place and why he'd saved a couple of missionaries from the lowland muck. It was clear that the judge cared for them. He'd brought many gifts to Mrs. Hinton and the boys over the years: finery like pewter trays, china vases, and new leather loafers that gathered dust and dirt after only a day. Arthur couldn't help but shake his head. What was the point of having such fine things in India?

He looked up through the leaves, the trees swaying in the breeze, and watched the smoke rise up to meet them, then spiral down with the streaming sunlight. He took the *bidi* to his lips, eyes unfocused in his bliss. He blinked several times before he began to register a faint movement among the trees. Not Moti, something larger—out there, just beyond his sight, blending with the dappled sunlight. Maybe just shadows of branches on the ground. He squinted, trying to make it out. Probably nothing, but last week he'd seen some men loitering around. They hadn't been trouble, but they hadn't been friendly either. He tried to recall their haggard faces, the wide eyes and bony frames, bonier than even himself. He had tried to approach them, but they'd moved off into the shadows by the time he made it out there. Maybe this time he should keep his distance. Still, he couldn't be sure what he was seeing in the first place. He took a step forward. A twig snapped behind him.

"Arthur?"

He jumped, whipping the *bidi* out of his mouth and hiding it behind his back as he swiveled toward the voice. Gene stood there with his topi on.

"Yes, sahib?" Arthur said. He squashed the *bidi* out against the stone behind him and instantly regretted the loss, the mangled bits of tobacco and temburni leaf falling through his fingers.

"Did you see something?"

"Out there? No, sahib. Only a monkey. I think." He kept his shaking hands hidden behind his back. Did Gene see the dog this morning? Or did it even matter if he did? To people like the Hintons, the pariah dogs were invisible, like gnats and other pests.

Gene scratched his leg and looked down at the ground. "Mother says you have to come with us on the hike. Uncle Ellis doesn't want to take his guards."

"The burra sahib is coming?" Arthur said.

"Yes."

Arthur didn't move. Neither did Gene. They stood there until Gene looked away, toward the forest.

"I like it here too," Gene said. He removed his topi and hugged it to his chest. "You know I won't tell anyone."

Arthur brushed the mangled *bidi* bits off his fingers. "I know you won't, sahib," he said.

The boy still lingered, as if he wanted to say something. Arthur began to feel uneasy; the longer he stayed, the more likely one of his brothers might come by. But the next instant, Gene's face broke into a grin. Arthur smiled back as the boy skittered off. Still, he worried if anyone else knew. He took one last look at the forest. There were times when he'd only been scared of what moved in the wild in the dark of the night. But during the day, the forest was like any other part of India, a place for living things to exist.

■■■

Gene had never expected the judge to say yes, but here they were, hiking in a line through the jungle. The guards had stood on the edge of the trail as they walked past, their unmoving faces not betraying whether letting the judge go without them was a foolish idea or nothing to worry about. With the pistol hanging from the judge's waist, Gene didn't think it was so dangerous. No one talked, and in a way it was good because that meant no one was complaining. They shuffled along the path, weaving deeper into the woods until they came upon the pools. Less than an hour's walk, but it was enough to make them sweaty and ready for a rest. The sun sparkled on the water and invited them to wade in. Many times, Gene had seen villagers carrying bundles of laundry along the path on the way to the pools, and he was tempted to take his own shirt off and soak it in the water. He settled for dipping his toes.

Gene was just peeling off his socks when Uncle Ellis cleared his throat, inhaled sharply, and said, "You know what I really want? A long nap on the verandah. All afternoon."

"But Uncle Ellis, you haven't seen—"

"It's too hot and I'm tired," he snapped. Strands of thinning hair reached after his pith helmet as he pulled it off. He wiped away the sweat from his forehead and put it on again.

"I thought you said he liked hiking," Gene whispered to Lee.

"He did."

"Damn it all!" The judge tore off his holster and thrust it at Arthur, who clutched it to his chest instinctually. Then, realizing what it was, he held it away, unsure of what to do. When the judge didn't take it back, Arthur bowed his head.

"You hold it. Even though the rest of you Indians want to kill us, you—you don't even know how to use one, do you?" Even so, the judge checked the safety. "*Precaution.* Ha! It's a ball and chain, is what it is." The judge stopped and looked at the boys, aware of their silence.

"Uncle Ellis," Lee said, "is everything . . . all right?"

The judge exhaled and bent over his knees. With his head down, he said, "Yes, my boy. I'm just tired." When he lifted his head up again, his previous scowl was rearranged into a sweaty smile.

Was that all? Just tired? Gene wanted to laugh. What an obvious lie—words to make them believe that all was well, that he was in control—but he wasn't fooling anyone, not even John, who had one eyebrow raised and arms crossed.

"What is it really, Uncle Ellis?" John said.

The scowl again. "I told you, it's a terrible day for a hike."

"That's not what you used to say," Lee said quietly. "You used to tell us there's no such thing as a terrible day for anything."

Gene squinted at the water. His socks were moist with sweat. One hung halfway off his foot like a deflated balloon. He yearned for the clear water, but the judge had already turned back down the path, the overgrowth swallowing him up.

"Keep up, boys!" he called. "There's plenty of jungle to sod through, and I've got enough mud on my soles to leave elephant footprints!"

"I don't know what's gotten into him," John said.

"There's not really much else to show him, anyway," said Will. He took a few steps forward. "Let's go, Arthur! Are you still there?"

"Yes, sahib!" came a pip from the back. The ferns were high enough to obscure the servant's figure. As the temperature climbed, the path stayed damp, shielded from the sun by the lush canopy.

"You said the people do their washing here? Pah. Just imagine the natives walking all that way for a chore," the judge called back to the boys. "The path is so muddy, if you dropped anything on the way home, you'd have to go back and do it all again." He seemed to be speaking to Arthur, although he did not turn his head to acknowledge him.

Arthur made the trip himself from time to time, at night, washing his clothing and then himself before walking back to the Big House naked, his wet garments draped around his neck, his body exposed only to the ferns.

"It's either that or sloshing pails of spring water back to the house. Far more burdensome to do that than to carry a bundle of clothes," said Lee.

"No. The mud in India is the worst. There's nothing like it. If you get a speck on your nice trousers, you can forget about ever wearing them again. It's already all over this pair!"

Gene frowned at the mud-splattered hems of the judge's pants. Everyone else was wearing shorts. "The judge is quite worked up about trousers. Don't you find it odd?" he whispered to his brothers.

"He's certainly got his in a bunch," Will said. The boys sniggered.

"All I'm saying is that there are things I have to worry about in India that I never needed to in England," the judge said. "Every day, I listen to these people's troubles, sort out the truth behind the lies, the flattery, the general stupidity of whatever these cases are invariably about, and get no gratitude for it. I want to come home and put my legs up on a good English-made chaise, not a bloody charpoy that could snap at any moment! Do you think I want to worry about my trousers being muddied by the washman, or a python finding its way into my bed, or the monsoons flooding the streets, or . . ."

Gene had never heard anyone complain so much in one breath, and as he went on, the judge's grumbles blended with the sounds of the jungle. Gene hung back, pausing on the trail to catch his breath. He didn't realize Arthur was following so close behind until the servant bumped into Gene's back, causing him to stumble.

"Sahib! I am sorry, sir, very sorry, sir." Arthur grasped Gene's shoulder to help right him, but Gene shrugged him off.

"It's all right, Arthur. You don't have to be like that with *me*," Gene said. "It was my fault."

"Of course, sir." Arthur put both his hands on the holster again.

"You can put it on, you know. It'd be more comfortable to carry."

Arthur stared again at the pistol like it was something he would much rather not be touching.

"Oh, all right, give it to me, then."

"No, it is my duty, sahib." Arthur pulled the holster around his waist and tightened it as much as he could, but it was still too large, and he had to keep holding it up. "Please carry on, sahib."

Down the path, the judge's voice droned angrily as ever. Gene wanted to turn around and go back to the pond, but it was only him and Arthur, and he didn't want the others to think they'd gotten lost. So he trekked on and began to hum to himself, brushing his fingers against the leaves and branches. His mind began to wander. What must it have been like centuries ago to walk through forests undiscovered? Were the trees twice as tall? Did flowers bloom longer? After a while, he noticed a humming coming from behind him. He smiled.

His brothers were still a ways up the trail, but they had stopped, standing still and looking off the path. As he came within earshot, Will turned to him. "Shh! Don't move." Gene turned and scanned the brush, but all he could see was dappled light and disjointed shadow, free-roaming vines and branches rustling in the breeze.

"Pistol." The judge held out his hand, his gaze still forward.

Arthur pushed past him, and Gene searched higher into the trees, hoping to spot the bird. A pheasant for supper from Uncle Ellis— that would be something. Maybe he did feel remorse for skipping all those dinners after all.

Arthur placed the pistol in the judge's hand and stepped back, bowing his head.

"Should have brought the rifle," Ellis said, though it was unclear if he was blaming Arthur or himself. He cocked the pistol and took aim, one-handed, legs planted firm. The barrel did not point very far up into the branches but only halfway or so up a tree, and still Gene couldn't see what he was aiming at. The jungle was too dense, too many colors to make sense of. He looked back at the judge. His finger was wrapped around the trigger, ready to pull. Everyone was silent, his brothers still. Gene focused on the pistol, small in the judge's hand, but all too large in the jungle. Beyond, Arthur stood behind the judge's other shoulder, looking pained, his eyes screwed almost shut. But the next instant they were wide open. A sudden movement in the trees. Arthur shot his hand out and grasped the judge's shoulder just as the gun went off. And there in the tree, Gene saw it now, not a bird at all but a leopard, falling as if in slow motion from its branch. But when it hit the ground, it didn't lie still as Gene had expected. It scrambled at first toward them, confused, alive, then changed course and tore away through the brush. Its pounding footsteps faded away in seconds, the jungle rearranging itself, fitting back together as if nothing had happened. There remained only the boys petrified, the servant terrified, and the judge smoldering.

"Idiot!" Ellis shouted, throwing Arthur's hand off. "I could have had its skin in my study!"

Arthur snapped straight like a jackknife and lowered his head, eyes to his naked feet. With a loathing glance, the judge snatched the holster out of Arthur's hand and fastened it around himself. He stuffed the pistol into its holder and stalked down the path home. But the boys lingered, curious to see the scratches on the tree trunk and footprints in the dirt. As they approached the tree, Gene turned back and saw that Arthur remained where he was, his eyes still on his dirtied feet. The sound of frogs in the streams and birds in the canopy began to retake the silence, but Arthur kept standing there, still and slight. Gene felt the weight of the humid air on his skin and sensed that he ought to not look anymore. Single file, the boys passed Arthur, Gene last.

"I am sorry," Arthur muttered. "It was not harming us . . ."

Gene stopped. He looked into Arthur's face, but the servant wouldn't meet his eyes. It felt strange to Gene that someone sought his forgiveness. He did not feel it was his to give, and so did not respond. He hurried along down the path, catching up to his brothers. They walked in silence, and Gene did not know what to say. No one was acknowledging that any excitement had occurred at all.

The jungle cover thinned away and a dense, low thicket remained between them and the house.

"Hideous statue," said the judge. "Want me to take her out for you? I need a new shooting target."

⬛⬛⬛

That night, under a ponderous sky, Arthur returned to the pools along the same trail they had all walked that afternoon. He couldn't remember the exact location the judge had shot the leopard; it had all been so sudden. But it had been right from this path, and he knew he would come to it. He tried to feel something, to sense a change in the jungle, but all felt how it had before. He realized that the leopard was still out here, too wounded to go very far after its initial frenzied escape. Uneager to let the thought fester into fear, he quickened his pace. He thought only of the water, the cool relief, the weightless feeling. In no time, he emerged from the trees and came to the pools, still and patient as though they had been waiting for him. Slowly he removed his clothes, hung them on a nearby branch, and fished a small pumice stone out of the pocket of his trousers. It was his usual custom to wash his clothing first and then his body, but on hard days, he found that his body could not wait to be cleansed back to its original state.

Arthur could not comprehend the short showers the *goras* took daily. They were so quickly in and quickly out, a few tosses of the bucket, as if cleaning one's skin and hair was the only thing bathing was for. Though he bathed only twice a week, he knew he was always cleaner than his employers. Just as any native, Arthur was accustomed to washing himself with the same scrupulousness as a monk cleaning a temple. He stepped tenderly along the hard stones that lined the pools, and climbing over the large rocks, he sank into a seated position on the edge, his feet anchored on the shallow bottom. As he rubbed the day's soreness away, he wondered if the leopard had been wounded. He hadn't seen blood, but he couldn't believe that any being in the way of the judge's gun could escape unscathed. He pressed his fingertips into the tight tendons of his feet, loosening them as he wiggled his toes to stretch them until they felt new again. When he was satisfied, he rose from the stones and strode farther into the pool until his body was submerged up to his torso, his tired limbs weighed down with hurt. He rubbed the pumice stone over his knees and his elbows and in between his hands until they felt smooth once more.

At last he continued farther into the deep until he could lean back and float, feet off the ground and eyes toward the heavens. The cool water lapped against his ears as the sounds of the jungle washed over him. All the sounds of India—the shrill chirping of the birds in the high canopy, the frenzied buzzing of the crickets in the elephant grass, the constant noise of the vibrating bazaar in town, the ever-flowing roads that led in and out of the city and connected the whole—all these leveled into a single note, low and rich and full, the steady hum of busy beings finding their peace at last. Arthur took it in, gazing upon the luminous sky, so full of stars. Around him, the pools glowed like molten silver poured from the moon.

He breathed in the diamond air and thought about the day. It had started innocently enough. It was too often that the sahib's way was not questioned aloud, but Arthur questioned it much, to himself. Why did they seem to always feel the need to show their power? Power is nothing if not quietly felt rather than loudly proclaimed. And guns were a necessary advantage in warfare, but an unnecessary hazard in everyday life. Had the burra sahib shot the leopard, a great and majestic animal would have been dispatched from this earth by a ball of lead smaller than its eyeball. Could anything be more unfair than that?

And what of the boys? They had so much malice for each other, for Gene especially, even though Gene was the only one who showed Arthur any kindness. The Padre Sahib gave sermons to all the natives about goodwill toward your fellow man, but the boys seemed to be exempt. Or was it Arthur who was the odd man out? The boys had lived in India their whole lives, same as Arthur, but it was a different place for them. For them, the world would be kind and attentive and full of possibility and adventure, and life would be long.

Arthur was not stupid. He knew what his territory was and what was not, where he held power and where he didn't, to whom he must obey and to whom he could be courteous through no obligation other than his own will. He understood that in the Big House, the burra sahib was superior to him. He had the pale skin and all the privileges that came with it. He had the large guest room in the house, had the right to make demands of Arthur, had the freedom to speak to whomever he pleased. He could let Arthur watch his hand linger on

Mrs. Hinton's waist and know he wouldn't say a damn thing. But here in the jungle, that all fell away. They walked the same path through the trees and came to the same pools and came back the same way, heard the same sounds and breathed the same air. Here in the jungle, Arthur was not a servant and Ellis was not a judge, and a leopard had every right to life as they did.

What was a judge worth anyway? Arthur wondered how Ellis came to be the one to pass sentences. He imagined him on a dark, wooden dais, in solemn robes, with that pistol in his hand, aiming it at the defendant as they hurriedly tried to explain themselves, and if they couldn't—*bang.*

Arthur lay on his back, his palms upward and legs outstretched as if to flatten against the sky. He felt the lightness of his being as he floated on the silent water. His skin did not know the caress of silk and his stomach did not know the warmth of fine drink, but his heart knew what true luxury was. Material wealth was for the few, but *this* grand show was for everyone. Would it be so bad to have someone to share it with?

He stretched a hand to the sky and closed his fist, imagining he could gather the stars in it. His thoughts turned to Neer and Neer's cousin Soni. Marrying had never been in Arthur's plans, and he didn't think it was even an option. But perhaps this opportunity was sent from the heavens. A chance at companionship, to grow a family before it was too late. He didn't dare think of love—that was something much too fine for his world, a thing of myth, of Radha Krishna. But it didn't have to be divine, this meeting with Soni. It could just be . . .

It could just be.

When his heavy bones felt light again, he knew that he was clean at last. Lowering his toes to touch the bottom of the pools, he walked renewed out of the water to retrieve his clothes from the branch.

He journeyed through the trees with nothing but moonlight on his skin. It was strange to think that this was the path toward his home. Long ago, when people still called him Arthin, he had known only the streets of Kharagpur—the little town across the river—and the opulence and austerity of the natural world was but a distant idea brought to the city in pieces, in the form of sal wood planks and indigo sold in the bazaar. How could he have once belonged anywhere else but this quiet paradise? He dreamed of a day when he could walk where and when he wished, to never again be the tool of someone else's life. But he should be grateful for the Hinton family. They treated him better than most sahibs would, he knew.

Perhaps it was the darkness or the excitement of the day that rattled his mind, but Arthur saw the leopard for a moment without seeing it, the eyes yellow, questioning, like something divine caught on earth. When he realized what it was, Arthur dropped to his knees, and in his nakedness, he begged silently for forgiveness, knowing that all the cleansing in the world could not wash away his guilt for not doing more, for not acting faster, for not thinking at all before handing the pistol over to a man like the burra sahib.

The leopard watched him, its gaze straight and unwavering. Only a few paces were between them. If the leopard decided to attack him, it would be fair. The more time passed, the more he willed it to happen, to right the balance that had been broken that day. They stayed like this, the supplicant and his king, until the leopard, seeming unaffected, stood and disappeared into the forest, but not before Arthur noticed a limp in its right front leg. So the judge hadn't missed.

Arthur remained a little while longer, feeling the cold of the coming morning and of the leopard's absence. Exhaling into the silence, he shouldered his garments once again and rose to his feet. Even in the Big House, he had never felt as small as he did now. He walked along the path again, down the gentle slope and out of the trees.

He found his way across the grounds and went straight into his hut on the edge of the forest. He did not see the dirt track or the tennis court, did not notice the dark figure who waited there, who watched him go inside and close the door, and who then stepped out into the moonlight and hurried away toward the village.

# CHAPTER 6

Gene lay awake, trying to piece together his memories of the leopard. His whole life, they had lived on the edge of the sal forest and he'd never seen one, and now that he had, there was no chance of sleep. It was without a doubt the most exciting thing that had ever happened here. Too often he had heard the stories of man-eaters prowling jungles all over India, be they tigers or leopards, and too often he had wished they lived closer to town for fear of an attack. And now they had seen one, so close, so alive, and Gene couldn't decide if it had made him less afraid or more.

The patter of rain grew stronger as the clouds broke. Gene's mosquito netting swayed with the gusts, and down in the wet grass the frogs babbled to each other. On most nights, it lulled him to sleep, but tonight it did the opposite.

A *tiktiki* scurried down from the ceiling and traversed the face of his netting, its tiny body a mere silhouette against the veil, its footsteps almost matching the rhythm of the raindrops on the porch eaves. Gene watched it for a while before slipping his left hand outside and extending a finger for it to climb aboard. It did, and Gene sat up to hold it in his palm. For such a small thing, it held a remarkable amount of energy as it scuttled up his arm. When it got to his shoulder, he transferred the curious creature to his other hand, and it hurried up again. They ran through this routine several times before Gene heard a sharp noise below, inside the house.

His brothers didn't stir. He held his breath and kept still, listening for it again. After a few seconds of silence, he couldn't shake the feeling that something had entered the house. He tried to remember the sound; what had it been? Not a crash, not an animal sound. Something more like a slap, a single thud, no reverberation, just a clean smack. Knowing he would never get back to sleep, he got to his feet and crept past his sleeping brothers and into the empty bedroom. As he maneuvered around the creaky floorboards and billowing netting, he felt the perverse hope of finding something dangerous waiting for him. It was his chance now, to rouse the family from their sleep with cries of victory against whatever was prowling in the house. He made his way through the dark to the corner by the door and groped around for the snake hook they kept there. Feeling the cool touch of the metal, he grasped it and held it close. The bedroom door was open, and a warm light glowed from downstairs. He stole through the empty room and out into the hallway, the gecko still in his closed hand.

As he crept down the stairs, voices drifted up from the sitting room, crests and troughs of a heated conversation. When he reached the bottom step, he realized that the voices were not intruders but his parents and the judge. He sank down on the steps, disappointed, the snake hook between his knees. For the first time, he realized how sore his muscles were from the adrenaline of the day. Relaxing his hand, he let the little gecko crawl between his fingers and up his arm again.

"So you were never there? Why would you lie to us, Ellis?"

"I didn't want to worry the boys," was the reply. "But I suppose the escort must have given away that something was up. But that's the thing—there's nothing *to* worry about. This is all just a precaution, and this business will all blow over. I'll return to Simla in a month or two, and all will be normal again."

"What do you mean?" Mrs. Hinton said. "What business is that?"

"Nothing, nothing."

Gene listened to the clinking of china as someone sipped their tea. The *tiktiki* hurried onto his other arm.

"Oh, come now, Ellis. You can't just turn up here the way you did and not give us an explanation. What on earth is going on?"

"I told you, it's nothing."

"Ellis!" said Mrs. Hinton. "I swear I will throw you out right this minute if you don't explain yourself. People will start asking questions soon! What do you think it looks like, soldiers surrounding the missionaries' house?"

"Oh, what does it matter now? It's done. And I don't care if it was the right thing to do. As if any Englishman there truly cares anymore about right or wrong. Who's going to stop you from having your way when you're the only one who's got the power? And frankly, that's the thing. I've realized that not only do I no longer care about these cases, but no one does. None of our kind, anyway."

"But *what* did you do?"

Gene held his breath. He heard no movements, no sips of tea. Even the rain seemed to lighten, waiting. The silence drew so long and empty, he wondered if they had all evaporated into thin air. Then the words came, low and weary.

"A man died in prison, awaiting trial. He was my case, and I made him wait. I wanted to make an example of him, that radical bastard. But I don't know, the prison guards got too enthusiastic, I guess."

Gene did not realize how tightly he had squeezed the gecko. Its tail swung frantically in the air, its only free body part.

"Oh, Ellis," Mrs. Hinton said. Gene had heard that tone before. "It's not your fault. Things happen like that sometimes. It's only part of your job."

"But that's it! I didn't care a thing for that man's life. It was all just a job. And now all the natives in Simla are after me. All I've ever done is try to help them." Gene heard a grunt, then the judge continued. "Oh, really, Hinton, don't give me that look. Don't act as if we're not the same. You tell these natives what they want, the one true God and eternal damnation, as if you're the one with all the answers! You pass out sentences just as much as I do. Except I don't cloud it in some false notion of charity and greater good."

"That's enough," Mr. Hinton said. "You need a holiday, is all."

"I need to retire. I'm old, look at me. Yes. Tomorrow I'll send word to Simla that I won't be coming back."

Gene relaxed his fingers. The gecko fell somewhere in his lap or on the steps at his feet; he couldn't see where.

"Nonsense," Mrs. Hinton said. "Let's just get some sleep. You'll think differently in the morning."

There seemed to be no argument left from Ellis, and as their footsteps neared the door, Gene realized that he had no time left to run back upstairs without being seen or heard. Jumping to his feet, he lost all hope of disappearing—the door swung open, and damning lamplight arrested his body.

"Gene!" Uncle Ellis said jovially. "I wouldn't think you'd be up at this hour. You've got some spunk. Couldn't get to sleep? Me neither, after today. But I'll try to get some now." He stepped out of the room and made for the stairs, then paused in front of Gene. "Ah, you've got one of those damn lizards on your shirt. Here, I'll get it for you." He gave the *tiktiki* a sharp flick of the finger, sending it into the dark corner of the hall. Patting Gene's shoulder, he carried on up the stairs.

Mrs. Hinton took the snake hook from Gene's hands and hurried him back up the stairs. "Gene? How long have you . . . ? You should be in bed. Don't you know what time it is?"

"I didn't hear anything—" he started.

"Sh! You'll wake your brothers." She pushed him into the bedroom and pulled the door shut.

Gene stood there, staring at the doorknob. His mother's footsteps faded away; the house quieted again. He swiveled on his heel and slipped back out onto the sleeping porch, his eyes adjusting to the darkness, picking his way past the bed frames and peeled-off socks on the floor. When he got to his bed, he gave his sheet a quick shake and climbed in. He didn't sleep for the rest of the night.

# CHAPTER 7

The next morning, the judge did not come down for breakfast or call for Arthur to bring him anything. Gene was sent up to check that all was well. He cracked the door and heard the rasping snore before he even saw the girth of the judge stretched beneath the sheet. Sunlight already splashed the entire room, but Gene let him sleep and left behind only a tray of naan and mango-sweetened water waiting on the nightstand.

Gene brooded about the house for the rest of the morning, trying to make sense of what he had heard last night. He stayed upstairs on the sleeping porch and looked past the lawn to the sal forest beyond. Though scattered and irregular like any wild thing, the thin trunks and the straightness of their architecture gave the illusion that they had been planted in rows. From the house, the forest did not appear dense or dark at all but in fact allowed ample sunlight through under the high branches. He had never thought of the forest as being anything other than welcoming, having hiked there with his father and brothers on many occasions. But now, in daylight, he felt last night's bravery wilting inside him.

"See anything?"

Gene jumped and turned to see John and Will in the doorway.

"The leopard's still out there, sis," Will continued. He walked over to where Gene stood and peered over the railing and down at the grass below. "You know, I bet it could climb up this."

Gene pushed past him and into the house, grabbed his shoes and topi, then hurried down the stairs. He sat on the bottom step to pull on the shoes, his fingers frantic, tangling the laces.

"We're going to reline the track today," Will said. "Mother doesn't seem to mind after what Ellis said about it. Want to come? You ought to train before the meet."

"No thanks," Gene said. "Where's Lee?"

"Last I saw, he was in the melon patch with Arthur," said John.

Gene left the house and made his way to the melon beds next to Arthur's hut. The servant's red cap bobbed up and down among the vines as he knelt and peeked under the leaves at the bloated cantaloupes nestled in the dirt. Lee stood over him, listening as Arthur reported the progress.

"Get your bike, Lee," Gene said.

Lee looked at him, startled. But rather than be angry, Lee appeared to be impressed that Gene was giving orders for once. "What are you talking about?" he said, but Gene didn't stop. He just looked back and raised his eyebrows, hoping they conveyed what he couldn't explain. Lee turned to Arthur and muttered an apology, then stepped over the rows to follow. They went to the shed to get the bikes as Arthur sat in the melon beds, pruning away the dying vines. It was only when they were out of earshot that Gene answered Lee's repeated questions about where they were going.

"To Howrah Station," he said.

"We can't go all the way to Howrah!" Lee cried. "That's an all-day ride! There's no way we'd make it back before dark, even if we left now."

Gene shook his head, unwilling to listen to reason. He wrenched the shed doors open and dragged out his bike, but Lee grabbed the handlebar.

"Hey!" Gene shouted. "Give it back!" He tugged it toward himself, but Lee held on. The bicycle wobbled between them, both grunting and struggling for the upper hand until Gene lost his grip and stumbled. The bike's momentum caught Lee by surprise. It fell on top of him, a tangle of spinning wheels and rusted framework.

"We're not going all the way to Howrah. If you're running away, I won't let you," Lee said through heavy breaths.

"Who said anything about running away?" Gene said, lifting the bike off his brother.

"Then why are you going?"

"I want to look at the papers." He thought how silly it sounded and mulled his next words over. "I think something's happened to Uncle Ellis."

"Well of course something's happened to him. You don't just show up with your own Afghan army if all is well." Lee pushed himself up and surveyed the dust on his backside.

"What do you think it is then?" Gene said.

"I don't know, but he certainly hasn't been in South Africa this whole time," Lee said.

"How do you know that?"

"We picked him up on the wrong platform. If he'd come from Bombay, he would have been on Platform 8. But we met him on Platform 1. Platform 1 serves lines to and from Simla."

Gene looked at him, amazed. "Why didn't you say anything before?"

"Oh, come on. You think he would have told us? He's hardly said a word to anyone this whole time. And I'd rather not ask just to hear another lie from him."

"Well, you could have told me. I would have asked him."

"No, you wouldn't."

Gene glared at his brother. But he was probably right. "Last night, I heard Uncle Ellis talking with Dad and Mother. He said something about sentencing a man to death—or a prisoner dying on his watch—I don't know. And now people are searching for him, like a criminal." He looked down at his hands, his dirty fingernails. "But if he's a judge, then why would he be in trouble?"

"And . . . you're going to Howrah to find out?"

"What would you do? Just ask him yourself, then?"

"No, but if I wanted to read the papers, I wouldn't go all the way to Cal. Let's just go down to the bizz and see what we can find."

"But what if that kind of news doesn't make it to Midnapore papers? We only get the big news here—like that fellow Gandhi and his Dandi march." He sighed and gazed into the distance toward the city. He could no longer deny how isolated they were, in their house among the sal trees.

"Midnapore is larger than you think. Let's see what we can find," Lee said. He fished his own bike from the shed and mounted it, nodding to Gene to go ahead. Somewhere in the yard, Gene could hear the hoots of John and Will as they raced each other around the track, and suddenly there was nothing he'd rather do than pedal as far as he could away from them. He led the way down the drive, the sound of rubber on gravel drowning out his brothers, except Lee of course, who stayed silent behind him. As they rolled past the frangipani trees, Gene caught sight of a lone figure coming up the drive. He slowed, dragging a foot in the gravel. Lee pulled up next to him, breathless.

"New boarder?" Gene said to him.

Lee shook his head. "Are you kidding? Look at her. She doesn't need help."

They pedaled toward the woman, close enough that Gene could make out her face. Indeed, she didn't fit the description of their usual boarders, whose dirty clothing could never quite obscure their bony limbs but instead looked as though it would slip off with any movement. She looked a healthy weight, her sari draping surely around her form. As they passed her, she gathered the fabric and drew it across her face, leaving only her eyes uncovered, piercing. She held Gene's gaze until he could not look back anymore, turning toward the road again.

"She must be lost," Lee said. "Maybe we should—"

"Come on," Gene said. He sped up, anxious to get to the bazaar before the morning papers were all sold.

# CHAPTER 8

**B**ack at the house, Arthur tended to the melon beds, running his fingers over the scaly cantaloupe skins and pressing to feel their ripeness. Their large leaves shaded them from the baking sun, and underneath, the soil stayed moist. He pinched the dirt between his fingers and rolled it back and forth until every grain and pebble dropped back to earth. Then he straightened up and faced the house, assessing its white cement walls stained from weather and years. One Afghan soldier kept watch at every corner, and two at the entry. Somehow, they seemed to match the Big House, as if its faded grandeur wasn't complete without tired guards to protect it.

Arthur scanned the edges of the forest for signs of Moti. He hadn't seen her since yesterday, when the soldiers' gunshots had sent her fleeing into the bramble. He wanted her to stay away, and yet he also wanted to know she was all right. He found himself inspecting the dirt when he walked now, looking for pawprints. But there was no trace of her.

He heard the footsteps first. They were softer and quicker than the guards', determined in their need to get somewhere. Suddenly, they stopped. He turned and saw the woman standing just up the road, looking not at him but at the house, at the top-corner window. He noticed her sandals first and tried to recall the last time he had seen an Indian woman without bare feet. Then he studied the outline of her slight body, visible through the thin silk of her sari. He had never seen a sari so light, so ethereal. She held the fine fabric over the bottom half of her face, but her eyes were visible. He approached a few paces and asked her in Bengali if she would like to come inside, and when she did not answer he repeated the invitation in English. At this, she looked away from the corner window of the house and acknowledged him. She bent her head, then straightened. "Yes, I would," she replied. Thickly accented English, Arthur noted, as he guided her toward the house.

But the two soldiers at the entrance moved to block their path. One stood tall with a rich curved mustache above his jet-black beard, while the other had remarkably light skin and mismatched eyes, one a mellow brown and the other striking green. Their wordless demeanors kept Arthur on edge.

"She is only a woman," Arthur said.

"It is memsahib who must give permission," the soldier with the green eye said.

"Then I shall get memsahib." Flustered, Arthur slipped past them and climbed the steps onto the verandah. He hurried around to the other side, where Mrs. Hinton lay dozing on a chaise longue under the porch eaves, close to the railing and just ever so slightly in the sun. Her hair, which she usually restrained in a bun, hung down the back of the chaise. One arm rested on a stack of cushions, loose and fluid like syrup poured over hotcakes.

Arthur straightened himself and cleared his throat. "Memsahib, a woman is here and wishes to come into the house."

Mrs. Hinton's eyes fluttered open. "Did she say what she wants?" she said.

"No, memsahib, but she is not from Bengal. She speaks with an accent. I do not recognize it."

Mrs. Hinton sat up with a sigh, pulled a handful of hairpins from the folds of her skirt, and began twisting her long locks into a low chignon. Then she rose and walked to the front of the house. There, the soldiers parted for her, and she came to stand a few paces in front of their new visitor.

"What is your name?" Mrs. Hinton said.

"Jaya, memsahib." The woman's voice sounded raspy and low—older than she looked.

With a hand on her hip, Mrs. Hinton looked her up and down. "That's a very fine sari, Jaya. You're not from the village. Have you come for a place to stay?"

The woman glanced up at the corner window again and then at the soldiers, who looked straight ahead and did not meet her gaze. Arthur noticed the dust on the hem of her sari.

When Jaya did not answer, Mrs. Hinton cleared her throat and said to Arthur, "She's clearly been traveling for some time. Show her inside, and I will bring her something to eat."

"Certainly," Arthur said. He gave an awkward nod to the woman, indicating for her to follow him. When she remained standing there, the soldier with the mustache stepped forward to take her arm. She jerked away and followed Arthur into the house. She walked with little steps that didn't make a sound. The soldier, expressionless, took up his post again.

Inside, Mrs. Hinton brought a tray of naan and mango-sweetened water to where the woman sat in the living room. Jaya sipped it once, then set it down and didn't pick it up again. The naan, too, remained untouched.

"Are you a Christian?" Mrs. Hinton asked, as she always did.

Jaya looked away and gave a minute shake of the head.

Mrs. Hinton sighed and leaned back into the sofa. "We don't like that. All the same, we will help you. What is it that you need? Food? A place to stay? Medicine? We can show you where to get these things."

The young woman did not answer. She sat stiffly on the couch, wary. Arthur stood by, watching her shiver even as the sweltering air wafted through the house from every window and entryway.

It wasn't unusual for visitors from the village to be guarded when asking for help. Shame was a common trait, but unlike the others who had come seeking help in the past, this woman did not seem embarrassed. Uncomfortable, perhaps, but Arthur saw nothing desperate or urgent in her. *Cold* was how he would have described her—not that anyone asked his opinion.

At last Mrs. Hinton leaned forward and whispered, "Are you pregnant?"

Jaya looked at Arthur, who lowered his head, suddenly acutely aware that he was a man. She nodded.

"She's going to be here a long time then," Mrs. Hinton said to Arthur. "She's not even showing."

The woman seemed to relax now, leaning back on the sofa and letting her clenched hands fall into her lap. Her eyes flicked around the room, pausing at the carven flute on the bookshelf and the photographs.

"We have an extra room." Mrs. Hinton examined the woman up and down, then continued. "People usually stay for just a few months, until they get back on their feet. We'll call a midwife when it's time, and you can come and go out of the house when you like, but don't go into the other bedrooms. And don't go upstairs. We have another guest staying with us, and you should try to stay out of his way as much as you can."

"Another guest."

"Yes, but not like you. He's a British judge visiting us from . . . well. It doesn't matter. He's visiting for, I don't know, another week or two. Should you ever need to, you must refer to him as 'burra sahib.' Well, you shouldn't need to."

When Jaya did not say anything, Mrs. Hinton called, "Arthur, ready the downstairs room. I'll draw a bath for her." She rose and stepped toward the door. "And one more thing, Jaya." Her voice was gentle and soft. "We would like you to come to the sermons with us. Every Sunday morning, we go to the church in town. My husband is the minister there. I think you'll find it may help you more than anything else."

With that, she left the room and Jaya behind on the couch, next to the tray of untouched naan. Arthur turned to leave as well, but the woman called out, "Wait!"

He stopped for her to speak, but she did not. Instead she seemed to think better of it and, bending her covered head, began smoothing out the peach silk of her sari.

Finding the words to try and help her, he said, "Memsahib is very kind, *na*? You should do as she says." Then, lowering his voice, he added, "Stay away from the burra sahib."

"What is he like?"

"He is not like any *ingraj* you have ever met."

She laughed, a little puff of breath in the humid air between them. She turned to gaze out the window, the warm sunlight highlighting her frown. "So strange, these guards. Do they ever leave?"

"I don't know," Arthur said, backing toward the door. "They go wherever he goes, *na*?"

He left then, his words echoing in his brain. After drawing a bath for Jaya, he straightened the downstairs room with a kind of giddiness that he had never felt for the other guests who had visited, and there had been many others before this woman. Wanting her to feel welcome, he went out into the melon beds, picked a ripened one, cut it into slices, and brought it to the room so it would be waiting for her. When the woman finished with her bath, he showed her to the bedroom, where she promptly made for the small charpoy in the corner, closed her eyes, and fell asleep on top of the blankets. It was his instinct as a servant to retreat and shut the door, but something about the way the sunlight from the window fell across her face made him linger. He could almost say she sparkled, her skin oily, healthy. If he had caught one of the boys sleeping in the sun, he'd have woken them to keep them from burning. But Indian people did not burn so easily.

# CHAPTER 9

Arthur saw his father's face everywhere. Here in the bazaar, among stalls wedged together like a mouth with too many teeth, Arthur liked to imagine bumping into him in the middle of doing his shopping for the Hintons. He could be any of these men—the ones that were tall and thin, a full head of graying hair all dusty and scraggly from the river breeze, with the blue khadi shirt he had been wearing the last time Arthur had seen him. It could happen so quickly, right here among the sacks of cardamom seeds and *arbi*. A tap on the shoulder, a moment of recognition, an apology for leaving that night when Arthur was just a boy. And he could ask every question he had ever thought of since his father disappeared. *Did you have no choice? Could I have helped? Did Ma know what you were going to do?*

It had taken him years to realize that his father had left for Arthur's sake, to make a better life for him. And it had taken even longer for Arthur not to blame him for what eventually happened. It had turned out all right for Arthur in the end. He'd found the Hintons—or, they had found him.

He watched the seller weigh his rice on the scale and wondered how many sons the man had. Again and again the man's weathered hands scooped more into the metal dish until it drew even with the other, then Arthur held out the empty ghee tin and watched as each grain disappeared into it. Money passed through hands, and then he shouldered the tin and used it to nudge aside the other customers, who scrambled to fill the space his body left. Though Saturdays were always busy, it seemed there were even more people than usual at the market today. The square seemed to swell with bodies, and the air hummed with an energy that set Arthur's skin tingling. He spotted a man passing out pamphlets to anyone who would take them, and Arthur was surprised to see many did; usually people ignored anyone offering anything but food or goods at the market. Before his eyes, the space packed more and more people. Arthur sighed through his nose in frustration—he wished that he could leave before whatever this event was, but Neer had told him to meet here.

That was the last of the memsahib's list, and he had finished the shopping with more time before the meeting with Neer and his cousin than he intended. Sometimes Arthur worried he spent too much time with the Hintons and was losing himself. He would never be like them, could never, and yet they were the people he surrounded himself with. He could hear Neer's voice: *Is that what you want for the rest of your life?*

He dropped the ghee tin in the shade of a spice stall and sat on it, watching the passersby. A woman, who could be his mother's age if she were still alive, met his eyes and grabbed two young girls—grand-daughters, most likely—tighter to her. Arthur straightened himself in response. He patted the dust off his shirt and smoothed his hair. But they had moved on to another stall, and Arthur peered around the shoppers to watch them. The girls were school age, with long, braided hair and pierced ears to highlight their youthful faces. They pointed at the things they wanted, and the grandmother smiled at them, granting their every wish. Arthur could tell from their dress that they were more well-to-do than most, and the leisurely way they browsed the goods made it obvious they did not have the desperate need to haggle every last anna. Arthur wondered where they got their wealth. A mother's good dowry? A hardworking father? Decades of money passed down, moving houses every generation to something bigger and better? Was that the normal trajectory of life? Arthur knew he should want this, too—it was the purpose of every man—and yet, he caught himself afraid. More people in his life meant more people depending on him.

His thoughts drifted to his father again. What would he do about this business with Neer and his cousin? Would he want Arthur to be married? He looked down at his hands and, tracing the wrinkles along his palm, dared to wonder something else: Was it too late for him? He squeezed his eyes and opened them again. What was he worrying so much for? Neer had said this would be a casual meeting. "Courting," he'd called it. He would just meet Soni and see what she was like, and if the worst thing that happened was he went home and never saw her again, well, then it would just be like life had never changed at all. So why was his heart pounding so much?

"Arthur!" Neer called out from the crowd of shoppers. He looked flustered, sweaty, but his face alighted at the sight of Arthur. He held a small, wrapped box, which he thrust into Arthur's hands.

"What's this?" Arthur said, standing up from the ghee tin.

"Sweets to give to Soni," Neer said. "See, I knew you wouldn't bring her anything."

Arthur squeezed the box to his stomach and hoped he hadn't offended Neer. He was about to ask why he would give a box of sweets to the daughter of sweets sellers, but his friend had moved on and was looking over Arthur's clothing with a frown.

"Is this your Sunday best?" he said.

Arthur glanced at the other people in the bazaar. "I'm no worse looking than most people here doing their shopping," he said.

"But this is my cousin and her—never mind, this will have to do."

"Where is she?" Arthur asked.

"She's waiting at home, come on."

"I am going to her home? I thought you said we will meet in the bazaar."

"No, I said *I* would meet you in the bazaar. Come, I will take you to her."

"But my things," Arthur said, gesturing at the sacks of vegetables and spices.

Neer sighed and lifted the largest one. "You had to tack on the shopping as well?"

"Memsahib doesn't just let me leave in the middle of the day, unless for shopping," Arthur felt his face grow hot. He hadn't planned on having to defend himself.

"OK. Just . . . let me take all this. You take the sweets. And try to smile, *na*? Girls like that."

He led Arthur down narrow side streets, ducking under clotheslines and dodging bamboo fishing cages, the smell of burning paddy husk permeating the air around every corner. In a few minutes, they stopped at a long courtyard, the entrance to which was so small and unadorned, Arthur might have passed it altogether. The walls were plain; he wondered if he'd even remember this place should he ever return.

"I'll just go up and get her," Neer said. He dropped the sacks against a wall and disappeared into a darkened stairwell. Arthur listened to his footsteps recede.

He didn't know what to do with himself. He looked down at the box of sweets as if it could reassure him that this was all right. Instead, he felt absurdly intimidated—the sweets were more presentable than he was. He took a deep breath and looked around the courtyard. He was surprised to find it wasn't empty at all. A pile of hay sat in one corner, where a pair of goats slept to escape the midday heat. They had the right idea; the walls were just high enough to keep the courtyard cool. He took a few steps around, noting the dead marigolds strewn here and there. He nudged a cluster with his foot and revealed etchings in the dried clay floor, an egret and mangrove tree, a moon— or perhaps a sun?—shining over them. Though footsteps and debris had smudged their edges, Arthur could still tell they were done with remarkable skill.

On the opposite side was a cluster of earthen pitchers and a damp spot in the dirt where Arthur guessed the family did the washing. His eyes followed the well-trodden path from the gate to the stairwell and tried to estimate how many family members lived here.

Arthur looked up and was surprised to see a group of children peering over the walls from the rooftops. They didn't look away when he spotted them. Instead, they grew bolder in their curiosity, whispering and giggling to each other. Arthur was about to pay them no heed, except a pair of faces in an upper window caught his eye. They were older than he was, and it seemed they regarded him not so much as an oddity, like the children probably did, but in the way one might inspect an ox at the market.

Arthur backed away, step by step, until he felt the cool wall against his back. He wished he could melt into the clay, entangle himself in the dead vines. He was sweating now and cursing Neer in his mind. What had he walked into? He looked down at his feet and had the mind to walk away right then when he noticed something. Another etching, a perfect lotus flower there in the hardened earth beneath his feet. It was so small and faint, he might never have spotted it at all had he not been waiting in this courtyard with nothing to do. He stepped to the side and took a few seconds to comprehend what his eyes were seeing. The flower was one of dozens, all etched in a circle as some sort of frame for what was at the center, a woman's face, round like the moon, with a straight yet delicate nose and deep, long brows. The lips were full and symmetrical, and unlike the rest of the etchings, which showed signs of smudging and trampling from footsteps unaware, the lines of the lips seemed fresh, as if just done recently. It was evident they had been made with great care.

Arthur wanted to kneel lower to examine the work more closely. But then his friend ducked back into the courtyard, a sheepish grin on his face. Neer turned around and reached a hand back into the shadowed stairwell, and a small, bangled hand settled in his palm. He helped the woman down the last of the steps, and all the while Arthur just watched without trying to look too irritated at this less than casual setup.

"Soni-Bai, this is my friend, Arthur." Neer nudged her forward.

Her simple undyed sari was draped over her head, and she held one edge over the lower half of her face. She cast her gaze to the ground as she bowed to Arthur, who had the urge to stop her, he felt so foolish. Instead, he pressed his palms together and said, "*Namaskar.*"

They stood an awkward distance apart, each not knowing what to do next. From over Soni's shoulder, Neer was springing his eyebrows up and down at Arthur, clearly trying to tell him something.

"Oh!" Arthur took the box of sweets from under his armpit and held it out to her.

She took it with her free hand and bowed again, whispering, "*Dhanyavad.*" This time she chanced a glance upward, and Arthur felt nothing at the sight of her plain, brown eyes and the too-wide space between them.

Neer cleared his throat. "Soni-Bai, tell Arthur here what you were cooking, just now inside."

She bent her head and murmured something Arthur couldn't make out.

"*Muri!*" Neer said. His loud voice startled her, for Arthur noticed she took a tiny step backward. "See? She loves to cook, just like you."

"*Muri?*" Arthur echoed. His mind felt stupefied, and repeating the word was all he could think to say. He was still trying to work out what was happening.

"Yes. She makes them with dates and sesame. Delicious."

In fact, Arthur could pick out the scent of toasted sesame and burnt jaggery in the air. "Smells lovely," Arthur said.

A beat of silence. Arthur wondered why Neer would bring it up if they weren't going to offer him any. "You live here?" he said after a few seconds. Though it might have well been a rhetorical question.

"Yes," Neer answered again for Soni. "My cousins have both floors."

They all three looked at the upper windows as if it just occurred to them that they existed. The same faces were still watching as when Arthur first arrived. He took a deep breath and resented how nervous he was feeling in this moment, in this courtyard.

"They can afford it very comfortably. Their shop has done very well." Neer wobbled his head as he spoke. They both knew his cousins' sweets shop was just a cart they could pull anywhere from the bazaar to the ghats, but Arthur didn't know why Neer was calling it a shop now.

"Do you make garlands, Soni?" Arthur asked. He kept his voice soft, but he searched her face; that is, the part he could see of it.

"Pardon?" she said.

"The marigolds over there," Arthur nodded at the floor where he'd seen the dead flowers.

"Oh, yes." She pulled the sari closer around her. "Sometimes I gather the ones left behind after the flower market. It is just to pass the time."

"What? No," Neer laughed. "Only the freshest. We get the freshest; we can get the freshest flowers."

Soni shook her head. "No, it's really—"

"And do you draw?" Arthur continued. He had a hunch about the etchings in the ground and wanted to see if it was true.

Soni hesitated, glancing at Neer, but his expression was empty. "No," she said.

Arthur blinked. "No?" He had felt so sure, so satisfied in himself for making the connection.

"What would I draw with?" Soni murmured.

Arthur almost pointed at the drawing on the ground to catch her in her lie—he was so sure it was a lie—but he stopped himself. Why would she lie about drawing? He was being ridiculous. He took a deep breath, not knowing what else to say.

"Arthur works for the Padre Sahib. The Baptist family," Neer continued.

"You are Christian," Soni said. It wasn't a question. Everyone knew Arthur had been baptized.

"The Hintons have been very kind to me. But I still attend Durga Puja every year. Habit, I guess."

"They allow it?" Soni asked.

"They have never asked me about it."

Another silence. Soni's eyes watched him over her sari, and Arthur wanted to ask her to lower it, though he didn't know how to ask politely. Despite himself and the annoyance he had with Neer for tricking him into whatever this meeting was, he was curious about her.

They exchanged more pleasantries—rather, Neer did for the both of them. His friend remarked on how thick and long Soni's hair had gotten, and Arthur had to take his word for it, for it remained concealed under her sari. Neer talked about Arthur's hut at the edge of the Hintons' land as though it were something impressive. Soni showed polite interest, and Arthur did his best to do the same.

They talked long enough that the light changed in the courtyard. Arthur gave the excuse he needed to get home and start the cooking for supper. Soni bowed her head in farewell, and with her face still concealed, he couldn't tell if she was disappointed or relieved that the meeting was at a close. Nothing was said about meeting again, but that didn't mean they couldn't. Neer was the only one who showed any excitement that the meeting had happened at all.

Outside on the street, as Neer handed the shopping sacks to Arthur, Arthur stopped his friend and looked him in the eye. "How come I've never seen this cousin?"

"What are you talking about? Of course you must have seen her in all the years we've known each other."

"Never. I come by the sweets cart almost every time I'm at the bazaar. I see her parents—and don't think I didn't notice them watching from the windows, by the way—but never Soni."

Something flickered behind Neer's eyes, but he swallowed and straightened his back. "Soni-Bai isn't there every day, and only at the busiest hours to help her parents. Perhaps you have just never caught her at the right time." He must have noticed the doubt on Arthur's face, for he softened and said, "What's this all about?"

"What's it all about! I really believed you and that silly business about 'courting.' As if that were something people like me could do. Instead you brought me to her parents' house!"

"Well, you didn't meet them," Neer said caustically.

"They were there all the same, and I was looked at and inspected as if I were hanging in a market stall."

"Come now, it wasn't like that. And I can tell Soni-Bai liked you. Please come and see her again."

Arthur felt his heat dissipate at the look of his friend's pleading face. He reminded himself that this was his oldest friend, and perhaps he did know things about life and love that Arthur did not. Would it really be so bad to see Soni again, to run out whatever matchmaking plan Neer had concocted? He thought of the Hintons and the judge all waiting at home, and it became more agreeable to spend another day away from them and with Neer and his cousin. Still, he was indignant at his friend and the way he was acting. What was he hiding?

"I have to go." Arthur gathered his things and turned away, but he chanced another look at the upstairs windows. The faces that had been watching him were gone.

# CHAPTER 10

The Midnapore bazaar was a cacophony of the whole of India concentrated into a restricted space. The high yells of hawkers pierced Gene's ears, the low grumbling of hagglers answering in turn. The din reverberated off the cement of the British-built structures, softening as it reached the mud walls and roofs of villagers' huts. Malnourished horses waited outside the stalls, flies humming around festering sores on their backs. Iron pots clanked together as vendors cooked *gulab jamuns* and *jelabies*, the ghee swirling noxiously with the syrup. And folded into the center of it all was the pounding sound of rice-husking machines, their mechanical heartbeats pumping life from private chambers throughout the veiny network of streets.

The smell of mud mixed with cow dung stuck in the boys' clothes. Mr. Hinton always joked that if he went to the bazaar and didn't buy anything, he'd still come back with the smell of manure. Gene could usually tolerate it, sometimes not even notice it, but today all the smells and bodies and carts in the streets seemed exceptionally irritating to him. He flicked the bell on his handlebar several times, but its cheerful *ding ding!* made no headway. To his side, Lee had hopped off his bike and was walking it through the narrow street.

Gene got off his bike, too, and stepped over the shallow puddles of unidentifiable fluids. Damp hay marked where droppings lay. He smelled the bitter aroma of tea leaves, and up ahead he could see a tea stall, old and blackened with smoke, with a squatting shopkeeper straining tea through a dirty cloth next to his foot. The shopkeeper held the cup out to the boys as they passed by, and when they did not take it, the old man tipped it back and enjoyed it himself.

They flowed with the river of people until at last they reached the newsstand. At the dizzying sight of the newsprint, Gene realized with a sinking stomach that this was going to be harder than he'd thought. Mr. and Mrs. Hinton read the Bengali papers and often left them lying around the house, but Gene could not decipher the wayward tendrils of the characters the way his parents and even his brothers could. He couldn't read it, and he knew how to say only a few phrases. It hadn't mattered that much—their boarding school taught in English, and their parents knew enough Bengali to get them by without Gene ever needing to learn it himself. He wiped a bead of sweat from his temple and cursed himself that he had never picked it up even with his whole life spent here in Bengal.

He rummaged through the English papers instead, searching among the block letters for headlines of Simla. As he lost himself in the lines of text, the sounds around him melted together until he couldn't make out anything from the muddle streaming through his mind. It was the heat, too, that blurred his vision as he skimmed each page, his gaze snaking up and down and over the words. *Prince. Policeman. Punjab.* Frustrated, he flipped the page over and scanned the photographs, Gandhi taking up the spread, Nehru on the next. This ship arrived carrying this official; that train arrived carrying that actress. He paused on a photograph from New York, with long lines of men dressed in heavy, wool pants. One man looked at the camera, his worried face frowning up at Gene from the page.

Suddenly, a hiss came to his ear. "*Angrez!*"

Gene whirled around and straightened as he clutched his handlebars with both hands, crushing the newspaper around the curve of the metal. He scanned the crowd but did not see a face that conceivably matched the voice he had just heard. People were milling about the streets, pushing against each other and crowding around this stall and that. Everything looked ordinary.

He had never heard the word spoken to him, but he knew what it meant. Telling himself it was nothing, he looked away and straightened out the paper in his hand.

"I went through that one already," Lee said, grabbing it from him and placing it back on the stand. "Try this one."

"But it's today's," Gene said, grabbing it back.

At this, Lee sighed and threw his paper down in the dirt. Sweat showed under his armpits as he raised his arms in exasperation. "This is ridiculous," he said. "Why'd we come all this way again?"

"You didn't have to come," Gene shot back.

"Then why'd you ask me?"

At that moment, Gene hated Lee for his immovable sense of logic. There was no winning arguments with him because everything he did was right. He noticed the way Lee's bicycle leaned purposely against him, his hip jutted out just so to prop it up, leaving both hands free.

The overflowing crowd jammed every available outlet. A massive oxcart waited outside the tea stall of the old man—the whole street stopped for the driver's tea. It would be impossible to get through again, especially going against the current this time.

Lee read Gene's face. "We'll just get an officer to escort us," he said.

Gene peered as far as he could down the street, but not a single British topi bobbed over the heads of the people. It was the same in the opposite direction.

"There aren't any," he said. The crowd had taken on a strange sense of order, all faced the same way down the street away from them. He looked at the people straining over shoulders and heads to see what had drawn everyone's attention. In the distance he could see signs with Bengali words but couldn't make them out.

"Something's happening," Gene said.

"I don't think we should be here," Lee said.

The beating of the rice-husking machines sank under the roar of chanting voices and stomping feet. Gene climbed onto his bicycle pedals for a better view. As he craned his neck toward the source, the shrill *ding-ding!* of his bicycle bell startled him and he lost balance, stepping a foot down. An Indian boy as scrawny and dirty as the old tea seller stood in front of him, flicking the bell *ding! ding! ding!* and cackling at the sound.

Out of the crowd stepped two more boys, larger and older. One had long, ruffled hair covered in dust, a drooping dhoti too big for him, and a clear outline of his protruding sternum. The other had wide eyes and blinked often, almost continually; Gene did not like to look at them. One of them slapped the boy's hand and the incessant ringing stopped. The boy with the wide eyes walked around Gene's bike, reached out, and slid his hand over the padded, leather bike seat and the wicker basket on the front.

Gene hoped someone in the crowd would notice, but the wall of people paid no attention. He should have shouted something but did not.

The boy with the large eyes stopped and crossed his arms, blinking firmly at the bike. He glanced up at the other older boy and gave a quick nod. Suddenly he seized the handlebars and flung an elbow at Gene's head, striking him on the ear and knocking him to the ground. Gene could only watch as the other boy lunged for Lee's bike and shook it violently as Lee tried to hold on but failed.

"Hey!" Gene finally broke out, his voice barely audible over the chanting. "Help! Thieves!"

No one turned around. There was no end to the chanting. The younger boy gave his raspy cackle again, hunching over as if the spastic motion of laughing hurt him.

Lee reached out for the bike, caught in a ridiculous tug of war, holding tight to the back wheel as the Indian boy grasped the front and pulled. Then the Indian boy swung his fist into Lee's eye and sent him staggering to the ground. The other one stepped toward him and kicked him in the back.

"No!" Gene cried out. "He's the minister's son! *Padre Sahib ka beta!*"

Scrabbling through the dirt, he tugged at the thief's ankle. It was slippery with sweat, so he dug his nails into the skin. The boy whirled around and smacked him in the face. As he pulled back for another blow, a hand reached out from the crowd, grabbed the arm, and held it back. Next came a sack of potatoes swung forcefully into the boy's chest.

The cackling boy had stopped now and yelled something in Bengali. The thieves grabbed the bikes and pushed through the crowd until it swallowed them.

"Please, sahib," came a familiar voice.

"Arthur!" Gene almost cried. There his savior stood, braced against the current of people. Arthur extended a bony elbow toward Gene—all he could offer as his hands were full with bags.

"We've got to stop them!" Gene said, refusing the elbow.

Arthur dropped the sacks of groceries and knelt where Lee lay crumpled up. "Lee-sahib!"

Lee groaned and rolled onto his back. Gene saw for the first time his brother's swollen eye, the bruise deepening quickly, and the blood trickling from a gash in his eyebrow. Lee coughed into the swirling dust and grimaced. He reached to his back, and Gene placed his own hand on it, only to make Lee flinch away at the touch.

"He's not well," Gene said to Arthur. "We must get him home. Can you walk, Lee?"

Lee groaned again. Taking this for the answer, Gene slipped his arm around him and attempted to pull him up but lost his grip. Lee's body felt like a tub of bathwater, limbs wet with sweat sloshing this way and that. Arthur grabbed an arm and raised the boy to his feet. Gene marveled at the servant's strength. He picked up the fallen produce, and the three of them hobbled toward a side street.

"Wait," Lee panted after only a few steps.

"He can't walk," Gene said.

"No. The newspaper."

"What?"

"I dropped it in the dirt. We should pay for it. Or at least put it back."

Gene was speechless. He couldn't believe Lee wanted to do something so ridiculous when all he could think about was getting out of here. But he knew his brother.

"Arthur, please do it," Lee said.

The servant appeared torn between obeying and saving them. He took a deep breath, his face grim, and surveyed the crowd. "Sahib, we must go now. It is getting more dangerous."

"Please."

"Please, sahib!"

The crowd had started to move with considerable force, jostling around them in an unstoppable tide. If they stayed any longer, they would be trampled. A cluster of protesters with arms linked, bodies tight together, was coming their way. There was no time to argue. No longer caring about the newspaper, Gene tossed it aside and heaved his brother backward, reeling under his weight. His head was locked in the crook of Lee's elbow, and he couldn't turn to see where he was taking them. He could only look back at Arthur as he snatched the paper out of the dirt just as the linked protesters stepped between them. When they had passed, Arthur was no longer there.

The boys continued back toward the edge of the street, making their way through the crowd. With all the jostling, their pith helmets had fallen into the depths, but they carried on until they were backed up against a wall. Gene looked around the corner down a side alley. It was empty. Just a few more paces and they were out of it, washed up from the moving body of people.

Gene listened to the muffled sound of the chanting. Sinking against a wall, he wiped the sweat off his brow and flung it to the ground.

"Do you see Arthur coming back yet?" Lee said.

"No," Gene breathed. "How do you think he found us?"

"Dunno. But don't you get the feeling he's always looking after us?" Lee sounded calm despite the purple shadows seeping to the surface of his skin. Gene examined him closely. Even though they were streaked with dust, Lee's socks were still pulled up to his knees.

Gene didn't know how to answer. For as long as he could remember, Arthur was always just *there*, so much a part of their lives as the very house they lived in. But it never occurred to Gene that Arthur cared about them or thought of them as anything other than his employers. At least, it never occurred to him until the judge arrived.

They waited in the alley for hours. But as the sun sunk below the rooftops and Arthur still didn't appear, the small relief of being free from the rally—and escaping the thieves—began to fade. Gene shook Lee's shoulder to make sure he was still conscious.

"Mm?" Lee murmured, not opening his eyes.

"He's not coming back," Gene said. "We should move on. How are we going to get home?"

"We'll get a rickshaw."

"We have no money."

"People know us." Lee pushed himself up and blinked his good eye open. "They'll help us."

"Lee, look around. Do you see anyone?"

Gene looked down the empty street and saw the outline of a woman sweeping her porch, clearing her home after the storm of people. He watched her swaying figure as it moved back and forth, the *shook shook shook* of the broom like echoes of the chanting. But she was there for only a moment. Like an apparition, she disappeared around the bend, the sound of the sweeping following her.

"There's got to be someone here who will help us." Lee shifted and winced. "Start knocking on doors. Someone will answer."

"You'd better come with me. If they see your eye, they'll be more likely to help." Even as he said this, Gene thought of all the crippled beggars and orphans whom no one batted an eye at, whom even he had ignored. People were too skeptical or too embittered by the suffering in India to care about it at all—there was so much of it. How foolish of him to believe help would come so easily; who should care about two American boys who had never begged for anything in their lives, or slept on newspapers at the train station, or picked up half-eaten morsels from the gutter to ease their aching stomachs? After each unanswered knock, Gene wished more and more for Arthur to appear, even more than for his parents or for Uncle Ellis.

"Uncle Ellis!" His voice echoed off the closed door in front of them. "Did he leave this morning? Do you remember?"

"His car was still in the drive."

"But he could have left after us, right? Which way to the club? He could be there! He was in and out of that place the whole first week here. And remember that woman we saw? If she's a new guest, I bet he'll want to get away from her. And where would he go?"

"The club," Lee said. "But they'd never let us in."

"They will if we mention Uncle Ellis." Gene turned and faced back toward the route of the rally. The dirt lane was trampled with footprints, and everywhere scraps of paper littered the ground and scattered in the wind. Gene slung Lee's arm over his shoulder and pulled him a few steps forward, then reached down and plucked one of the papers out of the dirt. He folded it and stuffed it into his back pocket.

"I know you know where it is," Gene said. "Just tell me where to go."

■■■

The British Officers Club of Midnapore was barely a tenth the size or luxury of the one Gene had glimpsed in Calcutta, but its wide steps and pristine white-cement walls were still enough to intimidate him as they approached. Hobbling step by step under the weight of his brother, he made slow progress up the drive and wished that it were after dark so people wouldn't be around to stare. He knew he and his brother were out of place; he didn't need the curious faces of the valets and the departing guests to confirm it. He searched among the cars for the judge's, but they all looked the same. Continuing on, he kept his eyes on the murky light spilling from the windows and did not stop until he reached the entrance.

Two doormen in white kurtas and red pagris opened the doors for them, their faces registering no opinion whatsoever on the boys' appearances. Gene realized, for the first time, what a kindness it was to open doors for other people. He was greeted by the smell of tobacco mingled with perfume, a sickly combination that made his head ache. Straightaway he settled Lee on a couch in the foyer and checked that he was still breathing. He tried to open one of Lee's eyes to be sure someone was still there behind them, but Lee batted his hand away.

"Get up from there!"

A short, stout man at the front desk frowned at them. Gene managed a smile. "It's all right," he said. He regretted his American accent. Thinking it would be proper to shake the man's hand as his father would, he walked over, wiped his palm on his shorts, and extended it. The man blinked.

"You're not members," he stated with no sign of a question.

"No," Gene said, trying to peek through the glass doors into the parlor, but potted palms everywhere blocked the guests. "But if we could just step in there for a moment—"

"I can't allow you to do that. Members only. And get *him* off of there. Both of you are filthy."

Gene glared at the man. Was he new to India? Everyone knew there was always some degree of filth everywhere and on everyone. Even this man's shirt collar was dampened with sweat, and bits of gravel were scattered on the entry rug from the drive. But that wasn't the point.

"He's injured," Gene said, careful to keep his voice level. "There's been trouble in the bazaar. We came looking for our uncle. You know him. Everyone knows him. Mr. Ellis, the judge."

The man raised his eyebrows and glanced toward the parlor, then back at Gene. The sweat outline grew larger. He stepped around the desk. "One moment, please," he said. He disappeared into the parlor, and Gene rushed to its door. The room was long and lined with plush sofas and low tables laden with teacups steaming in the evening heat. Servants manned the punkahs, fanning the guests in a synchronized rhythm. Down toward the end, the man had come to a stop before a seated gentleman facing away. The man murmured something. The judge made no movement. The man bowed low and spoke again. This time, the judge started and, turning in his chair, looked at Gene. He fired off a remark at the man and in no time was out of his chair and striding toward the door. As he came closer, Gene couldn't help but notice how at home the judge looked here in the parlor of the club, the smoke swirling around him with each step, his small, blue eyes sparkling amid all the crystal and ladies' jewelry.

"Good God, what's happened to you?" the judge said, taking in Gene's dirtied clothes. Then he caught sight of Lee, who looked as though he'd roll off the cushions at any moment. "Bloody hell!"

"There was a riot," Gene said. "Some boys stole our bikes."

"Did you report this to the police?" the judge said. He pulled out his handkerchief and dabbed at Lee's brow, but the blood had dried. "Never mind. We'll call a doctor straightaway."

"No, it's all right," Lee insisted. "Nothing's broken, I don't think."

"That's it," said the judge. "You can't let a bunch of ruffians weaken you. Carry on like a man; very good, Lee." Even so, he pulled Lee to his feet and guided him to the door, getting dust all over his suit.

Outside, Gene made out a gleaming, black car waiting in the drive, headlights glowing through the dying daylight. He saw the red turban of an Afghan soldier in the driver's seat. He and the judge eased Lee into the back, and Gene slid in after. As the car roared to life and rolled down the road, Gene thought of the stolen bicycles and their pith helmets left behind. There was nothing to be done; he leaned against the door and shut his eyes. His legs stuck to the soft leather of the seats, the smoothest he had ever felt. He looked at the judge next to him, examining his evening suit with the finely tailored jacket and pressed shirt, white as the Himalayas. Gold cuff links peeked out from his sleeves. Though the judge was not exactly fat (despite the weight he'd put on), he commanded a huge presence within the cab. Gene never thought of him as someone who could keep a low profile.

Gene no longer wanted to know the truth about where Uncle Ellis had been before arriving in Midnapore. In fact, he thought, perhaps the judge hadn't been lying at all.

"They called us *Angrez*," he said to the judge. He glanced at the driver, who kept his eyes on the road.

"Who?" the judge said.

"I couldn't see. Someone in the crowd. But why would they call us that? *English*? We are American."

The car took a sharp turn around a corner and at last was out of the city, the silhouette of the hills rising before them against an orange, tiger-striped sky. The judge wound down the window, and the whapping sound of air pouring through the narrow slit filled Gene's ears. But he still heard the judge's answer.

"They don't care if you're American or British. You're white, is what matters."

# CHAPTER 11

Gene helped Uncle Ellis ease Lee from the car as soon as it pulled up to the Big House. When he realized that the judge could manage Lee's slight frame on his own, Gene ran ahead to the front door to open it for them. The incessant buzzing of the flies as they hovered around the porch light greeted him, swarming his ears as if sensing his exhaustion. It was all he could do to lift a hand and swat them away. He squinted at the porch light to which they returned, and despite how weak it was, it blinded him. *So glad to be home*, he thought.

There was a chill in the air, which Gene had not felt for what seemed like ages. He stuffed his hands in his pockets and braced against the breeze. There, still in his pocket, was the folded pamphlet from the rally. He pulled it out and tried to read it under the porch light, but there wasn't much to read. On the front was a large image of Gandhi, a thick *X* over it, and the Bengali words he could just make out: *No violence, no change.*

Soldiers marched past Gene to assist the judge. Gene stuffed the paper back into his pocket and prayed the soldiers hadn't seen it as he went inside, where Will and John sat at the dining table. Metal spikes stuck out between Will's lips as he hammered one through his running shoes. The metallic clangs echoed through the room. John's form slumped over on the table, head down between his folded arms. Mr. Hinton sat in the glow of a reading lamp, turning the ruffled pages of the Bible. He did not look up.

"Lee with you?" Will said through the spikes.

Gene took a shaky breath and started to think of how he could explain what had happened that day. But all that came out of his mouth was air, weightless and inadequate. He settled for a single nod.

It seemed to do the trick. Will grew serious and looked to the door, where Uncle Ellis and Lee filled the frame. His eyes widened. He spat the spikes out on the table. "Mother! They're home!" he called, then pushed his chair back and brushed past Gene. "Why didn't you say he was hurt?"

"Goodness!" came a gasp from the stairs. Mrs. Hinton flew to her son and, in her urgency, grabbed his face and examined it. Lee winced but stayed put, his one good eye barely open and blinking at her.

She examined him like a rare artifact. Lee had never been hurt before, not really. The more her fingers quivered over the bruises and dried blood, the more Gene's tiredness turned to worry. In the dim light of the club, Lee had looked a little better already, but now, in the harsh frame of his mother's hands, his face had never looked worse.

"That's a shiner coming on," Will said, cocking his head as if looking at the bruises from another angle would help.

"So? I've had one loads of times," John said. "You'll be fine, Lee." Still, his tone was not so assured.

"He says he's all right," Uncle Ellis said from the doorway as he struggled out of his smoking jacket.

"'All right!'" Mrs. Hinton cried. "What happened? Ellis, were you there?"

"Wish I had been. Bastards would've never gotten away."

"Some thieves stole our bikes," Gene murmured, finding his voice. "In the bazaar."

"But looks like Lee wouldn't let them go without a fight," the judge said. "And I say we still won't. I won't stand for this. They robbed you; they beat you. If they get away with this, who knows how much bolder they'll be next time."

"Next time! Oh, never mind. We've got to get him cleaned up. Where's Arthur?"

"He didn't come back by himself?" Gene said.

It was clear he had not, but no one answered him; they were too busy fussing over Lee. He looked out the windows half expecting Arthur to walk up at that moment, but night had fallen and all he could see was darkness.

■■■

It had taken Arthur a while to figure out that all those people in the bazaar were anti-Gandhi protestors. They had been so forthright in their yelling and marching, and Arthur felt that they'd tear him to pieces had he asked what it all was for. Shouldn't he know? Shouldn't any Indian-born know? He gathered from their animated faces and hoarse voices that they were livid. But Arthur still couldn't make sense of it. "Gandhi, Gandhi, what a dandy!" and other epithets were hurled at the white officers' quarters as they marched past. Arthur scooped up the boys' pith helmets and food purchases where they had fallen, then followed the march all the way down to the ghats of the Kangsabati River. A burly man, young and sparkling with well-organized rage, climbed on one of the pilings and started to shout, but Arthur was too far back to catch more than a few words. Civil disobedience was worthless; no change would come if the whole country still played by the Raj's rules. It wasn't enough to be against the British anymore; they were against Gandhi, too, and all his fruitless nonviolence. The hour was late, and something swifter must be done. The crowd of people all nodded their heads in rabid agreement, but Arthur was distracted. A trick of the light on the water had caught his eye, and he took a step down the ghats toward it.

And then, like a dream, the angry voices of the protestors diminished and were replaced by a far-off singing, and Arthur knew only he could hear it coming from down where the golden water lapped the steps. He could see them, too, in the sunlight flashing off the surface. There they were in the water, the Hintons, from that day years ago, when four brothers were only three, the pregnant womb of Mrs. Hinton just touching the surface, the bottom half of her body submerged as she reached a hand out to him. There was Mr. Hinton waiting in the lazy current, sleeves rolled up as if he weren't already wet. They were all singing in that slow but cheerful way, the same hymn they always sang at every baptism. *"There's power in the blood, power in the blood. Come to a cleansing of Calvary's tide . . ."* That was the moment that he waited, one more breath, before he was plunged into the gentle swell of the river.

He shut his eyes tight and held his breath, opening them again to the rally. What act of God had brought him back to this place? He could not shake the feeling of shame, the sense that he should not be here now, not with these protesters who wanted so much harm to come to people like the Hintons. He swallowed the tears that threatened to spring and knew he had to get home.

■■■

He walked the long way back in a daze, the boys' topis still in hand, piecing together all the time that had passed since his baptism. Even this road, the one he must have walked down a thousand times, seemed like something he had conjured out of a dream. It occurred to him then: Why did this place never feel like home?

Suddenly he felt something warm and wet at his fingertips. "Moti, not now," Arthur said. But she only nuzzled closer, trotting alongside him and pushing her head into his free hand for pets. Such barefaced devotion, the simple delight of dogs, was too much for Arthur to face right now. He snatched his hand away and gripped the topis close to his chest like a shield.

At this, she bounded ahead and snatched up a stick in her mouth, scampered back, and offered it to him to throw. When he didn't take it, she dropped it in the dirt as if it made no difference, then nipped his pant leg so sharply that he heard the fabric rip.

"Moti!" He stomped his foot like a child, like he'd seen Gene do at some indignity from his brothers, but he didn't care if he was being childish. It was too late for this. He was too tired. He picked up a rock, a large one the size of an orange, and yelled, "Just let me go *home*!"

On the last word, he threw it at her. She yelped as it hit her flank, the soft stretch of skin he had once rubbed with affection. The sound she made, the sound of shocked betrayal, echoed in the branches above as she fled through the forest. He walked on.

When the Big House loomed into view, he could just make out the soldiers keeping watch, visible there under the glow of the porch light, which had stayed on all night, every night, since the judge arrived. They stood at attention when they spied him coming up the road, then relaxed when they saw his face and let him slip past and into the house. Inside, the darkness covered all, but he knew the lay of the furniture in every room. He walked with ease through the hall to the stairway. He stacked the topis one inside the other and hung them on the banister post at the base of the stairs, then turned to leave.

There stood the outline of a woman in the hallway, the peach glow of her sari illuminated from the porch light outside. She blocked the way to both the front door and the door to the back porch, so he stood still, unsure what to do or where to go. He could see in the dark and was accustomed to it, night wanderer that he was, but he wondered if the woman could see him as well as he could see her. Could she make out his face or sense his fear? Was it even fear that he felt or excitement? She did not seem threatening, but he thought it was common sense to be cautious of anyone who came upon him in the night and blocked his escape.

"You know she waits for you," Jaya said. As she stepped closer, Arthur could smell cantaloupe on her breath.

"Memsahib?" Arthur said. A panic rose in his chest that he had done something wrong.

"That dog," she said.

At this, his chest sank. He shouldn't have lost his temper; she was just a dog. But that was it. "She's just a dog," he said, a hardness in his voice.

"You've been to the rally," she whispered.

He felt a tingling climb up his neck, an uncomfortable heat rise up to his ears. "No," he said, hardly able to hear his own voice. He cleared his throat. "Well, not really. I was just shopping in the bazaar, for you, but I got only the potatoes before it started. Oh no—I've left them!" He tried to steady himself as the sudden urge to knock her over and run out the door rushed over him. Why was he explaining himself? So what if he was at the rally? He stuck an arm out in the darkness, trying to feel for the wall beside him. "I just got swept up in it, sort of, taken away with them. The people, they were so determined."

He could see her downcast eyes through the dark and the slump of her shoulders. "I thought I had an ally in you," she said. "But I cannot call you a nationalist, then."

He dropped his arm to his side and tried to make sense of what she was saying. He was not used to anyone asking his opinion on any topic, and politics was certainly not the subject he wanted to begin with.

"Arthin," he whispered at last. "Call me Arthin."

And suddenly it occurred to him that he couldn't recall the last time anyone had said his true name out loud. It felt good to say it, to reacquaint himself with his old name. All at once, little memories flickered on and off through his mind, of his friends yelling "Arthin, Arthin! Jump in, Arthin!" from the river, of his father saying his name softly for the last time, of his mother calling him home.

Still, it hadn't been bad with the Hintons. He smiled, thinking of

waking up the first Christmas morning to see a little wrapped pack-
age on his doorstep, of helping Mr. Hinton carry two crates of newly
printed Bibles just arrived from Calcutta, of Mr. Hinton's gentle
hand on his head as he rose from the river, of the family standing on
the bank looking on, proud, in a way that no one had ever looked at
him before.

Arthur's thoughts returned to Jaya. Was *she* a nationalist? Why
was she asking him? How had she known he had been to the rally,
that there had even been a rally? He was aware again that she was
blocking his escape. He cursed himself for not being suspicious of
her before. But she seemed uninterested now and slumped against
the wall with her hands behind her back, opening up a way for him to
pass. He stepped forward, slowly so as not to make a sound. He was
almost clear of her when out of the darkness she reached out a hand
to grasp his. Her skin was hot. She pulled him closer and kissed him
on the cheek, then pulled back and looked him in the eyes. Yes, she
could see him just as well as he could see her, he was sure of it. As
quickly as she had caught him, she let him go again and ran down
the hall, so lightly that all he could hear was the swishing of her sari.

Arthur stayed where he was, dumbfounded, in the middle of the
hall. He had never had any female interaction even remotely like
that—he relinquished any lingering suspicions about her. She was
gentle; she was kind. Oh, that one little kiss had quelled all the ten-
sion in his limbs and mind. But now they had a secret, bound to come
out in some shameful way, and he looked around out of paranoia that
someone had seen them. But the top of the stairs was empty, as was
the living room and dining room, and the soldiers had not stirred
from their places on the porch.

He leaned against the wall and could feel the warmth of her body
still there, a little piece of herself she left behind. He inhaled the lingering scent of cantaloupe, let it fill him up to bursting. There on the
wood floor, in the gleam of the light, her half footprints remained,

just the balls of her feet and the toes, each one separated like individual planets orbiting a half moon. He could almost believe she was not of this world, that he had made her up somehow, because how could someone like her pay any attention to someone like him?

He shook his head, breaking the spell. She was too beautiful, too young to honestly think of him that way. And he, in his age and status, was meant for people more like . . . well, more like Soni. Plain, hardworking, meek. Willing to take a man graying in the temples and toiling in a house owned by other people. And his friend Neer was obviously working so hard to make this match for him, to bring some happiness and companionship in Arthur's life. Jaya, on the other hand, was a complete stranger. And with child! Arthur slapped his face for being so naive. She was simply looking for a man to provide for her and her child. Well, it wouldn't be him. Absolutely not. And yet, his body burned for her.

He exhaled, slow and steady, and stood there a while more, listening to the crooked ticking of the grandfather clock in the other room.

# CHAPTER 12

"**W**here did you say you found it?"

"In the hallway, on the floor."

It was early the next morning when Gene heard the voices from the sitting room as he crept downstairs on his way to the toilet. He stopped as soon as he heard the judge and John. No one else was awake. The day was just light enough to barely make out the steps on the staircase.

"I don't like the sound of it," the judge said. "Things are getting dangerous."

"I agree," John whispered. "But what should we do?"

"You can start by keeping an eye on your servant. And that Indian woman downstairs. This must have come from one of them."

So the woman hadn't been lost—she'd come for a place to stay. Gene slid down a few steps so the sitting room was in his view. He could make out the silhouettes of the judge and his brother. In the judge's hand was a slip of paper. Gene's eyes widened. The pamphlet, from the rally. It must have slipped out of his pocket.

"We've got to protect ourselves," John said.

"Correct." The judge put his enormous hands on his hips and, in doing so, pushed up the edge of his jacket to reveal his gun glinting at his side. "Between you and me, I've been waiting for this. It was only a matter of time that things would break."

At this point, Gene was bursting with his need for the toilet. But he couldn't go down the stairs without them hearing and putting together that he had heard everything. He felt a pang in his stomach, knowing that the judge suspected Arthur for the pamphlet. But he didn't have time to worry about that now. How was he going to get down the stairs?

"Gene?" his mother's voice came from beside him, and a gentle hand rested on his shoulder. "Goodness, you're up early. Just as well, we've got to get to the sermon."

"I know," Gene stammered. "I was just looking for my shoes."

The conversation downstairs had stopped. Gene felt safe enough to go down, his mother right behind him like they had just happened to wake up at this time. As he passed the sitting room, he stole a glance at John and the judge. But he could see nothing in the pre-dawn light except their darkened faces, gazing out the window.

■■■

An hour later, just after dawn, they left the house with everyone but Ellis and Jaya. It was no surprise to anyone that the judge wasn't getting out of bed that morning. Yet Gene couldn't help but ask his mother, "Why isn't the woman coming?"

Mrs. Hinton looked startled at the question. "Oh. She said she's feeling a bit sick this morning. It's normal for—well. It's all right."

As they shuffled down the rocky road, Gene took a hard look at the purple smudges around Lee's eye.

"I still think you should've stayed home," Gene said.

Lee shook his head. "We can't show that we're afraid," he answered, although Gene couldn't tell if he was talking to himself or not.

"So you are afraid?" Gene whispered.

"No."

"I don't think the thieves were from the village," Gene said. "You're just going to look strange. The villagers will be curious. You might even scare some of them."

Lee turned his head and gave a worried look. But it lasted only a moment; Lee set his lips in a line, determined to continue on. So down the road they went.

Mr. Hinton kept pace at the front, a Bible in his hand. Ants had torn up the edges and eaten right through to the center of paragraphs, but Mr. Hinton knew it front to back and brought it along out of habit. Sometimes he would open it, but Gene never saw him actually read from it. He had come to the conclusion that his father simply liked for the villagers to see him reading, even if he wasn't really.

The Hintons did not have a church; they had many places of worship. Every village that would welcome them was their church. Not for lack of funds did they find themselves without their own church but rather for lack of success. Almost from the start, the Hintons found that Hindus did not come to a church of their own accord, so they realized they would have to go to them. Their purpose as missionaries was to preach not to people who were already convinced of the power of Christ but to nonbelievers. And nonbelievers were all around them, as the Bengal-Orissa region was home to Santals, Lodhas, Mahatoes, Koras, Goalas, Urias, Kols, and other aboriginal tribes.

Away from town was a Kora village in which lived the Hintons' first convert. The woman's name was Kamala, and she had journeyed up the hill to the white-washed house, newly renovated and painted a brighter white than the other houses of its kind around it. Seeing the open doors and windows, she walked right in, where Mrs. Hinton found her in the late morning, naked in their living room, disturbing the furniture with every touch. Shocked and afraid, Mrs. Hinton had called for the young Arthur to have her removed. She always contended that if her sons had been born at that time, she would have dumped the woman out in the road herself without a second thought. But Mr. Hinton insisted on helping the woman, who did not balk as they walked her down to the Kangsabati River that afternoon to be baptized.

When her people refused to take her back after they learned of the baptism, it interested the Hintons to learn about her tribe. Mr. Hinton had walked down with his flute one morning before dawn, found the general center of the village, and began playing a cheerful tune. Faces peeked out of doorways and around corners; bodies crept out of the shadows to see this ridiculous figure in his pith helmet the size of the moon. But something about him had evidently stuck, this white man who had somehow landed on their doorsteps, and he kept at it every week, strengthening his Bengali—which only consisted of a handful of words then—until he was giving full sermons to a rapt audience. Now, almost twenty years later, all the villagers were baptized Christians and could even understand his sermons in English, and Kamala herself sat in the front row every Sunday.

■■■

An animal shriek shattered the still morning air, but Gene knew the sound. Minnie leaped off John's shoulder and dashed on all fours after Arthur, who stumbled to the side, then zigzagged down the lane, trying to get away. Gene heard his brothers' laughs as they watched him try to fend off the monkey, but Minnie soon tired of the game and turned back to her owner. John knelt on one knee, and she hopped back onto his shoulders.

"Oh, leave him alone," Lee said.

"We are," John said.

Arthur glanced back at the monkey to make sure she was securely on John's shoulders and wouldn't come after him again. Arthur smoothed his cleanest white dhoti and tunic, then dusted off his leather shoes, which were handed down to him from Mr. Hinton himself, seeing as Arthur hadn't had any of his own. Mr. Hinton had given them to Arthur almost twenty years ago, but since Arthur wore them only on Sundays, there was hardly a change in condition from their previous owner.

When they reached the village, the center was empty except for a pair of roaming goats, which paid them no mind and continued to forage among the dirt for scraps of food and grass. Minnie hissed at them, the sound of water drops on a hot pan, but they did not lift their heads.

Arthur walked to the middle of the gathering place and laid a reed mat down in the dirt. He folded his legs under him and sat patiently. All the boys sat facing opposite him some distance away. Then the melody of the flute fluttered in the air, the tune picking up here and there, then slowing down to remind itself of the time.

A few figures appeared in the open doorways, their glossy faces looking out curiously. They were descendants of the Kora tribe, or what was left of them anyway. The name meant "earth digging," and their village was surrounded by bountiful crops carefully cultivated for thousands of years. Before the people converted to Christianity, they were Hindus, and many of their traditional customs still remained, having never been stamped out by the British or the missionaries.

The tribe was unusual in that it was the only Kora tribe to convert. If a single individual had converted all by himself, Mr. Hinton would never have been welcomed back to the village. That was why their method was on a larger scale, village by village, not person to person. Take them all out one day to the river and get it done. Mr. Hinton always told Gene he didn't know how exactly he convinced the whole tribe to convert, but he suspected it must have been the change that came over the woman once she had been baptized. If, in his youth and recklessness, his father ever doubted the Holy Spirit, he believed in it now with every bone in his body for the way the woman had emerged from that river completely new. Such a thing had never been witnessed since. He hadn't converted another tribe in all those years.

But this village was loyal to them every week. Gradually it awoke to the music. The villagers' faces and limbs were the darkest brown, gleaming with oil and sweat. They wore traditional outfits in saffron and fuchsia, adorned with silver beading and stitching. As much as the Hintons attempted to dress down on Sundays in an effort to be more relatable, the villagers liked to dress up. As a result, the Americans in their colorless outfits and cross-legged positions on the ground appeared as beggars to their elaborately dressed hosts. Mrs. Hinton even carried a small silver collection plate, which she placed far out in front of her. The plate was engraved with the emblem of the American Baptist Foreign Missionary Society: an ox with a plow on one side and an altar on the other, and *Ready for Either* on a banner above.

Children ran to the boys where they sat, going for John and Minnie most. Even though the monkey hissed and ran around the courtyard, the children laughed at all of it. Minnie climbed on roofs and scurried between people's legs, which woke everyone up far more than Mr. Hinton's flute ever could.

Gene wanted to believe that his oldest brother liked the village children. John's smile looked genuine, not like the sneer he'd seen so many times. He seemed to act especially kindly to anyone brave enough to approach Minnie, even encouraging them, though everyone knew how sharp her bite was. She dashed just out of reach of the crowd and climbed up a teak tree on the edge of the courtyard. A small boy, perhaps not even three, tugged at John's shorts and pointed at the tree.

"You're a brave one," John said, reaching down for the boy. "Up you go!" He pulled the boy onto his shoulders and walked him toward the branch where Minnie perched. Her slender tail hung down, and the boy reached out to pet it. The tail swung from side to side, almost in rhythm with the melody of the flute. After a few tries, the boy grasped the tail. Gene could tell immediately that the boy pulled too hard. With a sharp howl, Minnie clawed the air wrathfully, just above the boy's head, her pointed teeth gnashing at him. Terrorized but laughing, the boy jumped off John's shoulders and ran to his friends, who clapped him on the shoulders to congratulate him.

"Well done," John said, though Gene didn't know if he was speaking to the boy or to the monkey. He turned and caught his mother grinning.

The music stopped. Mr. Hinton took the flute from his lips and knelt at the center of the crowd. Everyone quieted. He never stood above the people while he gave his sermon, but instead preferred to bend on one knee. Years ago, when all the boys tried to be like their father, they'd bend a knee too. But now, they sat at the edge of the circle, legs crossed and backs slumped.

"Today, I'll speak on forgiveness." This was Mr. Hinton's way of starting every Sunday sermon. Forgiveness, kindness, family, love, humility, wrath. Always in a voice as smooth and soft as smoke.

"Forgiveness of a certain kind, forgiveness between each other. For we know that the Lord forgives our sins, but can we say so much for each other? Our sins should be between ourselves and our God, but sometimes they come out among us. Violence, for one."

Gene couldn't look away from Lee's black eye, lumpy and dark, like a too-ripened plum. He could still see the thieves kicking, and the way Lee had done nothing but put his arms up to his face, ineffective to block the blows. He couldn't imagine kicking anything so hard with his bare feet, but they had seemed undeterred by it, and probably didn't even own shoes. With the reminder of the violence so fresh in his mind, so too was his anger renewed. He hated the thieves for what they had done. It was not their stealing the bikes or kicking his brother or shoving him to the ground that was so hateful, but the way they had done it so confidently, as if they knew they would get away with it. He felt something tickle his knee and looked down to see an ant crawling on his skin.

His father continued. "'As far as the East is from the West, so far has He removed our transgressions from us.' But have we removed them from our fellow man?" His gentle voice gave the impression that he was in intimate conversation with a single person, and the whole crowd leaned forward to hear his words, their faces like flowers to the light. Gene crushed the ant under his thumb and flicked it into the dirt, where he noticed a line of them heading straight for the seat of his pants.

Mr. Hinton held the Bible open and gazed around at his listeners, his head tilted so that his eyes looked over his spectacles. "As Gandhi preaches nonviolence, so do I, but on a smaller scale, that of our single interactions with each other. And these are just as important. What good is a community if we are fearful of every person we meet? An attack on an individual is an attack on the whole, and it is nothing more than an admittance of one's own weakness, for true strength is in the spirit, not the body. And how does God say to treat the weak?"

He hadn't noticed it before, but today it bothered Gene how much Mr. Hinton seemed to talk to them all like children. Some stern admonition for a crime no one here committed. What good was this sermon going to accomplish? It didn't change anything, he thought, as he crushed more ants with the side of his shoe. The thieves weren't here to listen, and even if they were, would they set things right? He was no longer just angry at them; he wanted something done about it, and his father wasn't doing a thing but saying simple words to people who nodded along, like ants following each other without knowing where they were going.

The people did not answer, so Mr. Hinton glanced at the page and continued, "'Now we who are strong ought to bear the weaknesses of those without strength.' It is our duty to raise those weak in spirit to see the light of goodness." At this he adjusted his spectacles and pulled his topi lower; the sun was beginning to rise now, as if Mr. Hinton had planned the timing of this line with the dawn.

"Too often people mistake violence and dominance for strength, the fist struck out as a symbol for power. But true power is with the open palm, reached out toward our brother. For then, power flows through the two beings, rather than one. Think of the person who last helped you. Perhaps they carried something for you or walked with you to the spring. Gave you a bite of their food or wood for your fire. You think well of them, don't you? Did you know that they think well of you too? Because they helped you, they knew that in you, their help would not go to nothing, and that someday, somehow, you will repay the favor. You see, our relationship with each other is based on this kind of give and take, a wheel that turns itself on the good deeds we do for others. But sometimes, someone decides that that wheel does not work for *them*."

Here Mr. Hinton's tone changed, his voice deepening on that last word. He shifted his weight from his back foot to the fore, practically leaning into the Bible in his hands.

"Those people take things without asking, things to which they have no claim, things that someone else has worked hard for. And it may not be a thing that you can hold in your hand, but something else intangible, your place in line, for example. What is to stop us all from doing this too?"

The courtyard was quiet except for his voice, soft as cream: *God* was the definitive answer. It was the word that, even after all these years, Mr. Hinton said cautiously around the village, as if still unconvinced that the people accepted him and his God. Especially when said so suddenly like that, an answer to a question, a single word dangling alone, an offering that the people were supposed to take. They could leave it if they chose to. What if, Gene wondered, one Sunday the family arrived at the village and no one came out of their huts to listen to them?

"God has commanded that we love one another, if not for each other, then for Him. Always remind yourself of God, and remember that when you hurt your fellow beings, you hurt Him too, for we are made from Him."

Now Mr. Hinton closed the Bible and pushed his topi up on his forehead. Gene could see sweat on his father's skin. He wiped his own brow with the sleeve of his button-down. The dark smear left on the fabric didn't worry him—the heat would make it disappear in a matter of seconds.

Something tapped his elbow, and he turned to see a white hand-kerchief extended toward him. Along with his leather shoes, Arthur also brought his only handkerchief on Sundays, made from coarse cotton but cleaned well enough so that it looked brand new, week after week. Arthur smiled at him, but Gene refused, whispering, "I'm all right."

As the sermon continued, Gene wanted to shout that he knew exactly what his father was talking about—what happened to him and Lee. He didn't know why his father didn't just come right out and say it, as it was obvious that "some people" were the thieves and "evil deeds" were stealing bicycles and assaulting strangers. But he waited patiently, as everybody else did, until the last words came.

"That is all for this morning, and now we'll say amen." Everyone said the word at once, like a gentle welcome for the sun that had risen above the rooftops. People began to stir, and some dropped coins onto the collection plate with a metallic *ting!* But mostly everyone walked back into their huts or out of the village to go about their day. No one acknowledged Mr. Hinton, who stood straight up with hands folded around his Bible, watching the people retreat from the courtyard.

"Wonderful. Now let's go home," said Mrs. Hinton. She struggled several times to get her folded legs out from under her. John helped her to her feet. "Thank you, dear," she said to him. "How much did we get?"

"Looks about the same as usual," said Will, giving the collection plate a shake.

"Hmm," she said. She emptied the coins into her purse and gave the collection plate to Arthur.

Mr. Hinton rubbed his glasses with the hem of his shirt. He gave Gene a foggy smile, but Gene just turned his head. He couldn't look at his father now, not after that tepid speech on forgiveness. After all that had happened yesterday, he couldn't believe that his father's solution was to go about the day as normal, always so calm.

As he walked past, Mr. Hinton put an arm on Gene's shoulder. "What's the matter, son?"

"That didn't do much to get our bikes back," Gene mumbled.

A pause. "Say that again."

Gene knew he should keep his mouth shut, but he couldn't help throwing an angry glare at his father. A sharp slap met his cheek quicker than he could blink. Gene put a hand up and felt the growing sting.

Mr. Hinton pushed his glasses back up his nose and looked down at him. "Let's walk back," he said.

# CHAPTER 13

As the family meandered through the sal forest toward home, Gene kept to the back, walking with Lee and Arthur. The canopy above them smelled of new leaves and oil, rich and earthy. The crunch of broken seeds followed their every step. Arthur took off his shoes, wiped the dust off them, and carried them the rest of the way.

"'One thing I ask of the Lord,'" Mr. Hinton began to sing, "'this only do I seek: that I may dwell in the house of the Lord all the days of my life, to gaze on the beauty of the Lord and to seek him in his temple.'"

Gene listened as his father hummed in response to his own words, a low and winding melody punctuated by short breaths. He flicked the flute against his hip in time to the rhythm, the scattering leaves on the path his accompanying percussion. So they journeyed down the lane, and Gene began, without realizing, to let his anger fade.

He noticed Will dropping back from his usual position in the front, away from John and Mrs. Hinton, away from Minnie, until he was shoulder to shoulder with him. Gene didn't know what to say, when suddenly Will stopped altogether and looked off the path into the woods.

No one seemed to notice except Gene, so he stopped, too, and watched him. Will ducked low to see among the underbrush, then shot up to crane side to side, looking around this tree and that.

"What are you doing?"

Will didn't answer but instead gave him an annoyed glance. He picked his way among the trees, slipping deeper into the brush. Gene looked down the path to see that his family still had not turned, except Arthur, who was waiting for them. He gave the servant a wave to go on ahead, then turned to follow Will.

"What are you doing?" he asked again.

"Shhh!" Will said. "You'll scare it!"

Gene tensed. The forest looked empty, just leaves and branches. He crouched lower as he kept moving, looking under the bushes and bramble for any movement. Then he remembered—the leopard. Suddenly he was alert, adrenaline vibrating in the back of his throat.

"Scare it?" he croaked. But Will kept on.

Then, as Gene drew nearer, he could see a pile of white on the ground. Small feathers lingered with the fallen branches. Dried blood spattered the leaves at their feet and led them to the wrecked snare, nestled in waist-high bramble. A mangled chicken foot was still caught in the rope, but the rest of its body—

"Gosh darn it!" Will pulled up suddenly, causing Gene to bump into his shoulder. There in front of them, not ten paces away, the chicken's carcass hung out the side of a stray dog's mouth.

The dog froze upon seeing them too, her ears stiff, eyes wide and surprised. Blood from the chicken ran down her snout, wings and beak clamped between her teeth. She pounced toward them, swinging the carcass into the air, then snatching it back, wriggling her head as if to break the chicken's already limp neck. Then she stilled again, gazed at them with large pupils, tail swaying invitingly.

Neither Gene nor Will moved. They'd encountered enough pariah dogs to know they were impossible to catch unless you offered food, which this one presently had plenty of already. All they could do was stare at the dog with the brown patch of fur around one eye and the mischievous grin on her face.

"Curse these dogs!" Will threw up his hands and made a

half-hearted lunge to take the chicken away from her, but she side-stepped him easily and bowed, ready to spring away at the next attempt. This time Gene tried to catch her off guard by reaching from the side, but she escaped that too. Will lost his balance and stumbled into the leaves where she had stood a moment before, coming up with a handful of twigs.

"That tears it!" he said, hurling them into the dirt. "We can never do anything without these filthy dogs shoving their snouts into everything and ruining it!"

Gene wanted to point out that this was the first pariah dog they'd seen in a long while, since they'd come back from school in Mussoorie. But he bit his tongue and let the dog go; she was already wandering off into the trees, chicken still in her maw, apparently grown bored of them and their refusal to play with her.

"Damn," Will muttered. He knelt to gather the snare rope. "Mother's going to kill me."

"What are you talking about?"

Will swallowed and looked down at the matted feathers in disgust. "I was using it as bait."

Gene spied a handmade structure poking out from among the sticks. It was made of wood and formed the shape of a 4. "You wanted to catch the leopard!" he said.

"Well, obviously."

Gene didn't know anything about leopards, but he figured that a small snare made of thin rope and wooden boards would be no match for one.

"It's a killer," Will said. Although, the leopard hadn't actually killed anyone, as far as they knew. But Gene didn't detect any fear in the way Will said that word. *Killer.* He said it more like a compliment.

"That's one less hen in the coop," Gene said as he stared at the snowy down feathers strewn around their feet.

"You take it," Will said. He held the rope out to Gene.

Gene almost took it, reaching his hand out instinctively. But he stopped himself. "Why don't you just let Arthur take the blame," he said, letting his hand drop.

Will was taken aback, yet looked amused, as if impressed by this suggestion. "That's not like you," he said.

"It's like *you*." And when Will—for once—didn't have a retort, Gene continued. "You're just as bad as John, always pinning things on Arthur, running to him, all, 'Arthur! Arthur! You clean up my mess for me.' And you think I'm too stupid to not do the same. Well, *I* think it's stupid of *you* to get yourself into problems you can't solve without blaming someone else. Aren't you a little old for it?"

He had thrown that last bit in there, knowing it was a risk. Will wasn't as explosive as John, but still, neither of them liked to be insulted. But it just felt *so good* to say it for once.

"Look at you, all grown up," Will said, taking a step forward, bloody rope in hand. It was a menacing movement, but Gene stood his ground. "Do you want to know what I think about you? Acting so virtuous all the time, as if you're any different from us. Oh, sure, you try to be chummy with Arthur. 'That's all right, Arthur! You don't have to be like that with me!' Guess what? You're a spoiled foreign kid in his eyes, and you'll always have it better than him no matter what you do. Me and John, we just don't fight it. It's the natural order of things. And I'll let you in on a little secret. Life would get a lot easier on you if you'd just accept it too."

"That's funny, because what really makes my life hard is you and John."

"Oh, please. Quit your whining. What makes your life hard is that you try to be better than us. You're never going to be. You're no different from us. We're brothers. If you started acting like it, then maybe things would be better for you."

"So it's my fault, then."

"Afraid so."

Blood was pumping in his ears now; Gene narrowed his eyes and searched his brother's face. He couldn't tell if Will was really speaking his mind, or if he was toying with him, trying to get a rise out of him.

"Seriously, I'm proud of you, sis. I think that's the most I've ever heard you talk."

There it was again, that *sis*. It was like a command whistle. Suddenly Gene lunged at his brother. Caught by surprise, Will went down easily, the feathers exploding into the air as they hit the ground. For a few moments, Will didn't struggle, and Gene got in all the punches he could before his brother effortlessly flung him off. It was over in seconds. Still, fresh blood sprung from Will's busted lip, and Gene couldn't deny how pleased he felt.

"Jesus! All this for a chicken? You've lost your mind."

"What?"

"Fine. We won't blame anyone for our little accident here. But we got a problem. I know and you know that Mother never misses a chicken in her coop."

"We're back to the chicken again?"

"One of these days, she's going to notice it's gone."

"So go down to the bazaar and buy another one. Uncle Ellis will give you money," Gene said. "Won't he?" He stalked past the mess of feathers and made for the path. It wasn't his problem to solve. He took one look back at Will, who was brushing the leaves from his hair. Then he turned around and allowed himself a smile. Rubbing his knuckles as he picked through the brush, he reveled in their soreness.

As he walked back to the path, Gene couldn't stop thinking about the dog. It was rare that pariah dogs came all the way to their house, what with all the smells and rubbish to keep them happy in town. It was even rarer to encounter a lone stray—they always kept in groups, pack animals that they were. Except the outcasts. The ones treated lower than everyone else, the ones who had no claim to anything, no territory to call their own, because if someone bigger and meaner pushed them to move, they'd have no choice, unless they wanted to be caught in a fight they could not win.

And the forest was dangerous. It wasn't a place for docile dogs used to roaming the streets without care to other animals lying in wait. It was a place where things went to hide. Where people went to get away from the clamor. Did dogs know that too?

Though he tried to put it out of his mind, Gene couldn't deny the feeling deep within his bones that something in the dog felt like himself. Call it reincarnation perhaps, but it wasn't hard to imagine his soul in another life, wandering alone, scrounging for scraps in a world inhabited by larger, more powerful beings.

∎∎∎

"Ah. The happy family returns," Uncle Ellis greeted them from the verandah. He sounded cheerful, for a change. A large plate smeared with gooey egg yolk and bread crumbs sat on the edge of the table next to him, pushed all the way to the other side.

"She kept to herself, I hope?" Mrs. Hinton asked as she climbed the stairs. Arthur followed and took away the plate.

The judge snorted, then rearranged himself in his chair. "Bring me another cup of tea. This one's grown cold." Arthur nodded and went inside.

The judge leaned close to Mrs. Hinton and said, "See for yourself." He jutted his chin toward the side of the verandah. Through the railings, Gene could see something lying on the grass. It was the woman, flat on her back with eyes closed and arms folded behind her head.

"What is she doing?" Mrs. Hinton whispered.

"I don't know. She was like that when I came down this morning, after you had all left. I haven't seen her move. Just been sitting here."

Suddenly the sound of spikes against wood clamored through

the house as John and Will sprinted out with their track shoes on. "Let's go! Come on!"

"Training again, eh?" the judge said, following them to the grass.

"Every day," Will said. "We've got to keep up the family name again this year."

"I think I'll come watch," the judge said.

"I'm coming too," Gene said. "Wait up!" But his brothers rushed down the steps and sprinted toward the track. He took the stairs two at a time with his laces tied carelessly. They came undone not two steps out of the house, and he knelt to retie them.

"Please, sahib." He heard Arthur's voice from above. Gene looked up to see Arthur reaching an arm out toward his head. It drew back holding a white feather. Thankfully, no blood on it, Gene thought. "It was in your hair, sir."

Gene tried to think. "Must have been from my pillow," he said.

He got up and ran for the track. His shoes pinched every toe except the little one on the left foot, which burst through the leather.

▪▪▪

When the burra sahib had been served his tea, Arthur peered over at the woman, still lying motionless on the grass. One side of her sari swirled up to her side, exposing a few inches of her calf. The skin was dark, darker than his own.

From the railing, he could see that the skin on her face glistened, radiant in the sunlight. Her tongue poked through her cheek every once in a while, felt around, then switched to the other side. Arthur watched it like a guessing game of where it would pop up next.

"Kindly, miss," he said, sorry to break the silence.

She opened her eyes and turned her face toward him but said nothing.

"What are you doing?"

Taking a deep breath, she unfolded her hands and dragged them, palms down, fingers wide, in a sweeping arc up and down like wing-beats, unhurried and even, hands, rough from the sun, in perfect unison. She smiled widely and closed her eyes again.

"I've never felt green grass."

"What do you mean?"

"Haven't you ever heard of *purdah*?"

"Veils and screens?"

"And never going out unattended."

"Even just to feel the grass?"

"Mmm."

Arthur tried to imagine how someone could live like that, how feeling green grass could be a freedom. If that was the case, then her whole journey here must have been exhilarating. Or terrifying. But she didn't seem scared at all, not even of the burra sahib.

"A letter arrived while you were gone," Jaya said.

"I'll take it," Arthur said, meaning to pass it along to Mrs. Hinton.

"It's for you," she said, slipping a hand into the waist of her sari and pulling out a small, folded note. She held it in the air and turned it over in the sunshine, examining it like a seashell.

It could only be about Soni. Worried that she would read it—or that she already had—he took it from her with as much coolness as possible, though his hands were shaking. He remembered the kiss the night he came home after the rally. What would Jaya think if she learned he was receiving letters from another woman?

He hunched his shoulders and turned away. As he suspected, the letter was from Soni. He opened it and recognized Neer's handwriting, but it was clear the words were from her.

*I know we have known each other only briefly, but by now you must know my cousin's intentions to make us a match. I am a hard worker and have helped my family's business since I could walk. I can cook and keep a clean house. I am obedient to my*

*parents and will be obedient to you. Please don't be angry, but
Neer told me about your reason for not taking a wife the traditional way. I don't hold this against you. I only wish to humbly
say that my purpose as your wife would be to bring you happiness in the ways God has given me. It would please my parents
and Neer very much to see me happy with you.*

    *Soni*

There was a second piece of paper folded with the letter, this one
with charcoal portraits on either side, a man and a woman. He realized the man was himself, the same long and wavy hair style anyway,
and the subtle but carefully sketched wrinkles around eyes that were
certainly his. He felt a sinking in his chest at the realization that
he must appear so much older than he felt. Perhaps Soni was even
being kind in her portrait of him, for surely his skin sagged and hair
thinned more than what was on the page. It wasn't a perfect like-
ness, but then she had barely looked him in the face at their meeting.
Besides, who else could it be?

The other face was one he had not seen before: A woman with a
sari over her head and eyes downcast, dense lashes concealing her
gaze. A thick braid swooped over one shoulder, disappearing at the
bottom of the paper. But whereas the drawing of himself was cleanly
sketched with crisp, confident lines, the one of the woman was less
sure. There were faint lines where perhaps Soni had started but abandoned, and there was an unfavorable smudge right in the middle of
the face where the nose and lips should be. Arthur wondered if it had
been damaged by the messenger. He turned the page over to look
again at the one of himself, marveling at the talent Soni possessed.
He couldn't help but feel flattered at the gift, but also confused at this
woman courting *him*. And for the first time, he felt suspicious of not
only Neer but of Soni herself. Why could *she* not find a husband in
the traditional way?

"Is it bad news?" Jaya asked. She held a hand over her face to shield it from the sun. Her eyes were on the letter, which quivered in his hand.

"No," Arthur said. He folded it and tucked it in his pocket. "Not at all." But his words ached in his throat as he looked back at her.

# CHAPTER 14

When Gene made it out to the track, he found Will bent low dragging a chunk of chalk along the faded line, following the old with the new. The track sloped downward on one side, thanks to the curvature of the yard. It had been measured out one afternoon a few summers ago, when Will decided they needed more precise distance markers than the landmarks they'd been using. They could only run so many times around the tennis court before they lost count. So Will had measured his steps, one hundred large paces from one end of the straight to the other, then one hundred paces in a graceful arc.

The track still had remnants from when it was relined a few days ago, but winds and animals had left their mark on it, scattering the chalk.

Now that Mrs. Hinton had given her reluctant approval for it to become a regular fixture in the yard, Will made a point of keeping it well drawn. Even though he passed his other chores on to Gene, drawing the track was something he never let anyone else touch. It was too important and had to be precise. In their wild land, something so precise and well cared for looked like it didn't belong. Still, it offered something to do on these long, dusty days. The lines gleamed white, three lanes drawn evenly together. When Gene had asked why there wasn't a fourth for him, Will had said, "You've got to earn it."

Soon enough they began warming up. Will kicked his knees up like a soldier, with nothing less than military precision: toes pointed, knees at ninety-degree angles, back perpendicular with the ground, chin level, eyes on the horizon. His hands were rigid straight, fingers glued together. It was like admiring a war horse; Gene felt conscious of his own ungainliness.

In the very center of the track sat John, stretching his arms. Gene never really made sense of this. Wasn't running all about the legs?

"OK, I'm ready," John called.

Will answered right away. "Right. Let's go."

Ignoring Gene, who was not at all ready, they bounced over to the far end of the track, where Will had nailed wooden blocks into the ground. They were custom fit to their starting positions, which was fine for Will and John, who had stopped growing. The blocks in the outer lane didn't fit Lee anymore, but they looked like they might be right for Gene. With his muscles still tight, he lowered into them, staggered behind his brothers. *Just jog this one*, he thought to himself.

"Aww, we have to wait for Lee to start us," John realized, rising from his blocks. He shook out his legs.

"Gene can do it," Will said. "He's not warmed up, anyway."

"I'm fine," Gene said, irritated. He hated when his brothers spoke for him. "We'll wait."

Suddenly, a voice boomed at them from the direction of the house. "What are you doing just milling about? Get on with it!" The judge walked toward them, his giant form standing out among the tall grass and shrubs.

"Care for a run yourself, Uncle Ellis?" John called. Gene thought he was joking, but his brother's face looked so hopeful, it unsettled him. He shook his head and stared at his mark in the dirt, making sure his fingers were right on the line.

"Ah, I don't think I've run in twenty years," the judge said, adjusting his trousers.

"We use the boards over there to start. Just clap them together—"

"Nonsense. Only one way to start a race off properly." He pulled the pistol out of his waistband and stepped across the chalk lines to stand inside the track. With a grunt, he planted both feet and stood straight on, his crisp linen suit almost blending in with the dust. It was Sunday, and even though he hadn't come to the sermon this morning, he still looked more dressed up than usual. Although, Gene didn't really know what *usual* was for the judge. Everything about him seemed unusual.

"Right then, let's get on with it. On your marks."

Gene teetered on his fingertips, the hot dirt burning underneath. He could feel a pebble below his kneecap; he wished he could move it or shift his position, but he knew Will would get annoyed if he delayed the start for even one second. He waited in pain for the judge to say the next word.

"Set."

The boys rose onto their toes. The movement loosened a drop of sweat from Gene's brow. It fell onto the line of chalk with an audible splat, turning it a milky white. As his fingers began to weaken and shake, he felt his stomach rumble, and he realized he hadn't eaten anything since the day before.

With his arms shaking, Gene listened for the gun to break the silence. Straining his head up, he peeked at his brothers, their tensed calf muscles ready for the start. He didn't even know what distance they were running.

*Bang!* And the boys exploded forward. Gene snapped off from the blocks, straightening his back too soon, all the way upright before he even came to pass John's starting blocks. Already, a dull pain bit at his heel, on the ridge of his left Achilles tendon. With every step, it grew, and his brothers pulled away more and more.

He felt a drowning sensation in his lungs after only a few strides. Every inhale was a gasp, every exhale not long enough. His breathing and the pounding in his ears were all that he could hear, and as he rounded the curve to the straight, he shut his eyes against the pangs in his chest and imagined how effortless running must be for his brothers. Will probably didn't even think about it. His legs just moved of their own accord, at top speed, no pain, fluid like man's worthy answer to wings.

He opened his eyes and saw that the judge had moved to their side of the track, cheering John and Will as they sped past him and entered the next curve.

"Catch him, John! Catch him!" the judge barked, swinging his arms as if he could wind them up to make the boys go faster. Something terrifying lurked in the judge's motion, his animation, so enthusiastic and intense. Gene ran harder.

Will had passed John, who was losing form quickly. John's head bobbled on his shoulders, which tensed up and restricted his arms from swinging back and forth, which in turn prevented his legs from moving any faster. Before this, Gene didn't pay much attention to the way his brothers raced. He always assumed that John and Will were equally fast, but now that he was racing just the two of them, he could see the difference clearer than ever. Will ran like it wasn't hard at all, like his lungs never knew the drowning sensation, like this pulsing and whirring was the natural state of his muscles and being at rest was the true pain for him. John, on the other hand, obviously tried harder than any of them. But the more he tensed up in an effort to run faster, the more it actually slowed him down. The way Gene saw it, the harder he tried, the slower he ran.

As Gene rounded the next curve, he tried to mimic Will's form. He unclenched his fists and flattened them like blades, then lowered his chin. He imagined himself as a machine, with a metal breastplate attached to his chest keeping it stable, his legs reinforced with iron rods as bones, a motor whirring faster and faster on his back, his gasps no longer the breathing of a weak boy but the turning of hundreds of tiny gears inside his body. And machines didn't feel pain.

Remarkably, he was closing the gap between himself and John.

He tried to not think about it as the two of them barreled out of the curve and into the home stretch, with Will already halfway down. Gene pushed on harder, feeling like he'd never felt before when running, that it could actually be fun. He shut his eyes and tried to think like Will. *This is nothing. I'm not even running.*

Then out of the darkness of his mind, he saw the backs of the thieves running away with his and Lee's bikes. The bazaar came to life in his memory, the people who didn't see, the boy kicking Lee on the ground, the old shopkeeper drinking his tea. He wanted to run and run and run, back in time to that day to prevent it from happening, to turn it back and never go to the bazaar, never question the judge, never care about things that shouldn't concern him.

His eyes flashed open, and he saw his toes suddenly at John's heels. He swerved to keep from tripping, and as he stumbled to the side, the machine turned back into a boy. His armor crumbled and fell away all around him, and he threw his arms forward to break his fall. Rolling in the dirt, he saw his brothers upside-down, pushing through the finish line and slowing to an easy jog.

"All right, sis?" John called.

Gene brushed himself off and sprinted the last fifty meters to the finish line like it still mattered. "Don't call me that."

"Whatever you say, sis."

"Let's jog around, then go again. Eight hundred this time," said Will.

Whatever strength or hope Gene felt before had fallen away with the armor. The pain in his Achilles tendon flared up again, and his lungs felt stretched out. The little toe poking out of his left shoe was covered in dirt. He wiggled it to make sure it was still attached.

"Again," said Will.

And so they passed the day. Gene didn't come close to John again, and Will stayed out in front on every interval. Uncle Ellis's voice whipped them along as they moved round and round the track like hands on a clock. If Will was the second hand, Gene was the hour. As he watched his brothers slip farther and farther ahead of him, he simply couldn't make himself go any faster.

Their last interval was a 200-meter dash. When Ellis fired the gun, Gene's thighs seared in pain as he lurched forward from the blocks. Will's pace remained immaculate, keeping long strides and even breaths.

"That's it, John, catch him! Catch him!" Ellis bellowed again from behind them. But Gene could see John's head wobble back and forth as he dropped his discipline and his form. His hands flopped loosely as if the tendons were just barely holding on to the bones, the opposite of Will's razor-straight hands.

"Use your arms, Gene!" A different voice. From the corner of his eye, he spotted Lee, walking up the hill from the house. Lee was right; his shoulders were tensed up and his arms stayed close to his body. He wasn't using them at all, really. As he swung his arms farther back and farther forward, he found that his legs did the same, lengthening their strides to match his arms. The faster he moved his arms, the faster his legs would go.

And then, as they came out of the curve and into the straight-away, Gene realized he was gaining on John. It was all the encouragement he needed, to know that what he was doing was actually working, actually making him run faster. A fire burned in his chest, yet he drove through the pain. Will was practically at the finish line by now, but there was still enough space to catch John. He pumped his arms, punching the air in front of him as if breaking down a wall with every step. Drowning out the cheers of Lee and Uncle Ellis, his rapid breaths sounded more like the whirring of heavy machinery at full power than a twelve-year-old boy's lungs. But he was so close. Just a few more steps and he would be on his brother, and for one frightening moment, he had the animal instinct that he was actually *chasing* John, hunting him rather than racing alongside him.

Could he *smell* John's skin? *Feel* his body heat? Gene didn't know if he was imagining it, but something was overriding his human mind and taking control of his body. He'd never run this fast. He'd never thought it was possible. He was so close, just a few more strides until—

Suddenly, a blur of fur darted in and out of his peripheral vision. He didn't register what it was, but it was enough to snap him out of, well, whatever place his mind had gone off to. Then he felt a nip at his pant leg, the cloth tugging him back and causing him to stumble. He put his hands out to stop the fall, but instead of dry dust, his touch met brown fur and slobbery tongue.

A pariah dog had stormed the track and seemed to think she could herd Gene into a game of chase, by the looks of her playful bouncing and feinting. Half catching himself, half fending her off, Gene reeled to a halt as John slipped away, running to the finish line, unaware.

"Get off!" Gene stood with one knee up like a shield to protect against the dog's jumps. He was pretty sure she was only being play-ful, but it seemed her idea of play involved nips and clawing all the same. He looked wildly about for some fallen branch to distract her; spotting one to his right, he risked letting his guard down just long enough to lunge for it. In one swift movement, he snagged the branch from the dust and flung it as far away from himself as he could, and she was off like a bullet after it.

"Bloody hell!" Uncle Ellis shouted as he marched toward Gene.

"I'm all right—" Gene began to say, lifting up his unscathed arms as proof, but Uncle Ellis didn't even look at him. He walked right past, and Gene realized the dog was his real target. The dog, who had caught the branch and was now trotting back to them, the dog not knowing or understanding what Uncle Ellis still had in his left hand.

The gun.

Gene's eyes grew wide at the realization. He scrambled in the dirt, crawling like some pathetic insect, powerless against the judge's forceful footsteps, which shook the earth.

"No! Don't!" Gene's voice was so feeble, it couldn't have possibly carried to the judge's ears, let alone stopped him.

The dog had switched her attention from the branch to the man who was approaching her. Her tail wagged with aching eagerness at this new human playmate. Gene saw the gun twitch in Uncle Ellis's hand, and turned his face away, bracing for the bang. He looked for his brothers, who all stood still as stone at the finish line, the same shock on their faces. Nothing could be done. Gene, still in his cowardly crouch in the dirt, squeezed his eyes shut and waited for—

Laughter.

Uncle Ellis's gruff yet jovial voice, cackling with joy. Gene dared to look, and there was Uncle Ellis on one knee in front of the dog, an arm hugged round her head, the other tugging the branch from her. The gun was tucked in the back of his waistband, decommissioned. The look on Uncle Ellis's face was so disarmingly soft. Boyish. Innocent.

"Ha ha! She's a firecracker, isn't she?" Ellis said. He finally snatched the branch out of the dog's jaws and teased her with it along the ground. "Yoohoo! That's it! Fetch!"

He tossed it, and she chased it happily. When she returned with it, she bounded straight to Ellis's feet and dropped the branch, waiting.

"She's played this game before, looks like," John said, running over.

Gene's brothers had shaken off their shock and approached. Gene stood up and brushed the dirt off his clothes. As he looked more closely, he realized this must be the same dog he and Will had seen in the woods on the way back from the sermon.

"I wonder . . . ," Uncle Ellis said. He took the branch up and dangled it just out of her reach.

"Sit," he said. The dog did nothing. "*Betth*," he tried again. And she sat back on her haunches.

"Oh!" Lee said. "Someone must have trained her."

"Perhaps she belongs to someone, then," Gene said. "If someone cared enough to train her?"

"Doubt it," Will said. "Look how dirty she is. I'll bet she sleeps on the streets."

Gene watched as Uncle Ellis pulled something out of his pocket. It was a tea biscuit, the kind his mother had been making every morning since the judge arrived. The judge snapped off a piece and tossed it in the air. The dog jumped gracefully and caught it, crunching merrily.

"I worked with dogs in the army, ages ago. Ha! I was practically as young as you," he clamped a meaty hand down on Gene's shoulder. "Marvelous minds, they have. And they'll reward you if you put in the work with them. In fact, I have half a mind to work on her . . ."

He patted the dog on her head and brushed his fingers along one floppy ear. She responded with licks and wagging tail.

Something about the sweetness of that gesture made Gene uneasy. He looked away, back at the house. In the shade of the verandah, he spotted Arthur, running a rag along the banister. He looked not at all concentrated on his task but rather wore a look of concern on his face as he witnessed what was happening on the track.

"In fact, I think I shall." Uncle Ellis's voice brought Gene back. "We'll clean her up, give her a proper rags-to-riches life. I'll name her Ella. What do you think, boys? She's bold like me, so she may as well be named after me!"

"Fine choice, Uncle Ellis," John said.

As his brothers all crowded around the dog as if she weren't a flea-infested stray only a moment before, Gene glanced again in the direction of the house. Arthur was still watching, and Gene couldn't mistake the darkness in his face.

# CHAPTER 15

A week later, an oxcart came down their lane. Gene had watched it pull up in the late-morning light, the frangipani trees swaying overhead as he paused on his way to the latrine and caught the movement in the distance. Two men in simple white dress walked beside it, the cart itself too laden with objects to allow a seat. The ox ambled to the side as one of the men whistled, not at it but at the house, and Gene wondered if Arthur was around. Sure enough, he heard the shuffle of running feet in the dirt as Arthur jogged from some corner of the yard to the lane, calling in Bengali and waving a hand to come closer.

Gene decided he could wait a little while longer for the latrine and went after Arthur, glancing back to see if anyone else was coming. But the verandah was empty, everyone inside to wait out the day's heat.

"Arthur, what is it?" he called. "What are they selling?"

But his voice hadn't carried far enough, and Arthur continued to banter with the men, laughing and gesturing at the cart's contents, patting the ox on the rump. As the cart pulled closer, Gene made out tires, spokes, and metal frames all polished and gleaming. Brand new bicycles, bought by the one person who could afford them.

Gene gasped despite himself. "Uncle Ellis!"

Arthur helped the men take the bikes down from the cart, wheeling one toward Gene to inspect. Gene shook his head as Arthur handed it over, as if in disbelief at the luxury of it. They only ever had rusted, donated bicycles from the mission, and this was by far the most extravagant thing to be in his possession.

Gene marveled at the workmanship, the soft rubber handles taking perfectly to his grip, the buttery leather seat curving elegantly. The body was painted a dark green, with a yellow RALEIGH logo spaced out across the chain guard. A large light was attached to the front, next to a shining chrome bell.

"Woohoo!" Gene couldn't help his excitement at such a thing. And soon enough there were whoops coming from behind him as his brothers all rushed up the lane to see.

"It's so sleek!"

"It's *new*."

"There's another one in the cart!"

"Where's mine?"

Gene gripped his handlebars tighter, anticipating his brothers taking it from him at any moment.

"Well, Lee and Gene, you can't go on without a bike."

"Uncle Ellis! You shouldn't have." Lee was quick to be modest. The judge wasn't.

"Nonsense. I had to get you the latest after what happened."

"How did you even get them?" Gene asked.

"Fellow at the club just had a shipment come in from England. I told him right away to set two aside for me."

Gene didn't know how to react to such an expensive gift. He relaxed his grip on the handlebars and lifted his eyes to meet the judge's. "Thank you," he said.

"The least I could do," Ellis responded in a tone that was surprisingly heartfelt.

"But you said we'd get them back," Gene said. "The old ones, I mean. You said we wouldn't let those thieves get away with it."

"And we won't." The judge's grim voice carried so that all the boys and even the cart men looked up, listening. "But there's no reason you have to go without a bike in the meantime."

"Let's go show Dad and Mother!" Will said. "Won't they be impressed. I'll set them up next to mine, so they see how beat up mine is and get me a new one come Christmas."

"Go on, then," Lee said, handing his bike over to Will. "Test it out for me. I'm still too sore."

"Still? It's been a long time, hasn't it?" Gene said. And he hadn't seen Lee do anything very taxing in the past week.

"Go ahead, Will," Lee repeated.

But Will didn't have to be told twice. He was already swinging a leg over the seat and pushing off, the seat a little too low for him, but still, the dark-green bicycle paired well with khakis and a topi and made a rich picture as he sped down the lane toward the house. Gene took his time mounting his own, the bike wobbling under him as he got used to the smooth pedals. It felt firm and true, the wheels solid against the dirt road. He kept with the others as they walked back to the house, leaving the oxcart and the men behind. Gene thought to take his topi off and wave a thanks, but they were already back to conversation with Arthur, paying no attention to the boys.

Back on the porch, Mrs. Hinton took one look at the bikes and gave Uncle Ellis an embarrassingly affectionate kiss on the cheek.

"What on *earth* have you done!" she gushed, as if the evidence was not there in front of them all. "You spoil them."

"Always have, always will. Don't I keep telling you these boys deserve more?"

"Much too kind, Ellis," Mr. Hinton said from the doorway, where he had approached unseen.

For a moment, Gene thought his father would tell the judge to take the bikes back; they'd never accepted—or been offered—anything so grand as these, and the look in Mr. Hinton's eyes was not exactly that of approval. The bikes went against everything their father preached, but then again, they were a gift, not a purchase.

"Can we ride them to the Old Gope, Dad?" Gene said. He gave the bell a small *ding!* as if it were in agreement.

Mr. Hinton gazed around the yard, where sunlight caught in the long grass. "Nice day for it," he said.

"Take Arthur with you!" Mrs. Hinton said.

"Aww geez," John muttered. "She never lets us go there alone."

"It's a shame you're not feeling well, Lee," Will said. "You don't want to go, anyway. That place is a pile of dust. But I'll take good care of your bike for you."

Lee looked at the bike and swallowed, and Gene realized that his brother was afraid. Afraid of getting hurt again, of being jumped again, or of losing something so new, he didn't know. But enough time had passed since the bazaar that surely Lee couldn't still be affected. Could he?

"Come on, Lee," Gene said softly.

Lee moved toward the bike and let his fingertips rest on the handle. He glanced at Gene. "All right," he said.

At that moment, Arthur came around the house. He stepped lightly and wore a curious expression. "Memsahib says I am to go with you?"

"Can't see how," John said. "We're going on our bikes."

"I will ask the Padre Sahib for his," the servant said. He swiveled on his foot and scurried back into the house.

"Just go without him. I won't tell," said the judge. He'd taken a seat on the verandah, sipping his tea, feigning innocence.

John grinned and gave a mock salute to the judge, then swung a leg over his bike and pedaled off down the hill without saying a word to the rest of them.

"He's right. We're old enough to go alone," Will said, following suit. "You'll tell him we left, won't you, Uncle Ellis?" he called back.

Their wheels kicked up little murky clouds that hung in the air, good-bye notes to Arthur.

Gene didn't think it was right to leave Arthur behind without telling him, but then he wasn't missing much. As Will said, the Old Gope was a pile of dust. All that Gene knew of it was that it once served as the fort of a Biratnagar king during the Mahabharata War, but he found it hard to believe that anything so old could still be standing. Of course, the Old Gope wasn't its real name, but that's what the British called it. He liked the way it sounded like *goat* and the end of *antelope*, and every time they biked to the fort, he thought the whole way of animals grazing among the ruins.

■■■

A few years had slipped by since they had last been to the Old Gope. The road leading up to the hill had a bright rusty color with over-grown topiary trees lining the way, making for a grander entrance than the minuscule fort commanded. The fort itself was made of old brick and stone, with mottled patches of green grass and moss from the rains. It was an oasis of shade and cool air, the surrounding sal trees seeming smaller than Gene remembered. Or was it just that he had sprouted taller himself?

He remembered that British soldiers used to have shooting practice on the grounds around here. He could still see the clouds of smoke from their guns and hear the cracking sounds of shots as they echoed off the old stone walls. But today it was quiet, with only the sounds of birds as they flitted back and forth over crumbling win-dowsills and doorsteps.

"Let's go around the back," John said, dismounting from his bike where the smooth road ended.

They circumnavigated the ancient world in just a few steps, and they came to the open back of the ruins. The front actually looked well-preserved and almost completely intact, but the back offered better access and a view of the lazy river not far off. Plus it was a discreet place to leave the bikes.

"It's unfair, honestly," John said. "If I knew being taken for a sissy in the bazaar would get me a new Raleigh, I'd have done the same."

"Not me. I'd be damned before I let some natives jump me and get away with it," said Will.

Their words swarmed around Gene like buzzing flies; he felt like being alone. He wandered the ruins and wished he could get lost in them, but they made a poor maze. They were too logically made out. No winding hallways or stairways to nothing, like the great forts in Amer and Agra.

In only a few paces, he was at the outer wall, tall and silent, the voices of his brothers absorbing into the moss around him. Tapestries of gnarled vines shielded the walls, so tall for their tremendous age. They opened up to the sky—there remained no trace of a roof ever existing. Still, the sunlight could not reach the floor unless it was directly over the ruins. At this time of day, it was not, and so the ground still kept a uniform cover of moisture from the previous night's rains. It gave the place a lush atmosphere intensified by the dryness surrounding it. This was a capsule of halcyon days, and the boys knew nothing of its worth. Gene put his hand out to the ancient brick and imagined a hand on the other side of it, as a man carefully put this single brick into place centuries ago. Did he know then that it would still be here after all this time? He took his hand away and felt the grains of dirt and moss fall through his fingers, where perhaps they would lie for centuries more.

■■■

Gene returned to his brothers and found a comfortable pile of stones to sit on. His muscles still ached from a whole week of running, which practically qualified as professional status compared to his usual regimen of not doing much at all. And the bike ride hadn't made things better. But he thought it worthwhile to leave the house and see what else could be found among the rubble. For now, he rested his back against the cool stone and pulled an orange out of his chest pocket. He punched a fingernail through the peel and tore it away piece by piece, discarding them into the weeds.

"Give me a piece," John said.

He tossed a slice to him, then to Lee.

"Will's right," John said. "This place is a pile of dust."

"It's not dusty at all," Gene said.

John rolled his eyes. "It's just an old spit of land, is what I mean."

"No one cares enough to maintain it," Gene said.

John seemed to give it a second thought. "Swell place for climbing though," he said. Then he turned. "All right, Gene. I want a rematch for last week." He nodded toward the wall of stones.

"What, the race?" Gene faced his brother straight on. "Aw, come on," he said when he saw that John was serious. "I only came close to catching you, but you still won in the end." He hoped that was enough for John to leave it, but he thought some flattery might help too. "Gee, I couldn't climb that high even if I was as tall as you."

John gripped his elbow and pulled him up off the rocks. "I'll give you a head start."

When faced with the wall up close, he could see crumbling dirt between the bricks and a thin layer of moss on each one, just like the outer wall. He reached out to touch it. It crumbled away at his fingertips and gave him an idea.

"You know what?" he said. "You're on."

He put a hand on a protruding ledge and grasped it tight, hoping his body was still light enough for it to support him. He looked to Lee, but his brother's face remained smooth, betraying nothing. So he climbed up with only one thing on his mind: the top. Top of the wall, top of the ladder, top of the food chain. Whatever the word meant. Left foot placed here. Right arm reached there.

He trusted that the stones would not crumble and the moss would not peel away but that he would loosen them just enough for them to fall under John's weight. When he reached the top, he pulled himself to his feet and stood on the narrow wall. He could see what once were rooms along a stretch of hallway. Away to the west he spied the remains of some gardens, long dead from the heat and relentless sun.

From below came sounds of John's struggling. "Since when did you get to be so good at climbing?" he panted.

"Shh," Gene said. He could hear voices nearby, but he couldn't catch the words.

John scowled up at him. But he paused his movement and listened, too, evidently in need of a rest. Gene caught the voices again, this time more clearly. They sounded young, almost like boys their age. They bickered like boys, someone arguing with someone else. They were too far away to make out the words, but Gene could tell they spoke Bengali. He recognized the same short, clipped cadences, the way their voices stabbed the words on the initial syllable, then fell away to the end of the phrase.

"You hear it? What are they saying?" he asked.

"What are they ever saying?" John said. "All natives ever talk about is cows and Vishnu." At that moment, a sharp crack rumbled from somewhere in the wall. John caught Gene's eye with a look of horror. In an instant, a piece of brick gave way beneath his hand, and with a cry he fell to the ground.

"Damn!" John yelled, cradling his left knee. There was blood, but not a lot of it, not yet. Still, Gene's instinct was not to go down, but to move toward the voices and to catch the boys before they got away.

Gene's feet touched down in the tall grass on the other side of the wall. He dashed through the sal trees downhill, in the direction of the river. But the voices had stopped. No doubt they'd heard their shouts. He gripped a trunk and listened again.

"What are you doing?" Lee called, rounding the wall and catching up to him.

"I bet they're the ones who jumped us in the bazaar."

"Who?"

"The boys out there. Don't you hear them? John did."

"Oh, come on. You're not serious? Of all the people in all of Midnapore, they couldn't be the same ones." Lee stopped him, made him look in his eye. He searched Gene's face for something. "Look—would you look at me? I know it's natural to still feel angry. But you shouldn't seek revenge. Remember what Father said? Weren't you listening last Sunday?"

Gene wanted to say that of course he was, but all through that sermon he'd heard pounding in his ears as his heart churned out more blood and anger. And with the thought that the boys who beat his brother could be right here in this very place . . .

Suddenly, laughter. The arguing voices gave way to mirth. It bounced off the stones and carried through the grass to hit them square in the face. Gene walked toward it, crouching low. He followed the perimeter of the ruins, bent on finding the boys. Even if they weren't the same boys, he wanted to find someone, anyone, who could pay back what had been taken. But when he circled them completely, he saw nothing. He listened again. He couldn't let them get away.

*Ding ding!*

The bike. His new bike. He ran for the wall and skidded to a halt, expecting to find someone ringing the bell. But it was John, extracting his bike from the rubble. Will stood in the lane with his own, waiting.

"My knee's all busted up. We're going home," he called.

"The boys that jumped us are out there! I saw them!" Gene startled himself with his lie, but he wanted so much to believe it. And what if it really was them? It could be.

John stopped his struggles. "You think they're the ones?"

Gene didn't answer, not so much as a nod. But John didn't need an answer.

"Well, now, we can't pass up a chance to get even."

"But your knee," said Will.

"But nothing. Let's get them."

Lee stepped in. "What's gotten into you?" He spoke to John, but he gave Gene a serious look.

"Uncle Ellis told us to get even. I'm doing it," John said. He dropped his bike and rolled up his sleeves, making fists in a way that was almost comical.

"But it's not your fight," Lee said sternly. "You weren't there."

"I don't care. They'd have done the same to me."

"These aren't even the same guys."

"They're all the same, aren't they? Somebody's going to pay today." Without waiting for more protest, John was off into the trees, and Gene couldn't even tell if he heard the voices anymore.

"I don't know what's gotten into your head, Gene, but we've got to stop him before he does something stupid," Lee said, hurrying after him.

Gene knew it was wrong, but for once he didn't want to hear Lee's relentless levelheadedness. He could see that day again clearly in his mind, the faces of the boys, the brown finger flicking the bell right in front of him, the tattered clothes and the sternum protruding so grotesquely. Every kick in his brother's back that day only pushed Gene forward now as he ran to catch up. Will was past them in two seconds, his pace intent on missing none of the action.

When Gene's ears picked up the voices again, he did not hear that there were more than five boys, six even. Neither did he realize how far he had come and that at every turn, he had gotten more and more lost. With clenched fists and gritted teeth, he barreled around a crumbled turret and saw them, squatting right there in front of John and Will, who stood still, facing them. He jerked to a halt. They were old. Not boys, but men, and many. Perhaps ten. Not tattered rags, but tunics and dhotis that looked clean enough and black bands around their arms. One seemed to be their leader from the look of his hands on his hips and the light-gold eyes that reflected the sun like fire. As the man turned his body toward the boys approaching, his brows narrowed and lips parted, as if readying to speak.

The other men rose. They spoke in hurried Bengali to each other. Gene could only make out one word. *Angrez*. The two syllables stretched to fit all the horrible ways they could possibly mean it. It cut through his foolishness and sent his legs into action again. He stumbled forward and put a hand on John's shoulder, pulling him away.

"It's not them," he began to say, but John shrugged him off.

"Now which ones of you stole our bikes and beat up my brothers here? My uncle's a judge! We can bring it to him, or we can settle it here ourselves!"

The men continued speaking, and it was clear they didn't know English. One broke out into a grin, batting a hand at the brothers in a way that universally could be understood as dismissive.

"*Well?*" John yelled again, his voice cracking in the air like lightning.

The man with the fire in his eyes took a step toward them. John matched it. Gene made one last desperate attempt to restrain him, tugging at his linen shirt, but had no more success than a small child tugging at his neglectful mother.

"Leave it, John. You don't know what you're doing."

"The hell I do," John said. Faster than anyone could realize what was happening, he put a hand inside his shirt and, in one swift movement, pulled out a gun—a gun Gene had most certainly seen before.

A cry went up from one of the men as they all started and put their hands up. John leveled the barrel at one of them and stepped forward. For a split second, everything stood still like that, and nothing but the wind seemed to pass between the two sides. Then, faster than Gene could register it, the man at the farthest edge of the gathering turned and ran. The movement triggered his companions, who scrambled after him as if broken by some spell. A shot rang out—a single shot. Gene squeezed his eyes shut and waited for the sound of a body hitting the ground, but none came. John had missed. Gene gaped at the image of his oldest brother standing in the sun with the gun smoking in his left hand.

"It—it's all right," Gene said, breaking through the frozen horror. "No one was hit . . ."

"Thank God you missed," Lee breathed, as if the wind were knocked out of him.

John lowered the gun. "I knew what I was doing," he spat. "That was just a warning shot."

"It was a damn stupid thing to do," Lee said. "Where the hell did you get that?"

"From Uncle Ellis, of course."

"Does he know you took it?"

John was silent as he slipped it back through his shirt into the hidden holster. "Sure."

"You shouldn't have done that."

"Well, maybe if you had a gun that day in the bazaar, things would have turned out different!"

"They would have been a lot different," Lee said, his face grim. "But not in the way you think."

"We've got to get home," Gene said. "Dad's going to kill you."

▪▪▪

The whole ride back, Gene hung behind and let his brothers fade down the road. He felt filthy. Even though he'd never touched a gun, knowing that one of his brothers had and felt no shame or remorse after coming so close to killing another person with it was something he couldn't comprehend. What would people think if they knew the missionary boys had done something so terrible? Along the road, he passed no one, not the usual rickshaw or water buffalo cart; it was as though everyone knew what had happened and wouldn't go near them. He couldn't feel his hands, as if they too didn't want to touch him but would rather go unfeeling and limp. He stopped his bike on the side of the road and stared out over the river, the sun catching in the murky waters and turning it a striking gold. For a moment, the air was filled with a remarkable calmness, only the breeze rippling through the dry grass toward him, carrying up from the river the scent of mud and moisture. All at once he realized something; for all the terror and hatred John had invoked, he had done it for *him*, for him and Lee. John was willing to go this far to stand up for them, to do it unquestioningly, without all the facts, except for the simple truth that he was their brother and he was going to make things right, in whatever way that might be.

And then another fact occurred to him—none of them had so much as touched a gun before, and yet there John had stood pointing it so confidently. What else had Uncle Ellis been teaching him that the rest of them didn't know about?

# CHAPTER 16

When Gene returned home, he noticed that the Afghan guards were not at their usual standard. Ever since they had arrived, they'd given off a sort of superiority with every movement and every look. Gene thought they must see Ellis as some sort of royal. But as he approached the house and threw down his bike in the grass, the guards did not acknowledge him. They did not stand in their usual formation but instead huddled near the cookhouse.

"You made it back. Took you long enough."

Will leaned against the verandah railing, peeling orange slices apart from each other and popping them into his wide mouth.

"Yeah," Gene said, distracted.

Lee stepped up onto the verandah and tossed his topi over a chair. "What's going on over there?"

Will looked toward the cookhouse, squinting into the late-after-noon sun. "Oh," he said. "That woman's gone."

He sounded pleased about it, but Gene worried about the guards. He knew they wouldn't leave their posts for just anything. "What does that have to do with them?" he said, nodding in the guards' direction. Backing down the steps, he tried to get a closer look at them. But at that moment, the enormous mass of the judge stepped out of the house and knocked him aside on his way down the steps.

"Don't bother!" Ellis roared to the guards, who all snapped to attention. "She's already gone, and where she goes, I don't give a fig.

No, I need you all here with me. That's what you're all damn well here for, isn't it?"

The guards didn't answer. One gave an order to the others, and they all marched back to their posts.

Ellis grunted as he lowered himself into a chair on the verandah. "Ah, enjoying the new bikes, I see. How did they feel?"

Gene didn't respond. No guest had ever left so abruptly before, without saying goodbye. But it was too much to think about; the events of this afternoon took up all the space in his head, leaving no room for anything else.

"We went to the fort," said Will.

"Saw some men up to no good there." John pulled the pistol out of the holster and laid it on the table in front of the judge. The metal rang clear as the weight of it dropped on the wood surface. Ellis stared at it for a long time before giving John a clouded look.

"Hope you didn't do anything stupid," he said.

Mr. Hinton appeared on the lawn, coming from the forest with a bow in his hand from his afternoon hunt. From the looks of his other empty hand, he had been unsuccessful. The judge scooped the pistol into his jacket. "Ellis, what's happened?" Mr. Hinton said.

The judge's stern face broke into a grin, and he chuckled. He slapped his thigh and left behind a faint handprint of dirt. "Oh! This business with your guest? I've never met a woman who wasn't insane." He shifted in his chair and looked out over the grass, not meeting anyone's eyes. "I went to the cookhouse to . . . you know, scrounge around for an apple or something to hold me over until dinner. And there she was inside, brandishing a knife at me! Now, I'm never one to be afraid of a woman, but the look in her eyes made me keep well back. She had that long, black hair all roughed up, looked just like a monster. Ghastly. But I didn't even think of calling the guards over. If I can't keep safe from a woman, let alone an Indian one, then I have no business getting out of bed every morning. So I backed out the door and gave her plenty of space because at that point she'd started swinging. Then she came out, gnashing like a badger. The only sense I could talk into her was to drop that knife. It's still over there in the doorway. She took to the forest after that, and I say we're lucky she left us. I can't believe you let a thing like that into your home. Now you know to think twice before you let another one in."

"Why didn't you just ask my wife to get you something?"

It sounded so territorial. *My wife*. But the judge just shrugged and shook his head as though he didn't know the answer.

"Gene, get the knife," Mr. Hinton continued. "And put it away."

As Gene passed his father, he could feel the cold emanating from his gaze. He found the knife among the grass right in front of the cookhouse door. The blade was clean. He knelt to pick it up and heard Lee ask, "Where is Mother? Does she know?"

"No," Ellis said. "She's up in bed with a headache."

∎∎∎

Arthur spent that afternoon down in the bazaar. It was well after the morning rush, the time of day when you could see the bottoms of crates and barrels. He hardly noticed as a produce seller filled his basket with bruised fruit, for his mind was elsewhere. This past whole week, he had watched the judge domesticate Moti, *his* Moti, into practically another servant. Sit, stand, stay, come, beg—it must have pleased the burra sahib very much to order someone around endlessly. And Moti proved a worthy disciple, eager for all the bits of cooked chicken that the judge gave so readily. Arthur hadn't had to feed Moti scraps anymore; oh no, the judge was fattening her just fine with food off his own plate. She was as hungry as she was intelligent, and in no time at all, she was the picture of "man's best friend."

Truthfully, Arthur was grateful that the judge's attention had been shifted off himself. As much as it made Arthur sick to see Moti salivate over the judge, the burra sahib spent more time teaching her commands and less time berating Arthur.

Memsahib begrudgingly let the dog on the verandah, but never inside. "Even with a bath, she is still a street dog," she'd said. The Padre Sahib had no opinion at all. And at least the dog had the good sense to not outstay her welcome, leaving every evening to sleep somewhere in the forest, Arthur guessed, or on the sunbaked pavement in town. Still, Arthur couldn't shake off this edge, this feeling that the judge would do something nefarious, that surely the judge had not come all this way to sit around drinking tea on a cobwebbed verandah and training the first pariah dog he found to pay him respect.

As Arthur busied himself selecting bunches of spinach and bushels of limes and piling his woven basket higher and higher, he had only Jaya on his mind. He tried to guess the sort of things she liked to eat, a challenging game, as she had refused almost everything she had been given, except the fruit. Hers was a polite refusal, one that came after a few well-mannered bites, chewed once or twice, before she slipped the food almost whole down her throat as she set the foreign fork down on the napkin. Of course, it was normal for pregnant women, but Arthur recognized it as a refusal all the same.

So he picked something she hadn't tried before—*palak paneer*. It was vegetarian, simple. He had hoped that Mr. Hinton would be unsuccessful on his hunt, so that she wouldn't be surrounded by the smell of meat, if that was what disquieted her appetite. He knew how Hindus were.

On his return to the house, he stopped at the melon patch and picked a ripe one. He made sure it looked just small enough to tuck under his arm and be hidden by the draping of his oversize shirt. The rough rind of the cantaloupe didn't feel anything like Jaya's lips or the way he remembered them. He thought they should plant honeydew next year.

But before he could slip into the cookhouse unseen, two guards seized him. It all happened so fast. Without a word, one of them dumped the contents of his basket into the dirt, shook it with far too much force, and held it in his arms like classified evidence. The other guard punched his wooden baton through the loose folds of Arthur's clothes, knocking the melon free. It fell to the ground and rolled to join its other edible comrades. The guard raised an eyebrow but backed away.

The first guard thrust the basket back into Arthur's hands. Arthur knelt to gather the items. He would have to wash them.

The guards offered no explanation, and their stony faces and metallic eyes did not invite conversation. He used to think they were the same as him, service men for white masters, but from where he knelt in the dirt among his vegetables, he knew now where they stood. They were off again before he could get to his feet.

He set the basket inside the cookhouse. Mrs. Hinton wasn't there to order him around, so he took the cantaloupe into his open hands and strode out the door, in the direction of his hut. But a voice stopped him.

"Arthur!"

He nearly toppled back into the cookhouse again. He steadied himself against the door frame and realized he gripped the melon so tightly that his nails had punctured the rind. Up on the verandah, the family looked down at him through the slats of the railing.

"You'll have to do all the cooking tonight," called Mr. Hinton. "No luck on the hunt. But that's all right. What you got from the bazaar should be enough for us."

"Yes, sahib," Arthur said.

They all turned back to their conversation. He wiped his sticky hands on his tunic and entered the house through the back.

*Tiktikies* peppered the walls of the hallway, which led to the downstairs guest room. Arthur found his pocketknife in the folds of his clothes, cut a slice of the melon, and left it on the floor to the side. The geckos began to crawl down the walls, their miniature bodies wiggling cheerfully. He'd pick up the rind tomorrow morning. Then he continued to the door and knocked.

When Jaya did not answer, he put his ear to the door but heard nothing. He squatted and put his eye to the ground, trying to see in. He could detect nothing. He desperately did not want to open the door—he'd never opened a closed bedroom door without permission, and he didn't feel that he should now, not with a pregnant woman. He knocked once more, but when there was still no answer, no stirring sound, he decided he would come back later. It wasn't important anyway—he had forgotten why he'd come to see her. Maybe there wasn't a reason in the first place. He walked back down the hall, careful to step around the geckos.

He could count only a few times in the past when he had had to make dinner all on his own. Mrs. Hinton usually took care of it, and he was there simply to help and to serve the food at the table. But this evening, he liked the idea of being in charge in the cookhouse. He'd take his time, start early, and make something special. This would be the best meal they'd ever had. He got to work, whistling as he fished the produce out of the basket.

Onions were already frying to a perfect golden brown and the scent of cardamom and jeera wafting up to the rafters when he stopped. Mrs. Hinton hadn't even checked the basket. She always did—and made a point of it. ("The *boxwallahs* were always looking for someone to cheat," she would say.) He could have bought anything he'd wanted . . .

He looked at the basket in the corner, still laden with vegetables for the rest of the week. No one knew what was in there, no one but him. Wasting no time, he hurried over to it, forgetting the onions still on the stove. The best produce was at the top, uncrushed by the weight of everything else. He picked out the oranges, fresh mint, and dates. Oh, how he wished he'd bought some *jelabies*! He filled his hands up with more and more, then stepped toward the door for somewhere to hide it for himself. But if everyone was still on the verandah, he couldn't run out unseen to his hut. He glanced around the cookhouse and spied baskets of dirty linens along the wall. He tucked the food under the sheets.

An hour later, he was almost done cooking when Gene ambled through the door. Arthur looked up from his stirring, wondering what he could want. But the boy didn't say anything—he made his way around the room, peaked at the pot on the stove, and swiped some chopped nuts off the cutting board. Then he found a seat on top of the laundry basket and peered at Arthur with his blue eyes, eating the nuts one by one.

It was the crunching sound of his chewing that made Arthur sweat. Could the boy feel the food underneath the sheets? Gene shifted his weight, trying to find a more comfortable position. Arthur held his breath. Gene reached a hand underneath his buttocks and pulled out a single lime.

"How did this get in here?"

"Mmm, sahib, it . . ." Arthur thought quickly. "It is to feed Minnie, sir."

Gene looked down at the lime, frowning. "More than she deserves."

Arthur turned back to his cooking, but the boy still did not leave. "Is there something the matter, sahib?"

Gene shook his head and began swinging his legs. They were too short to reach the ground. With his mouth full, he said, "That smells good."

Arthur smiled. He hoped everyone would like it.

"Did Dad tell you there's one less mouth to feed?"

"No, sahib."

"That woman is gone. Uncle Ellis told us she left when we were at the Old Gope. And Mother isn't coming down to dinner. Said she has another headache."

"She's gone?"

"No, she's just up in bed, sleeping it off."

"Jaya—the woman, I mean. She is gone?"

"Yes."

Arthur knew that the rice would be done in two minutes, and the dal would begin to burn if he didn't stir it. He still needed to set the table and brew the chai and change out of his tunic. But all that didn't matter now. He bolted out of the cookhouse, scanning the porch for anyone still there. When he saw no one, he burst through the front door and spotted Mr. Hinton mounting the stairs.

"Padre Sahib!" he said, out of breath.

Mr. Hinton paused, his face alarmed. "What is it, Arthur?"

Arthur was suddenly aware what a sight he must look. He tried to calm himself. "Kindly, sir—is it true? Has the woman called Jaya left this afternoon?"

When Mr. Hinton did not answer right away, Arthur knew it was true. He cleared his throat. "Should we search for her, sir?"

"It is not necessary," Mr. Hinton said.

*Not necessary—vital,* was what Arthur wanted to say. "I will search for her, then. It is my duty, sir."

Mr. Hinton raised his eyebrows. He placed a hand on the banister and tilted his head. Arthur felt proud. He knew the Padre Sahib would encourage a good deed, and what better deed was there than to rescue a pregnant woman all alone in the world?

"Your duty," said Mr. Hinton, "is to serve dinner tonight."

# CHAPTER 17

There was nothing Arthur could do to get out of serving dinner—Mr. Hinton had made that clear. What could he do except his duty, his *real* duty, to be a servant to the Hintons?

As he prepared the trays to carry into the house, thoughts of Jaya swept through his mind. Where could she have gone, a woman like that? She wasn't from anywhere in Bengal, and she didn't know anyone. If she went into the jungle, she might last a few days if she was smart. But if she headed east toward Howrah, she could catch a train to anywhere. She would be out of his life, just another lost soul in the mass of India. His hands shook so much at the thought that he dropped a jar of chutney. He had no time to clean it up—he was already behind. The family would be pulling in their chairs right about now, and no food was on the table. He used his bare foot to sweep the refuse under the cupboards. The shards of glass only glanced off his calluses. He couldn't feel a thing.

When he returned to the dining room, everyone seemed quiet. A conversation about school took a few fledgling steps, then died. Arthur wasn't paying attention; his mind was somewhere else. For the first time, he didn't really care about what the Hintons needed of him. But still—his body went through the motions anyway, unable to break the habit. So he numbly shoveled *palak paneer* and *basmati* rice onto a plate. It looked horrible, overcooked and limp as mud. He was actually grateful that Jaya wasn't here to see it. He set the plate in front of the burra sahib and began to move down the table toward Mrs. Hinton, whose headache had ebbed just enough to come down.

"Arthur," said a voice from the other side of the table.

He looked up and found John staring at him.

"Yes, sahib?" he said.

"Uncle Ellis didn't get any *roti*."

Arthur looked at the judge's plate. It seemed perfectly full to him. But the boy was right—no *roti*.

"Well, don't make him say it again. Come back here," said the judge.

"Say please, Ellis; that's not polite," said Mrs. Hinton.

"I've had a hell of a day, you all leaving me alone with that woman."

"What about you, boys," Mr. Hinton said. "See anything interesting at the Old Gope?"

The boys were quiet, and Arthur caught a pointed glance between Gene and John. "No," Gene said.

"Arthur, some more water, please," Lee said.

"Yes, sahib." He quickly moved on from the judge's *roti*-filled plate. But just as he passed the judge, he noticed something strange about his silver hair. It was not smoothly combed as it normally appeared. Silver strands matted together in the back, and the slightest crumbles of dirt clung to the ends. It would have been imperceptible from the front. From the judge's place at the other end of the table, the back of his head was safe from everyone's gaze, all except Arthur's. He thought back to what he'd heard had happened between Jaya and the judge. There had obviously been some sort of a struggle. Or else, why would the judge be lying in the dirt?

"Darling, how's your head?" Mr. Hinton held a glass in his hand, full and still, as he looked pointedly at his wife. That word, *darling*—it sounded so unnatural.

She shook her head and tilted it in mock response to his affection. "Fine, darling. Just the heat is all. You know how it gets to me."

The meal didn't last long. For once, no one seemed much for talking. Arthur cleared the table quickly, and when he could be sure the family was deep in their own nighttime routines afterward, he slipped out of the house. He didn't know where to find Jaya, but something tugged him toward the forest. The only thing he knew was that the sun was setting fast and the evening rain threatened to fall.

Usually he followed the trail easily. He knew every uncovered root, every turn, every shadow. But he couldn't concentrate, couldn't focus. He could only see Jaya swirling somewhere in his mind, and nothing else. The clouds and the canopy let no starlight through. Every turn he tried to take proved wrong. Surely the path curved here, didn't it? But when he tried to turn, walls of leaves smacked him in the face. For a brief moment, he imagined the leopard waiting on a branch above him, ready to pounce. It probably still lurked in the area—leopards stalked their prey, and he'd been in and out of the forest often lately. But Jaya. If she were here, in the jungle, that was all the more reason to push on. She'd never survive a leopard attack all by herself.

He had never been afraid in the forest before, but everywhere seemed alien to him. His eyes tried and failed to focus—he felt sure he was going blind. A twig snapped somewhere up ahead. He turned every which way, trying to gain some sort of recognition of his surroundings. Something deep inside him flicked on, an animalistic fear, an ingrained urge to flee. He tore through the brush, straight forward, leaving the path behind him. He felt as though something were tugging him, reeling him through the darkness. The fear clung to every bit of his skin. His lungs turned to lead. Leaves and branches clutched his limbs and his clothes. He stumbled—somehow his body kept moving, darker and darker the jungle grew, closing in around him, and then—

There.

A light through the trees, a little pearl in the deep. It rippled. A single shaft of moonlight through the clouds on a lone pool of water.

And there.

A body floated on the surface. He couldn't tell if it was moving. The curves of the body could just be made out—upturned face illuminated by the emerging moon, hands at the sides, breasts . . .

She was still clothed, a relief for his embarrassment. But that made Arthur worry. Had she slipped on the rocks and fallen in? *Oh no*, he thought.

He hadn't moved from his place in the shadows. Carefully he crept forward, afraid of what he knew to be true. Now he could see that she wasn't moving, except for the dark mass of hair that clouded the water around her head.

He stepped out from the brush and onto the rocks that skirted the pool. Enchanted, he kept his eyes on her, forgetting his manners. But it didn't matter. The moon provided just enough light to see her.

He said her name. She remained motionless. "Jaya," he called, this time more loudly.

His heart lurched into his throat when she looked up at the sound of his voice. She came to life then, her arms skimming the water above her head. Arthur was surprised she could swim. As she came closer, he could hear her crying, from somewhere deep inside her. It sounded unnatural, or maybe it had been so long since he had heard such despair from one body. He waded toward her, worried that at any moment she might give up and sink straight toward the bottom. But the water was shallow, and soon enough she was in his grasp.

"Right there," she said through shaky breaths. "He was right there . . ."

"Right where?" Arthur searched her face. But she stumbled on the slippery bottom and dug her fingers into his flesh, hard. Startled, Arthur tried to gather her up, her dripping sari like sails from a sunken ship. "Right where?!" he said again, eyeing the surrounding trees for any movement in the shadows, listening for a sound.

He heard nothing though, just the mournful drip of water as it ran down her hair and fell back into the pool.

"You and I . . . we must be friends," she said.

Her randomness alarmed him. "We are," he said. He began to pull away to get a good look at her, to see if she was hurt. He couldn't tell if she was of right mind.

"No!" she sobbed and tightened her hold on his body, her arms like vines around his back. "Don't let me go."

He had no idea what on earth had made her act like this. Just the presence of her body so close to his own was enough to make him faint. What would the Hintons do if they knew? He looked at the sky, wondering what he should do. Above them, stars emerged from the clouds like concerned and well-meaning friends.

"We must be more than friends. You and I are of the same earth; don't you see that we must look out for each other? Save each other?"

"From what?" He laughed. But joy did not seem to have a place in this moment. He worried she might think him callous. He touched her matted hair, which had looked so soft that day she lay in the sun. "What has made you so . . . afraid?"

She started from him then, hardening herself against that word, and at once he knew he had said the wrong thing. But then she rearranged herself, adjusting to it.

"I'm not afraid," she said. She seemed to struggle with what to say next. After a long pause, she looked him in the eye. "How do you think they came to have such a nice house?"

Arthur grew angry at the accusation in her tone. He had never heard anyone speak against the Hintons before. Besides, she had come to them in the first place. It's not like they had forced her to stay in the Big House. She had asked for their help.

"Hmm?" she filled in his silence. "Or an automobile, when you live in such a small hut and sleep on a charpoy? The house is filled bottom to brim with nice furniture, and you, yourself an Indian, can't afford your own country's goods? Is that what being Christian is about?"

Arthur couldn't deny that the Hintons did have nice things and that he did not, but everywhere in India, things were that way. It wasn't unusual that Westerners had more than Indians. And no, they weren't his things, but he was around them and called the Big House home.

"They've made my life better. Not with things, but by showing God to me," he said.

"Is it really better? Better than it was before?"

"You don't even know what my life was like before." He felt his ears growing hot. "They are good people," he said, his jaw clenched. "People of God."

"Is the judge a man of God?"

Arthur didn't answer. He took one step away from her and tried to lead her out of the water. She was shaking, which worried him. He guided her toward a huge slab of rock on which he liked to lie after bathing. He knew its crevices well, its juts and recesses, the curves that caressed his body.

"I will answer for you," Jaya said after a time. "He is not."

"You don't know that. Besides, the faith of the burra sahib should not matter to you. It is not your place to judge."

"But it does matter to me," she whispered. "He . . . tried to undress me."

She took his hand and drew it to her waist, where he found the ragged fabric that ran all the way to her navel.

If not for the rock to steady him, he would have nearly fallen over. He simply couldn't believe what she was saying about someone so close to the Hintons. The judge had made it clear what he thought of Indians. Why would the burra sahib attempt such a thing with an Indian woman—a *pregnant* Indian woman?

She sat in silence next to him, still holding his hand at her belly. He pulled it away.

"Is this true?" was all he could say. She didn't answer. Everything felt so fragile now—the tear in her clothes, the shallow breaths coming from her mouth. Even the rock beneath them felt as though it would crack. Somehow he felt responsible. He had warned her to keep away from the burra sahib, but it hadn't been enough.

"For the past several days, when no one was around, the judge had . . ." She gave up on saying the words. "But I am glad. I can't stay in that house."

"But you must. Because of your . . ." He didn't know how to continue. "You need someone to look after you."

"There is no child coming."

The breeze had picked up, and the leaves were rustling all around them, as if murmuring their disbelief at what she had said. Even the stars seemed to widen in surprise. Arthur kept his eyes on the sky, too stricken to look at Jaya.

"You lie," he said.

"It's true," she said.

He cleared his throat. "You lie to the Padre Sahib. You lie to memsahib. You lie to me."

She had lied and taken advantage of their kindness. Surely this was the only explanation. Well, then, he thought, she deserved what she got. One sin for another. Wasn't that fair? But he knew the Padre Sahib would not think in this way. Still, how could he forgive her? And if she wasn't pregnant, why then had she come to the Big House?

"It has been such a weight, carrying this secret. A child that is not there," she said. She rested her small hand on Arthur's beside him. He did not move. Her voice was soft as starlight. "Thank you for taking it from me."

Arthur couldn't help but soften. He had never had a secret with someone before. He thought of the day when Gene had seen him smoking and promised not to tell, but Gene was a child. This was different. This meant something. Now, he would keep someone else's secret safe. Now, someone's safety depended on him. He rolled his head to one side, looking down at her hand on his. He squeezed it tightly.

"You know I won't tell anyone," he said.

■■■

What was there to do now? Hours passed unnoticed as they lay on the rock, and Arthur tried to imagine where to go from here. She couldn't go back to living at the house, but at least now she was not as fragile as he had thought. He supposed she could go anywhere, but he felt he should protect her. She wasn't from Bengal—in fact, he didn't have any idea where she had come from.

"Can you return to your . . . home?" he asked.

The word *home* had an unexpected effect. Even through the darkness, Arthur could see something burning in her. He had the immediate desire to get out of the way.

"There is no home to me anymore," she said.

Rolling onto her stomach, she drew her face close to his and hovered above him, a light in her eyes he couldn't interpret. Then, like something melting away, she peeled her damp sari off, and, sure that he must be in a dream, Arthur watched her rise up naked before him. She pulled him onto his feet, and taking no notice of the clothes between them, she pressed her hips into his. Arthur realized their bodies aligned perfectly. Her lips found his. He had no time to react.

Was this the sort of thing that happened between lovers? Was his mind supposed to go blank like this, the way it did when he nodded off to sleep, or the way it did that day down by the river, the Padre Sahib's gentle hand on his submerged head? Love was the sort of thing that let a mind rest, wasn't it?

For that was what happened to him in this moment. It didn't take long for her lips to not feel like lips anymore, but like air itself, breathing life into him. And her arms didn't feel like arms anymore, but like silk wrapped around his waist. There remained only the gentle ripple of the water and the whispering of the jungle around them. Too often he had heard these sounds and wished for someone to share them with.

But something felt wrong. Maybe it was the fact that he had never been in the presence of a naked woman before, or maybe it was the night air growing cold, sending a shiver through his body. He pulled away and gently unwrapped her arms from his body.

"This is not right," he said. "I should take you somewhere to stay." He thought of his hut, how the Hintons usually left him well enough alone there. But he couldn't risk any of the boys catching sight of Jaya, so close to the path that led into the forest. "We need a plan," he said.

She shrunk down to the rock and reached for some pebbles at her feet, then tossed them into the water with a forceful plunk. "Tell them I have left for Calcutta. Tell them I have family there to meet."

"Do you?"

"Of course not. But I can find my own way. There are plenty of ways for a woman to live in Calcutta."

"Not alone. Unless you intend to . . ."

"Don't worry about me," she said. She looked back at him, her face showing nothing in the dark.

But how could he not? Calcutta wasn't a place for a woman to be alone, without family, without friends. Even he knew this, and he hardly went into the city. "You said so yourself," he said. "We must look out for each other."

He could just make out the hard line of her mouth as she pressed her lips together, calculating. He waited for her answer—but she only kissed him again, passionately, expertly. And he could only give in to the gift she put forth, the idea that someone cared about him enough to make him feel wanted. Cautious hands became curious. Wet skin on skin exchanged body heat. Here in the jungle, she led him into new territory, not gently as one dips his toes into the shallow shore, but forcefully, holding his head under water until he learned to breathe without oxygen.

# CHAPTER 18

**B**efore first light, Arthur walked with Jaya to Midnapore where she would catch a bullock cart from there to Calcutta.

They walked in silence along the road, and despite everything, Arthur could feel an easiness between them that was real and true as sunlight. In another life, he could imagine them walking this road together just because, not to run away from something like they were now. If he could forget the goodbye coming at the end of the road and just focus on the sweetness of her sari brushing against his leg with each step, the sap-dampened air in his throat, the hazy light he could see on the horizon—if he could just stay in this moment for the rest of his life, then he could be happy.

But that wasn't how life worked.

They stopped at the farmers' carts that lined the road on the other side of town, ready to take their crops into Calcutta for better prices than could be had in Midnapore. They found a cart that wasn't too laden with jute and sugarcane and watched other laborers climb aboard. Arthur eyed the men warily and gestured at them to make room. When Jaya squeezed in between two ancient women who seemed only half awake, Arthur slipped her some rupees he'd been saving in an old ghee tin, plus the food he'd hidden in the laundry pile. There was no goodbye they could say that would make him feel better about seeing her go. Instead, he touched her face, only for a moment, before she pulled her sari over her head and the cart driver jolted the oxen forward. Arthur watched her go until the back of her head was just a dot lost in the traffic. He waited for her to look back, to show her face one more time, but she kept forward, floating away from him like a cloud on some unchangeable wind.

When he could finally will his feet to move from the spot, he turned and walked back through town. Kicking rocks and biting his lip into a pulp, he thought about what he should do next. She was saved from the judge for now, but where to go after this? She had made him believe in the possibility of life beyond the Big House, an identity other than as a lonely servant to a tiresome family. But what could they possibly build together? He thought of his childhood, the little shack nestled in the fields, waking up to impatient chickens and the plow waiting every day in the green, green farmland. Until it all turned brown in the famine.

He shook his head and let the vision fade. He took a few turns down alleys wet with wash water before he let himself think the question that had gnawed at him ever since he had made love to Jaya the night before. Could a life together even be possible?

The morning air bit at the edges of his mind, and he was brought back from his thoughts by the sharp cries of children spilling out into the streets to play. Smoke from simmering coals wafted from glowing doorways, and Arthur caught the scent of bubbling ghee in the air. He tucked his hands in the pockets of his dhoti. His fingers closed around folded paper. His first thought was that it must be an old grocery list from memsahib, but when he pulled it out, he saw Neer's handwriting.

It was the note from Soni, and the drawing of them both. He looked at it, held it with a dull dread in his limbs. There was a delicate devotion that came with a drawing of oneself, the understanding that Soni had spent time, perhaps hours, recalling his face and trying to draw it. His breath was thick as he stuffed the paper back in his pocket. He didn't want to deal with it, but he knew it was the right thing to do, to tell her that this wasn't what he wanted. After what had just happened with Jaya, he couldn't possibly entertain Soni anymore.

Yet he couldn't shake the creeping suspicion that he had felt the last few weeks. Why had he never seen this cousin Soni, let alone heard of her at all? He thought he knew his friend Neer quite well, well enough to know his whole extended family by now. But Neer hadn't had a sensible answer for it. Perhaps Arthur could find out more about this mysterious Soni himself.

He remembered the way to the courtyard where he had first met her. The scent of burning jaggery confirmed it was the house of the sweets sellers, her parents. Arthur crept to the wall, thankful it was a quiet street with no passersby. He looked up at the windows, but they were all dark. He realized that this house, squeezed among the others on the narrow street, was nothing like the Big House. There was no space, no openness, no interaction with the nature that was just outside the door. There were only cold walls, packed dirt, and the square of lightening sky above.

He couldn't linger much longer, and he was about to turn away in disappointment when he heard an odd scratching sound coming from the courtyard. It wasn't just the pecking of chickens or scraping of hooves. It sounded deliberate, careful. In the far corner of the courtyard, he saw a figure bent over the ground, a thin stick in her hand, tracing a design in the dirt. He remembered the drawings from the first time he had met Soni—well, the only time—and was mesmerized by the smooth, wide strokes she created now.

There was something preposterous about it. The too-crowded city would be chaos by midday; the rickshaws would be cranking down streets, cows mucking up pathways, children scrambling underfoot. Everyone would be busy, busy, busy. He himself would be rushing to be here or there, always at someone's beck and call. And yet in this darkened corner, someone was making a drawing. Someone was doing something . . . *slowly*. Someone was taking her time. Arthur tried to remember the last time he had ever focused so much or had used such care for anything that wasn't a part of his employment. And he couldn't.

Without realizing it, he had begun to move toward her. Like a boy leaning over a well to see his face, he was being pulled forward by his desire to see what she was drawing. Step by step he approached, his bare feet landing softly in the dirt, his movements so gentle they were almost imperceptible. He did not wish to disturb her, only to witness.

Soni continued drawing, her sari covering her head like a hood concealing her face. She appeared not to notice Arthur, for he came to a stop about five paces away and examined the drawing. It was unfinished of course, but it was clearly a woman's face, just like the one he had seen here before. A luscious braid curved around one shoulder, long eyebrows framed wide eyes, and a perfectly drawn pair of lips hinted at happiness.

He watched and listened to the cheerful sound of her bangles tinkling up and down her wrists as she moved. She seemed content drawing in the feeble light, and there was something undeniably alluring about her grace that tugged at Arthur. His heart faltered, and for a moment his feelings for Jaya were suspended.

He knew Soni had been the one who made these drawings, and yet, why had she lied about it when he had asked then? Suddenly, he felt emboldened. Well, why not ask her right now?

With a new heat in his chest, he stepped forward and knelt so that he was even with her. He must have still been out of her range of vision, for she continued as though she hadn't noticed his presence. He cleared his throat.

"I knew it was you who made these drawings," he said lowly.

As soon as he said the words, he felt a sudden pang of fear that he might scare her off like a feral animal. But she froze.

"Yes," she whispered. And then, perhaps sensing that she should explain, "Neer didn't think it was proper for a wife. It's a waste of time, he thinks."

"I don't think that," Arthur said.

"Besides cooking, it's the only thing I do very well," she said.

Arthur considered her words. He laughed to break the silence. "At least you do something well at all. I do everything only passably." *Am I flirting with her?* Then he grew serious. "Why haven't I ever seen you before? I've known Neer ever since I came to Midnapore, and I thought I knew his whole family. In fact, I'm sure I've seen your parents at their sweets stall before, but never you. Are they hiding you?"

He said that last part as a joke, returning to the playful tone again. But he saw her stiffen at it. She set the stick down in the dirt to the side so as not to disturb her work and rose to her full height. She came to about Arthur's shoulders, and though the folds of her clothing concealed her body, he could still sense its slightness.

"Wouldn't you hide me?" she whispered.

Before he could ask what she meant, she pulled the sari back from her head and lifted her chin so that the light of morning fell across her face.

Above the nose, it was a simple face. Nothing particularly beautiful, but everything in its right place. The same too-wide eyes he had seen before. The dark, dark skin he had noticed on first meeting. But Arthur didn't register all that this time. His gaze was locked on the rupture of skin where her lips should be. It was as if her upper lip were snagged on her nose, revealing the violent red flesh of her gums. Her nostrils were fused into one wide opening, and the end of her nose stretched as wide as her mouth to accommodate it.

"Oh." That single, stupid syllable was all Arthur could think to say.

Soni's eyes hardened, as though daring him to look away. And he knew it was wrong, but he felt ill at the sight. It wasn't so much that he'd never seen deformities or birth defects or red flesh or even missing limbs before, but it was the unexpectedness of it all. And what made it worse was finding out in this moment that he was the kind of person who would care about appearances.

"I tried to show you before," she whispered. "In the drawing I gave to you. I drew myself exactly as you see me now. But Neer discovered it and forced me to smudge out my face. I tried to show you."

Arthur's mouth opened and closed as he grasped for something more to say. When the words didn't come, Soni reached a hand to his face. He expected it to land softly on his cheek, like the way Jaya had caressed him, but the firm grip with which she caught his jaw shocked him. She held him there, forcing him to look at her face. And because he couldn't bring himself to look at her lips, he locked his gaze on her eyes. In them he saw all the years of pain and sadness she had endured, the grief of loneliness, the ghostly existence she had been forced into.

Panic mobilized him. He slipped from her grasp and backed away, trying and failing again to utter words—an apology, an excuse, anything. He turned with burning cheeks and walked swiftly out of the courtyard.

Immediately, he felt shame run down his whole body, like he had just been doused with it. By his age, he shouldn't be this shallow. And even if he did believe in superstitions like he once had, the bad luck of his past was far worse than whatever misfortune a birth defect could bring. He should have been kind enough to at least pretend that her face was the most unremarkable thing he'd ever seen, even if just long enough to think of a more graceful exit.

But the truth was, it wasn't the sight of Soni's deformity that caused this reaction in Arthur. It was the knowledge that his friend Neer had deceived him.

He took a deep breath. As he inhaled, he felt a heat fill his lungs. Closing his fist, he fought the urge to growl. He had to find Neer.

∎∎∎

Neer's green bike was tied to the banyan tree at their usual meeting place by the river, just as Arthur suspected. He walked right up to it and flicked the bell.

"*Are!*" he shouted. "Hey, Neer! Where are you?"

Arthur stalked down the bank toward the river, scanning the shore for his friend. The calm waters reflected the clear morning sky, and there were several men scattered around, some sharing a smoke or standing in the shallow water to cool their feet. He didn't care if they all thought him deranged. He needed to find Neer. He needed answers.

"Oh, are you hiding from me now?" Arthur laughed. "Figured out what this is about, *na*?"

"Arthur!" Neer called from behind him. He was sitting on a log, smoking a bidi by himself. He rose to his feet as Arthur turned and started for him. Guilt was written on his friend's face, and Arthur couldn't deny the satisfaction in seeing it there.

"Neer, my dear friend Neer, my *best* friend, Neer," Arthur spat. "I hate to disturb your morning, but there's been a *development* in your plan to trick me into marrying Soni. Surprise! I stopped by her home this morning and saw her face—her *whole* face—and the little detail you forgot to mention."

As he said the words out loud, he felt that stab of shame again that he should care so much about physicality. But his rage could not be stifled.

"Oh no," Neer whispered. His shoulders sunk inward in defeat, and he clasped his hands together in front of him, ready to plead forgiveness. "It's not like that," he said.

"What, did you think I wouldn't find out eventually?" Arthur said. "Or did you think I would marry her and go years without seeing her face?"

"Of course you would see her face, but I hoped you would at least get to know her and come to like her first, enough so that it wouldn't matter to you by the time you found out!"

Arthur huffed. "I cannot believe you would try to fool me like this. My own friend. My oldest friend."

Neer put out his hands. "Don't you see, it's *because* you're my friend. I know your heart, I know you could come to see past it. Another man would—"

"Another man would have higher standards, is that it? Another man would be smarter than to fall into this trap? You really thought I was this simple, *na*?"

"No, but I didn't think you were this heartless."

"Oh, so it's my fault. Poor, stupid Arthur found out your genius plan to marry off your undesirable cousin. Whom you had to *hide* from the world her whole life, but yes, I'm the heartless one!"

"It wasn't my idea to hide her! Her parents are very traditional! And Soni was resigned to never marrying, but I told them about you, and all your good qualities, and they really believed you would see past it. So we tried. It was foolish, I admit, to deceive you, but I meant to tell you eventually."

"Funny. I was resigned to never marrying either. I was perfectly happy living my life before all this. I have my own problems, but at least they are mine alone. I cannot believe I let you convince me that being alone was so horrible. It certainly beats this . . . whatever this deception was."

"Please, Arthur, be reasonable! Yes, the plan was idiotic, but Soni would still make a good wife! Just calm down and think about—"

"No, there's nothing to think about. That's the sad thing. She probably would make a perfectly fine wife. In fact, give my regards to Soni. She didn't do anything wrong. You—you were the one who tainted it."

As he turned away, Neer grasped for his sleeve. "Arthur—"

"Don't!" Arthur jerked his arm away. For a moment, he was reminded of Jaya, the passion of last night, and the easy way they walked together that morning, the heartache at seeing her go, and the impossibility that that had all happened barely hours ago. He had the mind to throw this in Neer's face, to boast that a far more beautiful woman knew him more intimately than, well, anyone—and that he didn't need Neer's insulting plan. But all he wanted was to get out of there. He spun backward and was struck by the barefaced curiosity of the other men around them who had witnessed everything.

"I have work to do," he spat as he walked back up the riverbank.

# CHAPTER 19

Jaya never told Arthur where she was staying in Calcutta. And when they met every few weeks at the pools, somehow she was always there before him, so he didn't even know from which direction she came. Nothing about her appearance gave a clue to her new living quarters, except that she looked clean enough to not be on the street. Or perhaps she cared enough about Arthur to clean up and look presentable for him. In any case, he was also forbidden from following her when she left. Jaya told him it was for their safety—they didn't know what malice the judge was capable of, and should the judge decide to tie up loose ends, it was best that Arthur know nothing. Still, Arthur felt the pain, the shame, of being unable to protect her.

In their meetings, Jaya also pressed on him the importance of appearing normal around the house, acting as though nothing of importance had happened to him. The Hintons didn't know about their relationship, and she cared too much about Arthur, she said, to risk his losing his job.

To keep his mind off her, he worked at his chores and kept his hands busy. It seemed to work well until midweek, when he realized, kneeling in front of the perfectly polished leg of the dining table with a rag in one hand and a worn walnut piece in the other, that there was nothing left to do.

As he stood behind his hut one afternoon, freshly lit bidi in hand, the cheers and whoops of the boys carried over from the track. He peered around the corner to see what was going on. The two older boys were the ones making all the noise, waving branches above their heads as Gene sprinted out in front of them.

"See?" John yelled, trailing behind. "He just needs a bit of persuasion."

"Yaw! Yaw! *Calo ya'i!*" Will hollered at Gene's heels. "The race is day after tomorrow, you know!"

Arthur shook his head and put the bidi to his lips. Its earthy taste enveloped his tongue. They wouldn't see him, not from all the way over there. Gene had his head down, chin glued to his chest as he pumped his legs. It actually worked—his brothers were falling behind.

Watching the boys chase each other all up and down the track reminded him of his own childhood in Kharagpur. Days were longer then, it seemed—empty and ready to be filled with play. But there was only so much a single child could do before he began to get bored—or lonely. As Arthur tapped the ashes off, he tried to conjure the faces of the children that had grown up along his country road. There was the boy who was pudgy around the middle, making him stand out among the other malnourished children. There was the girl with braided hair all the way down to her legs, around whom Arthur had been too shy to say hello. He had been so happy one evening when she shouted "Arthin!" from down the road. He had stood there, elated that she actually knew his name, when a cart *wallah* began hollering from behind him. He had leaped to the side at the last moment and looked down the street at her frowning face. She had meant only to warn him to get out of the way.

Was that like having an older sister? Someone to watch out for you, to call you by your true name and remind you of who you were before?

From all the days Arthur had spent around the Hinton boys, it was plain to see how horrible they were to each other. Not one of them seemed to have the fear of God in them to make them behave.

When the judge had arrived, Arthur noticed a brief change in their manners, but here they were, back to their tricks again. He watched as John took a whack at Gene's calves.

"Ouch!" the boy yelped. He stopped altogether and examined the back of his leg. Even Arthur could see it was nothing serious. But immediately Gene was roaring about it; he lunged for the branch, trying to tug it out of John's hands. The two older boys just cackled, fending him off easily.

Arthur laughed, too, even though he liked Gene. But couldn't he figure out, after so many times, that his brothers just wanted to get a rise out of him? How could he not know he was playing their game and losing every time? If only he stopped playing, he would win.

Through the clouds of dust in the air, Arthur could make out the judge at the center of the track, Moti at his side. He was dressed in what Arthur could only assume was a tennis ensemble, the kind he had seen other Britishers and even the Hintons wear. The crisp, white collar and creased shorts were apparently necessary for the athleticism of training a dog to beg at one's feet. Arthur watched the judge drag a piece of last night's mutton around his legs, luring her like a fish on a line, until she came to a stop between his legs directly underneath him. He still withheld the morsel, so Moti kept still, drops of her saliva sprinkling her paws. Then Moti's inner wildness overcame this new domesticated "Ella," and she jumped with both paws on the judge's rotund paunch, inclined to take the taunting treat by force.

Surprisingly, the judge was not angered at all. "That's the spirit!" he said with an encouraging pat to her chin. "No dog of mine will wait for things she has earned."

"Come on, Uncle Ellis, enough with the tricks," John whined. "Leave the dog for a while and help us train!"

The judge chuckled as he leaned down and grasped Moti's chin, then wiggled it back and forth in some form of affection. Arthur pulled again on his bidi.

"All right, run along." The judge dismissed her, but she didn't budge. Instead, she stared up at him, waiting for a command she could understand. "I don't know, boys, she's gotten quite attached," he said.

"Just tell Arthur to look after her," Will said. "I bet he can teach her something new in the time it takes us to run four 400s."

"Arthur!" the judge barked.

*Shit.*

Arthur pressed the bidi out against the wall, hid it under the crawl space, and wiped his fingers on his shirt. "Yes, sahib!" he called, trotting over.

"Take her and . . . teach her something worthwhile," the judge said, tossing him a piece of biscuit that Arthur assumed was his training material.

"Like what, sahib?"

"I don't know, come up with something. Something I can use. Now, hurry up, keep her out of our way while I whip these boys into shape."

The judge turned away and checked his gun to start their race. Moti, elated to see Arthur, was already leaning into his shins and lapping at his toes.

"She certainly took to you," the judge said, watching them.

Arthur thought he caught an edge to his voice, but before he could think of an explanation, the judge had turned away again.

"Come on," he whispered to Moti, who seemed all too happy to run away with him.

■■■

In the shade behind his hut, Arthur gave Moti the entire biscuit at once and then pushed her over to rub her belly.

"What are you doing with him?" he asked. A contented sigh was her response.

Though her wagging tail and pricked ears showed how eager she was to learn from humans, Arthur refused to believe it equated to love or devotion for the judge. He held on to the belief that she was simply a curious being, a hungry thing willing to entertain anyone who gave her attention, to savor life and all its opportunities. He had to believe there were still creatures as plain and good as that. He regretted not playing with her more when he had the chance—the chance to revel in her innocence before the judge stepped in and claimed her for himself and trained her for his own vanity. Arthur knew it was his fault for leading her to the Big House, unintentional though it was. She was trapped here—even if she didn't know it herself.

For all Moti's intelligence, Arthur could see no way to teach her that the judge was a bad man. It had always been said that dogs knew people from good and evil, but that didn't account for the juicy meat offered freely and the particularly ravenous bellies of Bengali pariah dogs. There was no way for him to teach her the danger of humans. After all, he himself was one.

They passed the time in play, Arthur tossing sticks and rocks and handfuls of leaves and Moti chasing after anything that moved, only occasionally bringing it back to him to throw again. She much preferred to chew the sticks to shreds after hunting them down in the grass. After a while, Arthur squatted in the dirt and rested his chin in his hands. It was the simplest of pleasures, watching her.

Time escaped them both, moving shadows across the ground without their noticing. Eventually, she tired of the game and came to lay at his feet. He took a velvet ear in between his fingers and caressed it, the softness like a salve to his roughened hands. "Moti, Moti, Moti," he murmured. "My Moti."

"Your what?" a voice interrupted them. The burra sahib stood not five paces away, his calm face betraying nothing.

Arthur stood up so swiftly that the blood rushed to his head.

"Sahib," he said, his throat scratchy. "It—it is only an endearment. Like *love* or *darling*. You know."

Then Arthur folded his arms behind his back and meant to walk away, eager to get far from this interaction. But the judge took a step and blocked his way.

"Show me what you taught her."

"Pardon?"

"Well, what have you been working on this whole time?"

"Kindly, sahib, we were only playing. She seemed not in the mood." Arthur attempted a weak smile in the hopes that the judge would find it funny.

"You didn't obey me?"

Arthur shifted his feet and looked stupidly at Moti, as if she'd know what to say.

But the judge continued. "I don't care if I ask you to train her or shoot her, I expect you to obey my order."

He knew what the proper response would be: *I'm very sorry, sir, it won't happen again.* But the words tasted bitter and would not release from his tongue. Maybe it was the loosening effects of the bidi or the diversion of playing with Moti or simply the heat of the late afternoon gone to his head, but something made Arthur clear his throat and say, without really thinking, "I don't work for you."

The air inflated between them. Arthur held the judge's gaze, waiting to see what he would do next. The recklessness was like a drug. It felt good not to think about the consequences of what he just said. He tried to ignore the pounding in his chest as the judge appraised him with fresh eyes.

"This is your hut, isn't it?" The judge, still with a blank face, gestured at the building that shaded them.

"Yes, sahib," Arthur whispered, enough sense coming back to him to keep his voice down, anything to appear submissive.

"Mm." The judge looked it up and down, the crumbling walls,

the thatched roof, the pathetic size. "A place of your own must be a luxury. You know, I see many officers' homes, and almost none of them have a dwelling like this for the help. In fact, I've no idea where they must go after their work is done. The streets, I imagine."

Arthur felt vaguely offended by this, but he had no intention of prolonging this conversation, so he simply nodded in reply.

The judge took a step to the side, almost enough to let Arthur by, but not enough to be sure. Then he drew another piece of mutton out of his pocket. "I suppose you remember the first time I visited here?"

The judge waited, apparently wanting a response. He dangled the mutton over Moti's head, just out of reach. She stretched her neck for it, drool glistening on her jowls.

Arthur swallowed. "Yes, sahib."

"Of course you remember me. I take great care to be someone people never forget. But what you may not know is that I remembered you."

His words made Arthur's hair stand on end, the back of his neck grow cold. For all the judge's cruelty toward him, his one comfort was knowing that the judge forgot him as soon as he was out of sight, that any given interaction would never last beyond the present. But if the judge remembered him, then that meant he had thought of Arthur—*retained* him in his mind like an animal caught in a trap.

"I remembered you had the cleanest pair of shoes for Sunday sermon, a rarity for people like you. And I remember watching you ride away on Mr. Hinton's bicycle one day, off to do some errand or other, and I thought to myself, *My word, they trust their servant quite a lot to let him do such a thing.*

"At first I was baffled that you brought the bicycle back, good as new. Why wouldn't you try to sell it? You could say it was stolen and pocket the profits for yourself. Or even those nice shoes—surely you could find someone who would pay good money for those, and again, you could say something happened to them. Dogs are always chewing shoes." At this, he knelt down to Moti and began petting her head slowly, so forcefully her eyes stretched back. In his other hand, the mutton remained just out of her reach. Moti let out a high-pitched whine.

"And the more I thought of it, the more I realized how intelligent you are. You have a good deal going here. The Hintons, they don't live lavishly like I do—they keep an automobile that will break if you so much as look at it, and they have no nice things save for what I buy them. But to you . . . why, this hut is practically Buckingham Palace."

Arthur's mouth had gone dry. He gulped a breath and felt his ribs tighten.

"So I decided to try something. I tried testing your loyalty. How far would you go to keep this deal going? At first I simply called you names, little insults I picked up at the Officers Club. When you didn't bat an eye, I had to start getting creative. Would you still do nothing if I . . . put a hand on Mrs. Hinton's waist when no one else was watching? Or follow her up the stairs after Mr. Hinton had fallen asleep in his chair? Let you listen when I called her *darling*."

Arthur's stomach was in knots by now, to hear such dark things he had known all along spoken aloud after all this time. For the judge was right: Arthur had seen everything.

The judge's face shone with sweat. He stood up again. Moti reacted by sitting straight in front of him, staring at the piece of meat.

"So you know my secrets, and hers as well. Hell—you must know everyone's secrets in this place, enough to bring the whole family to ruin if you wanted. You could tell everyone how *virtuous* the Hinton family *really* is. They would be expelled from their mission. They would be disgraced. They would leave India. You could bring all this upon them. But you won't. Because if they go, you have nothing. Do you see how that works?"

The judge teased Moti again with the morsel, almost allowing her to get it before snapping it back. She laid down on her stomach, trying a more submissive position to get her treat. "You may not work for me." He let go of the meat. In the split second it fell, Moti sprang from her haunches and snatched it midair, spit spraying, and devoured it by the time she landed on her paws again. "But I own you just the same."

The judge turned and walked back to the track. Moti didn't need to be called to follow. The taste of meat on her tongue was enough to lure her along. Arthur sank back against his hut, his vision swimming. He stayed still for some time, minutes or hours, until he finally willed himself to move and take on his usual duties. He passed the rest of the day in a haze. He served supper. He cleared the table. He retired early from the house. He lay numb on his charpoy, watching the moonlight stream through the cracks around the door of his hut. He had never felt more trapped in his life.

■■■

Everything was gray in the first light of morning. Arthur awoke to a world dry and dull; he yearned for the monsoons to come. He lurched out of bed and prepared for his Friday walk to the market, searching for his red cap and rucksack. What else was there to do but carry on? The judge's words played in his head all the sleepless night, and he couldn't wait to get away from the Big House and spend the day in town.

As he gathered his things around the hut, a shot rang out. The sound of it shook him. His eyes widened. Mind raced. A gun, that much was certain. But who? The judge had guns. Arthur could remember the pistol clearly. Suddenly he began to imagine every possible scenario. Oh no. Surely the boys weren't foolish enough to . . . ? Or the judge had been acting glum all these weeks. Could he have . . . ? It could also be nothing, just the guards practicing. But the shot sounded so close. Too close.

A sharp whistle jolted him as the shuffle of feet ran past his door. The guards. Could they have shot at someone? A trespasser. He remembered the men with the black arm bands, the streets full of them. But a trespasser could also be—

Arthur put a hand to his mouth, stifling a yelp. He flung the door open and ran out toward the house, thinking over and over in his head, *No, no, no.*

"Stop!"

A guard ran toward him, gripping his gun. He drew up in front of Arthur and said something, but Arthur couldn't hear it over the pounding in his ears. Without thinking, Arthur grabbed the guard's shoulder and pushed him aside, fleeing past him before the guard could steady himself.

As he approached the front of the house, he thought back to that day when he had seen Jaya's body lying in the grass, sunlight reflecting off her glossy hair like a mirror that showed him his barest self.

Fresh tears blurred his vision. He could see the spot in the grass now where something lay unmoving. He let out a sob and did not attempt to stifle it this time. All he could think was that he must look, see her one last time. But as he wiped his eyes, it all became clear.

The leopard.

There, in the dry grass and feeble rays of the dawn, the leopard's body lay crumpled like a pile of rags, the angles all wrong, the limbs splayed unnaturally, one giant paw held in front of its tired face as if in shame. And there, between the eyes, like a jewel fixed in the skull, the black hole where the bullet entered.

Arthur felt hands grab his body and force him to the ground, smash his face into the dirt. Arthur didn't feel anger toward them; they were reacting the only way they knew how when they hear a sudden gunshot. Get the native, take him down. From his sideways view, he watched the other guards rush at the leopard, pelting it with rocks to make sure it was dead. But couldn't they see all the blood?

"Don't touch it!"

Arthur squeezed his eyes shut. He did not want to see the horrible face of the judge. But there was his voice all the same, coming from the open guest room window. He relaxed his eyes and opened them.

The judge emerged from the front door barefoot, fastening his trousers, an unbuttoned shirt hanging off his shoulders and billowing behind him as he strode down the verandah steps, howdah pistol in hand.

"Damn good shot. *Damn* good. Ha!" he said, stooping over the leopard.

Arthur felt his legs move beneath him, attempting to stand up, but the soldiers gripped him harder and shoved him again into the ground.

"Payback!" shouted the judge. "To think those rajputlians put on those ridiculous hunts to bag one of these. And I shoot this old boy from my bedroom window!" The judge tossed the pistol into the grass and took hold of the leopard's paw, and for one horrific moment, Arthur thought the judge might begin waving it at him. But instead, the judge stretched the paw upward at the house, shaking it in the direction of the sleeping porch, where four heads peeked over the railing. "Wave hello!" he sneered, as the grotesque paw jerked in the air next to the judge's red face. "*That's* why you practice your shot, boys. You might just get lucky."

The judge began to laugh, a wheezing sound that emanated from his throat. But no one else said a word. The boys gaped, frozen in shock. The guards glanced between themselves, embarrassed to look at the scene in front of them.

Arthur wished he could sink into the earth, will the guards to push him harder until he broke through the solid ground. Because what else was there to do? What else mattered now but disappearing, leaving this earth where senseless killing could happen and be laughed about? Everything seemed to stand still. The pounding in his ears had stopped and there was a sudden clarity in the air, as if God had wanted him to see this moment plainly, arranged as though on a stage, the judge and leopard center, the pistol cast aside, the guards waiting in the wings.

But instead, the guards let go of him and retreated, finally realizing he had nothing to do with the gunshot. Arthur struggled to get up. His legs had gone numb, a thousand needles stuck all up and down. He sat back on his heels and did not attempt to get up again.

"Well, come on, let's get a picture," the judge said. "Hinton! Where are you?"

There in the front doorway, Mr. Hinton stood with his arms crossed. He bowed his head and passed a hand over his face. Mrs. Hinton stood behind, her disheveled hair and sleepy face just visible in the darkness of the house.

"Well?" the judge said again as he propped the leopard's head upright.

"Ellis." The Padre Sahib strode toward the judge, his leather sandals crunching in the dirt.

"Still have that Retina I gave you? Boys! Come down and—"

"Ellis!"

Arthur turned his head to look at them upright, the minister standing over the judge, who drew himself up. They were the same height. Arthur could just barely hear the padre speak, in a tone he had never heard before.

"What have you done?"

The judge reddened more. His eyes narrowed as he leaned in closer. "What do you mean, what have I done? What have *you* done? You've had this thing lurking in the woods around your house this entire time, and you never did a single thing to protect yourself. It could have attacked your children. Your wife!"

Mr. Hinton shook his head. "My wife?" He let out a small laugh. "You of all people," he said, "should know by now to leave things well enough alone." He stepped around the judge and knelt beside the leopard, examining its face. He sighed long and slow, letting the air out as though he'd been holding it this whole time. "What did it ever do to you?"

The judge faced the house, his back to Mr. Hinton and the leopard. He raised his head and gazed at the sky all afire with the dawn. "Do you remember," he said, "down in Contai, that first little house you lived in? There were cobras in your bedroom. And the grass roof had been whittled down by the cows to practically nothing. And when that storm rolled in and ripped the rest of that roof off and crumbled your walls, do you remember? Do you remember how frightened she was? How she begged you to let her go home after that—*home*, to America? And you almost said yes. You thought you should leave. You thought you weren't strong enough, didn't you? You wanted to go back. But I wouldn't let you. There's something in you this damned country needs, and I saw it when you wouldn't see it in yourself."

"Don't." Mr. Hinton's voice was softer than a whisper. He glanced up at the sleeping porch. "Don't you dare try to pretend you've ever supported my work."

"I put you up in *my* own house. For months! Do you remember!"

"Yes!" the Padre Sahib shouted, his face a surprising red. "But it was never because you *believed in me*. You may be able to convince yourself that your motives aren't selfish, but you can't convince me." Here his voice lowered to a snarl, as though he didn't want anyone to hear what came next: "Is that how it all started between you two? You stick around because of her, not because of my work. Do you think I don't notice? You've never cared a lick about God or sin, they're one and the same to you."

"I stick around for her because you dragged her into the jungle! She needs me, and *you* need me, and I'm the only one civilized enough around here to know it!"

"What do we need you for?"

"I'm a bloody high court judge—"

"You're disgraced. You've practically been banished; they don't want you back in Simla, and they don't want you here either. Perhaps you'll never work again. That business in Simla was too much trouble."

The judge stiffened.

"Tell me"—the Padre Sahib's voice kept low, like a snake in the grass—"where will you go when the whole country wants you out?"

Before anyone knew what was happening, the judge whirled and sprang toward Mr. Hinton, where he still knelt over the leopard. The judge's meaty hand closed around the padre's collar and yanked him up like a noose, but the padre's face remained still and stoic, as though in a medieval painting, waiting for the will of God to fall upon him.

"Enough!" Mrs. Hinton's shriek echoed from the house, where she stood in the darkness, ashamed, her blood-drained face like a ghost. Yet somehow her single word stayed the judge's hand. His purple face froze in its hateful sneer, allowing Mr. Hinton to extract himself from his grasp. He made for the front door, and she moved aside to let him through. He came out again with a white sheet and laid it down beside the leopard, giving neither the judge nor his wife nor the audience of guards any notice. They all stood in shock, the silence of these two men's cease-fire weighing in the air.

"Let's get it out of here," Mr. Hinton said.

The judge let out his breath. With a last glare at the padre, he flicked his wrist at his guards, gesturing toward the leopard.

"No," said Mr. Hinton. "You and me, Ellis. We'll take it to the shed."

Arthur, still kneeling, was paralyzed. The servant in him knew he should help, but the leopard had been young, not even fully grown. The guards all appeared saddened yet disgusted, willing to feel sorry for the leopard but not to touch its dead body. Arthur could understand that. Evil spirits were already flocking to the smell of death.

∎∎∎

After Mr. Hinton and the judge carried the body to the shed and covered it with the sheet, they still had not spoken to each other. They had already said enough. Not two minutes later, the judge had dressed himself and sped off in his car, not telling when he'd be back. But the judge's sudden departure could not undo the damage he'd caused.

Arthur put his hand on the shed door and nudged it open. He thought about all the times he had walked the woods without knowing the leopard had been there. Were there moments he had passed it, and it had let him go free? Had it watched him from the shadows as he'd run to Jaya? Had it seen him naked in the pools, bathing in the starlight?

The white sheet was larger than the leopard and covered the animal completely. The outline of the body was so much smaller than it had appeared out there in the grass. Arthur stood in the doorway, his shadow falling over the sheet. For a moment, he kept still, wishing that the leopard would move, show some sign of life. He laughed. Never in all his years had he wished so hard to be in a room with a live leopard. But there it was, at his feet, with nothing but drops of blood here and there as proof that it once lived. He bit his lip and suddenly found it hard to breathe. What was the point, he thought, of having such fine things in India?

After a while of just standing there in the doorway, it became clear that he did not have the strength to look under the sheet. He knew it was there anyway. And what good would it really do to see it? It was never coming back. He began to pull the shed door closed.

"Wait."

A little voice like a bird behind him. Gene.

"Sah—" Arthur's throat caught.

"You don't have to," Gene said. Then he inched closer and lowered his eyes. "I wanted to see it."

Arthur relaxed his shoulders and stepped back into the shed, opening the door again. He stood aside to let Gene in, but the boy did not come closer. He kept outside the shed, where it was barely possible to see the sheet.

Gene swallowed. "Will you lift it for me?"

Arthur couldn't tell if the boy was scared or fascinated or something else entirely. He thought back to the day they had seen the leopard on that hike and tried to recall how Gene had reacted. Had he backed away slowly, or had he crept forward? Had he screamed, or had he held his breath? Had he run away as soon as it was safe, or had he searched after the leopard as it tore away into the forest? It all seemed so long ago, and look how things had changed.

Arthur reached out and peeled back a corner of the sheet. When Gene seemed to have had enough, he gently placed it back. Arthur didn't look.

As Arthur stepped out of the shed, he felt the need to comfort the boy, though he himself was in just as much shock. But wasn't that what adults were supposed to do for children? He laid a hesitant hand on the boy's golden hair and removed it after a second. How much had the boy seen?

Gene looked up, his eyes wide and gentle. Not knowing what to say, Arthur took a deep breath and looked away. He continued walking from the shed, knowing only that he needed to get far from here, far from the house's curse he had been denying all these years.

"Arthur?" Gene said.

But he kept walking, his legs carrying him toward the statue on the edge of the lawn and past it down the winding trail that led into the trees.

# CHAPTER 20

Not long after the judge left, Mr. Hinton gathered the whole family to the shed to say a prayer for the leopard and for God's forgiveness. As his father's words filled the small space, Gene kept his eyes on the red spot where blood had seeped through the sheet. It reminded him of the shape Lee's black eye had appeared the night after the attack in the bazaar. Except that had faded into nothing now, and this stain would never wash out.

Afterward, the boys hung around the shed just staring at the leopard, with the sheet pulled back and its eyes closed as if someone had tucked it into bed. They marveled at how much smaller it was and even speculated that perhaps it wasn't the same one they had seen before. But leopards were solitary creatures, and Gene knew this was the one.

"I don't see what Dad is so upset about," said John, arms crossed as he examined the corpse. "Look at those claws. It's a predator. Could've had any one of us."

"How could you think that?" said Lee. "It's a beautiful creature. And just imagine what the villagers will think of us when they hear what we've done."

"Are you kidding? If anything, it'll win their favor. Uncle Ellis *saved* us. Did you see how close to the house it got? And we leave doors and windows open all the time. Frankly, I'm surprised nothing's gotten in before."

"But look at it," Gene whispered.

They stared at it some more in silence, knowing they probably would never get this close to a leopard again.

The longer Gene looked, the harder the pit in his stomach grew. The shock of the gunshot in the still morning, that single shot, coming from inside the house. He had never actually felt afraid of the judge before, but now he couldn't deny the feeling of dread at just the thought of him. If he could shoot a leopard straight between the eyes from his bedroom window, what else was he capable of? He was always armed. Evidently, he kept his pistol within arm's reach while he slept. Suddenly, it occurred to him. If what he knew of the judge was true—his weapons, his tenacity, his massive size—then how was it possible that the Indian woman had tried to attack him, as he said?

By the time the sun was all the way above the treetops, it was already deathly hot, and they all knew the leopard's body couldn't be kept in the shed much longer before it started to reek. John and Will helped Mr. Hinton move it out under the cashew trees behind the cookhouse, which wasn't much cooler. By midmorning, the judge returned in a small truck with a guard and two British officers. He directed them to the body; they appeared impressed, remarking on the straight shot and the leopard's figure, lean but muscular, with a healthy coat that would make a dashing skin. They shook the judge's hand in congratulations, then got to work moving it to the truck bed. As the judge got back into the passenger side, Mr. and Mrs. Hinton still did not come out of the house. The judge waved once at the boys as the truck drove away, but his face remained solemn, angry.

"Do you think he'll be back?" said John.

"He will," said Lee. "He didn't take his trunks."

■■■

Arthur hadn't the slightest idea what time it was, and frankly, he didn't care. He had been walking all afternoon on the same trail, one foot in front of the other, replaying over and over everything that had occurred since the judge had stepped off that train weeks before. What had been that first thing he'd said? Something arrogant and obnoxious, though nothing he hadn't heard from other British people before.

He had long passed the pools by now, following the trail farther than he ever had. For all he cared, he could just keep going until the Big House and the judge and those horrible boys were long behind him. He needed to see Jaya. She would understand. He stopped for a moment to catch his breath; all this fuming, the years of injustices all being realized at once, was making him exhausted.

The brush was so much thicker here, and the path was barely visible through the wayward branches of banyan and frangipani. The forest was no longer just sal. All sorts of trees flourished here, with vines dripping from high places. Arthur wondered when someone had last passed through. He wiped his brow with the sleeve of his tunic. It was so unbearably hot and humid today, more than he had ever endured in his life. Was it the way the canopy sealed in everything beneath it, so that there was no way for air to pass? Was it the steam rising from the moist earth like he had never seen before, as he'd gotten used to the dry dust back at the house? Or was it the way the heat seemed to be coming from inside him instead, as if his very stomach, empty and shrunken, was about to burst into flame?

He could take it no more. With a raw screech, he kicked a nearby branch clean off its trunk and sent it sailing into the jungle. The silence that followed sobered him. What had come over him? He kept picturing that singular paw waving in the air, grotesque and somber. How else was someone supposed to act after that?

He sat down in the middle of the trail and rubbed his swollen feet. It would take ages to wipe off all the dirt before dinner. But who cared about dinner now? Let them serve it themselves. They'd been living in India for almost twenty years; it was time they learned to do things themselves for a change.

All of a sudden his eyes began to water, his shoulders shook, and he felt so totally alone. He realized there wasn't one person who knew where he was or even cared, save a family that needed him only to scoop dal onto their oversize plates.

For the first time in a long while, he imagined what his parents would be doing this very moment if they were still alive. His mother would be down at the ghats, straining river water through the same clothes she'd worn for decades. And his father would be crouching in their doorway waiting for her to come home, rolling a bidi the way he'd taught Arthur. He felt a pang in his stomach at the thought that his life with them had been cut short.

He closed his eyes and leaned all the way back so he was flat in the middle of the path, the lowest leaves just brushing his arms and face. It was a little cooler so low to the ground, and he thought he might stay like this for a while. He cracked one eye open, and then the other, to gaze at the multitude of layers the jungle created above. The geometry of the forest never ceased to amaze him. Every leaf, every dangling berry, every patch of moss complemented the next, so that everything gave the impression of being arranged by an artist. And every bit of space was home to some living thing. Not a single ray of light made its way down to where Arthur lay on the ground, but the highest leaves were all glowing green from the sunlight on the other side. A leaf could never be that vivid on its own; only sunlight could make it so.

Eventually the tickle of ants became too much to bear. He stood and brushed them off along with the dirt—and there she was, staring at him from the bushes.

"Moti!"

The sight of her goofy ears and gentle eyes was enough to make the tears flow for real now. The relief at a familiar face flooded his whole body with warmth. "Moti, thank God, thank God."

She bounced over the branches and came to his feet, licking his toes. He didn't care that it tickled, like the ants all over again. He embraced her. She kept on licking. He thought, *Thank God thank God thank God.*

As he stroked her fur, he thought how fortunate it was she had not been around when the judge shot the leopard. What if he had shot Moti instead? Any animal, wild or not, wasn't safe near the judge. Arthur had been foolish to think the burra sahib really cared about Moti—*Ella.* It was only a matter of time before he inflicted some violent end to her too. He had to take this chance while the judge was away . . .

"Moti, come, Moti," he whispered, as if someone were around to hear him. "Come, I'm taking you home."

■■■

The door to his hut was still open from that morning when he had rushed out at the sound of the gunshot. He pushed Moti in and glanced back at the Big House. Lights were still on in the downstairs windows, and he could hear the clinking of glasses and cutlery. So they had served dinner themselves. Arthur felt almost happy for their accomplishment. He thought at first he should go in and apologize in case they had worried about him, but something about the way the glasses sounded so cheerful—*ding! ding!*—suggested they had not missed him at all.

Just as Arthur was going to shut the door, a light came on in the upper corner window. All he could really see of the room from below was the ceiling, but a distorted shadow of a head and shoulders in profile loomed across the window. Arthur could tell by the person's size that it was the judge. So they had taken him back in. *Like good Christian people*, he thought. Shaking his head, he pushed the door closed, dropped the latch in place. He would have to hide Moti here until first light, then figure out how to get her away before anyone woke up. He gave her a piece of stale bread from his meager stash, and she settled on the floor to chew it like a bone, it was that tough. He made his way through the dark to the little table next to his charpoy. He lit the lamp, and there on the charpoy was Jaya.

"How did you get in here?" he whispered. But he was so relieved to see her face, her long, black hair still silky and so, so feminine.

"It wasn't locked," she said. "And these guards, they are not earning their pay."

"But how did no one see you? No one saw you, right?"

She got up from the bed, ignoring the question. Shaking the folds of her sari, she stepped toward him and reached out, eyes shining in the low light.

"What happened here?" she asked.

Arthur couldn't think where to begin. "He—there was . . ." It was as if his mouth had gone numb, swollen with all the words he wished he could say. "I can't—"

She put a hand to his cheek, kissed him softly, barely touching her lips to his, but a kiss all the same. And he told her everything, not just about that morning but about the afternoon too, about the things he'd finally realized about the Hintons, how they were no better than the friends they kept; how the judge was back in the house as though nothing had happened; how perhaps they didn't need him, Arthur, anymore; how all the years he'd worked for them had been for nothing. They would never care about him or the people they so righteously "helped," and they likely never had.

It all came out like the Ganges, filthy but somehow cleansing, and when he finished, she said his name so sweetly—"Arthin"—like a release from a spell. And Moti, done with her supper, gave a contented sigh and closed her eyes.

"I barely know them, these Hintons," she said, "but they are just like the others. Better you realize late than never."

He let Jaya stroke his head. She smelled like smoke, like burning ghee, like the bazaar. He realized he hadn't eaten a single thing all day.

"Tell me where you go," he said.

She pulled herself away and looked at him with a kind of sorrow he might have seen somewhere before. He only just realized she looked a little like his mother. She shook her head.

"I cannot tell you," she whispered. "But don't you want to know where I came from?"

There it was, the accent in her voice, the way she spoke only Hindi to him, or English to the Hintons. Not a single word of Bengali. She had become so familiar, so intimate with him by now, that he had forgotten she was not from here. He wobbled his head in the hesitant affirmative.

"Do you know I grew up in a house larger than that?" She nodded in the direction of the Big House. She must have seen the surprise on Arthur's face. She led him to the charpoy, which creaked under their combined weight. Outside, the crickets quieted down like an audience holding its breath.

"We were zamindars of Himachal," she continued. "You know, in the mountains. Or do you even know? How large this country is? The highest peaks you've ever seen. Winding roads that disappear into the clouds. The birth of the Ganges. I bathed in pure crystal-clear water. And our home was beautiful. We ourselves weren't all that powerful, but my father dined with maharajahs, and my brother—" She swallowed.

Arthur could feel her start to tremble. Taking her hand, he leaned sideways into her. She seemed to have trouble carrying on, so he spoke.

"What is your brother's name?"

"Amarendra." She smiled. "Amar."

What must it be like to have a brother, Arthur thought, whose mere mention brought a smile to your face, no matter how far away?

"Do you ever hear about what goes on in Himachal?" she asked.

"No."

"Exactly. Because nothing goes wrong there. That's why the Raj moves up there every summer. Dalhousie, Simla, they are so quiet compared to Bengal. The people here drove the Raj away—you are so headstrong. I admire it. And my brother admired it. He wanted to do the same for Himachal."

She rested her head on Arthur's shoulder, and suddenly he felt so drowsy, listening to her story about places so far away. He closed his eyes, hearing only her voice in the dark.

"So charismatic, Amar. It wasn't long before he had a large following. He held demonstrations, supported native candidates in the elections. The papers said he was no Gandhiji. They said Amar supported bombings, violent protests, any means to bring down the Raj. But it wasn't true! You know how things get. People inevitably turn violent when they get together. And hadn't the British started it?"

She paused, perhaps expecting an answer or else checking to see if he was following. But it was all so much information at once, about a woman he hadn't dared to think too much about, lest this dream end. He knew she was a mysterious woman, and mysterious women were best left alone, but now he was in deep, so deep it was all he could do to nod his cheek against the top of her head—yes, he was with her.

That seemed to satisfy her. She inched backward from the edge of the bed so that now she leaned against the wall, as if telling Arthur all this exhausted her. Instead of joining her, he rested his head in her lap and shut his eyes again. When she spoke, her voice dropped so low he could just barely hear her over his own breathing.

"One day they arrested him. Some made-up charges that he was connected to a plan to bomb the magistrate. The day I saw an English officer's hands on my brother was the day it all changed. It was coming. Our zamindari, along with everywhere else in India where Indians still held power, was under more and more restrictions. But I had just looked past it, because my father had accepted it and it was happening everywhere. But when they took Amar away . . ."

"You couldn't stand by anymore."

"Hm." She seemed to be enjoying the fact that he had agreed with her. "And do you know who presided over his case?"

He saw fear in her eyes now, like she'd never said this out loud to someone else and was only now confronting it, and now it would be true if it was spoken.

"Judge Ellis." She said his name like a curse, *Ell-ees*, breathing the two words forcefully down to Arthur's face, giving them a physicality only the judge's name, of all people, could achieve. "Only, he never did put Amar on trial. Because Amar was so forcefully against the Raj and because he was making progress, they all took their time and made sure he waited in prison for a long, long time. Too long. So long that he grew sick."

"No."

"We heard barely a word from him, just what the officers told us, that he was fine, best treatment, the judge would see to it soon, any day now. But when he became sick, oh, my mother became a monster. She broke her *purdah*, she was at the courthouse day and night, demanding his release, demanding to see the judge, and my father couldn't stop her. You should have seen her. All her finest clothes, all her jewels, because she thought it would make a difference. But they didn't change a thing. I joined her on the day she came to the prison wearing the sari she'd borrowed from her handmaid. I borrowed one from mine. We looked so plain together. And they must have taken pity on us then because they let us see him in his cell. You are lucky you have no brothers, and you will never see what I saw. It was like he'd aged fifty years, he looked so much like our father. And my mother couldn't even say a word. She wailed all through the prison. Amar reached his hand out to me, and it was so filthy and pale. I said to him, 'Why are you in a common cell? They told us they were treating you well.' And his answer? 'Because I am a common man in this India. The Raj cares nothing for the zamindar any more than for the untouchables. All they see is that we are Indian.'

"He died a few days later. We never got to bring him home. And I didn't stay for his cremation. But there were so many riots against the court, against the British judge who would not let a zamindar home."

"So he came here. Judge Ellis."

"Yes."

"And so you did too. You followed him. But how could you stand to be around him?" And then, realizing the danger of what he now knew, he added, "What do you intend to do?"

"What anyone would do when their brother has rotted to death in a cell, when all the centuries of their family's history mean nothing anymore, when the man they so despise is so cowardly that he flees, as if things will all die down back there, as if Indians all around the country are not rising up."

Arthur wondered how much of all this could possibly be true. He could perhaps believe she came from a higher class, the way she held herself and spoke, how she managed to be so impeccably groomed. And of course he believed she was from another place. It had been obvious the first day he'd seen her. But how could he believe she had followed the judge all the way here? How could she have known that he was staying with the Hintons? And how convenient that this was a boarding house, so she, too, could stay under the same roof as the judge—if she could stand it.

"It is foolish to do what you're doing," he said.

"It is foolish to do nothing."

"Well, then, how?"

"You know where he keeps it."

"With his own!" He sat up and stared at Jaya.

"What better way?" She stared back. "You have changed since I met you. Your eyes are open. Think! There is so much that has changed."

If she were telling the truth, then it was indeed a tragedy he could never know, seeing your innocent brother die in jail, denied justice, care, or even the decency to die at home. And the judge was not innocent. In fact, all Arthur had ever seen of the judge indicated that the world would be better off without him. Still, it didn't add up to murder.

"I'll have no part in it," he said.

"You are already a part of it."

"Why?" he snapped. "Why bring me into this? I'm no young man. I know you did not warm up to me because you are so attracted to me. You bring me into this, you bring them into it. We did not ask to be part of your plot!"

"You think I have loved you falsely?"

"If you really are a zamindar, you wouldn't even touch me."

"Don't you see! Castes mean nothing. I left my caste behind when I left home. Our caste could not save my brother."

She paused and looked hard into the darkness. Then she stood with her hands on her hips, turning back to him. There were tears in her eyes, and now it mattered less to Arthur whether they were real or not. What *was* real was another person, here in this hut, sharing more about herself than anyone ever had with him before. They had met not long ago, but she had so quickly become vital to him, his one source of joy, the only person who cared about him at all, who thought him worthy of secrets, of tender touch, of equal conversation.

He stood to embrace her. She pushed him away. He stumbled back onto the bed. Moti stirred from the commotion and jumped onto the charpoy, licking Arthur's hands.

"Don't," Jaya breathed, a fierceness in her eyes. "You are not loyal to me."

The tears had stopped. She made for the door and reached for the handle. She was going to leave, and Arthur didn't know how to stop her. He couldn't bear to see her go. He looked around the room. His red servant's cap, in the corner. It transported him back twenty years to the day he first stepped inside this hut, tired and so proud to be here, a servant for that nice American couple, before their sons came. They had given him the cap, and he had cared for it like all his things, with more attention than it needed; it was just a cap after all. Except it wasn't just a cap; it was a sign of upward mobility, a step up from life in Kharagpur, a sign that he was going somewhere, doing something worthwhile in his life that perhaps would last long after he was gone. But what had it really come to? The Hintons knew and cared as much about him now as they had on that first day. And now the one person who might possibly love him was leaving. Faster than he had ever moved before, he pushed Moti away, bounded off the charpoy, grasped Jaya's arm with one hand, and shut the door with the other.

"Tell me your plan," he said.

# CHAPTER 21

The plan, once Jaya was through telling it, felt like a reckoning that had stalked Arthur ever since he left his childhood home in Kharagpur. He listened to her words in a trance, as if she were telling him his fortune.

After what his father had done all those years ago, Arthur had believed for his whole life that it was only a matter of time before the same would happen to himself. That's how he thought of it: something that had happened to him, like a prophecy passed down to him from his father, forged in the most desperate of times.

***

Arthin was twelve years old when the well ran dry on his family's plot. They owned a meager parcel just wide enough to walk 163 paces across. He knew the exact number because he had pulled the plow himself with his father most years, a plow that was meant for an ox that they could never afford.

In the good years, their home in Kharagpur was a happy place for a child. Afternoons spent in the tall grass, hiding from the world. Cold swims with his father in the irrigation ditches before sunrise, before the heat set in. The basket in his arms growing heavier as they harvested the barley together, the grin on his father's face when the year was a bountiful one. The walk to the market with his mother, the weight of coins in his pocket on the way home. The warm feeling in his belly every night as he went to bed full.

That summer, he watched the barley fields shed the green color of spring for gold, the natural order of things, of time passing, of the year ripening. But the monsoons that came before the reaping did not bring the rain that was promised. The clouds remained tethered to the mountains, not daring to push across the plains, leaving the ashen skies to rot into orange in some unbending cycle. Days that were once filled with whoops of neighboring farmers goading their livestock or the low rumble of wheels over pebbles in the lane now fell silent. Some mornings, even the birds could not be roused to seek the grub and seeds that might be found in the cracks of the dry earth. A tiredness weighed over all, and Arthin spent more time dragging water from the Kangsabati River ten kilometers away than he spent at home.

By September, Arthin watched as the whispered worries that came from his parents' bed began to wear themselves on everyone's faces as time marched toward a dry and brittle harvest. Some families abandoned their homes before it got bad. The ones that stayed spent more time loitering together than tending the fields, playing games on the roadside to pass the day, fending off the hopelessness in their minds.

One morning, he joined his father, scythe in hand, to walk the rows in the amber dawn. He stood waist deep in the field as his father knelt to examine the drought-ravaged stalks, the wilted heads turned downward in apology. And these were the rows that were still standing. The others, stricken white in their drawn-out death, lay crippled on the ground.

By then, Arthin was acquainted with the dull ache of hunger, which seemed to spread from his gut to his entire body, the empty feeling in his head, the weight in his feet. But he wasn't accustomed to the wasted look in his father's eyes, the tired way he rose in the morning as if the day had already exhausted him before he even went out the door.

Because despite the signs, his father still went out every morning to look at the crops. At first, Arthin went with him, trusting his father's silence as a good sign. They were to get to work. There would be work to do. But his father would only walk the tiny length of the rows and stand still, eyes fixated on nothing in particular. Eventually, Arthin just stayed in the doorway of their dwelling and watched with his mother's arm around his shoulder. He could feel her body thinning, wasting away from the soft and supple flesh that once comforted him.

"Would you believe it?" his mother said. "After all this, they'll still collect the land tax at the end of the month."

"What will we do, Ma?" he murmured, his lips dragging on the words. "What will we do if we can't sell the barley?"

"What will we do if we can't eat?" his mother said. Her answer to his question with another question was all the more awful.

In time, they had no choice but to go into town and look for scraps left behind by people who still had bellies full enough to discard food. It was unclean, and in a way, it changed Arthin. He began to wonder why people would spend what little money they had on clean, unblemished fruit when it could be found on the roadside, dust covering the rotten parts. Wilted vegetables and half-gnawed bones were still good enough to boil into a stew, so Arthin and his mother gathered all they could in their baskets and walked back home, as natural as if they had merely finished the shopping in the bazaar.

As they turned down the lane that led to their plot, Arthin sensed the sting of smoke in the air. White ash drifted in the light breeze, never falling to the ground, but catching on his sticky skin as he walked through. His mother yelped at what she realized must be happening and dropped her basket to run. But Arthin picked up the basket and stacked it on top of his own, resuming his slow walk. Because he guessed what waited at the end of the lane. And he preferred not to rush the horizon.

The dried stalks burned up so quickly that the fire was almost out by the time Arthin came upon the sight. His father sat on the ground with his legs straight out in the dirt, watching the embers that he had started. His bare chest moved in shallow breaths, and Arthin could see his lips move without a sound. A handful of barley heads lay scattered at his side as if they were worth saving, a memento of what could have been. Should have been. Thankfully, the empty ditches around their field were enough to break the fire and keep it from spreading to the neighboring plots. Not that they had anything valuable or living either.

It was such a small and inconsequential place, their barley plot, which was no longer a barley plot. No one but Arthin and his family would mourn the loss. One hundred and sixty-three paces. That was all he had ever occupied in the world. It was so little to lose, yet it was everything.

The next morning, Arthin didn't even rise from his sleeping mat. Now that there was truly nothing to do, no rows to walk, no scythe to wield, he felt the dread that ached at the back of his throat ripple like water to the wind. They had had tough years before, but they had always pulled out of it. Other farmers had lent a hand when their plow broke. Or when they had bought bad seeds one year, another family had taught them to test them in water next time.

But there was no test for drought. No test for rain that remained absent from the sky. No test for the empty well that once reflected light and showed Arthin his face. Everything was empty, empty.

One night, Arthin awoke to the sound of his father stumbling home in the dark. The stench of temburni leaves and betel juice followed him in, fouling their hut in a matter of seconds. His mother was up from her sleeping mat and smacking his father's ears before Arthin could even rub the sleep out of his eyes.

"Where have you been?" she screamed. "What are you doing, spending money on smokes? Didn't you do enough damage already? You ruined us!"

"You're lucky I came back, there are plenty of other places to sleep. Don't worry, I'll be gone again as soon as the sun rises. So you can keep telling all the neighbors you have a failure for a husband."

"What neighbors? Are you too brainless to see half of them have left? No one can stay here, no one is stupid enough to stay here!"

His father stumbled back into the hazy light of the full moon brushing through the open doorway. He took a sweeping look around the shadowed room, the corrugated iron roof, the rusted pot on the dead coals, the spare cotton kurta hanging on a hook on the wall, their one luxury. And he began to laugh. The sound was like broken glass to Arthin's ears.

"You think I ruined you?" his father hissed in the darkness. "We have always been ruined."

And just as quickly as he had come home, he staggered backward into the night again. Arthin scrambled to his mother and hugged her waist, certain that something awful would befall them now, if he hadn't been certain before. He felt his mother's shuddering breaths as they watched his father's receding silhouette, before he turned around and shouted, "We were ruined the day we were born!"

"I should go after him, Ma," Arthin said. "To make sure he doesn't get hurt."

"Let him get hurt," she spat. "Let him fall down in a ditch and choke on the dust!" But she didn't stop Arthin from running after his father.

He followed the sound of his father's dragging feet and stuporous hum past dead jute fields and diseased potato rows, past the watering hole that once brimmed with people splashing in the abundant depths. The empyrean moonlight glistened off the iron roofs, while crickets hushed as Arthin crept past. His father was not moving with much purpose, and Arthin wondered if he knew where he was going. But eventually his father turned off the lane and tramped over broken growth toward a tiny hut in the middle of a jute plot, one that barely stood taller than the stalks. A single candle flame flickered in the doorway, and Arthin watched as it was eclipsed by a dark figure stepping into view. Arthin ducked behind a cluster of weeds and watched as his father approached the hut. He couldn't make out the words, but he could tell that there were some five or six voices packed into the small space. Once his father disappeared inside, Arthin crept closer to hear.

"Our scout says they'll come through Lodhasuli Forest in two days' time," a gruff voice said.

"You have a scout?" his father asked.

"Another farmer like us. His rice paddy has been dry since the winter."

"The forest is far from here," another man whispered. "How will we time it right?"

"They collect the tax on the last day of September. They'll be on the way to the bank by then. We'll wait the night before, and if we must wait all the next day too, so be it. What else is there to do?"

"How do we split it?"

"I'll take half. I have the gun, and I'll do the deed if it comes to it. The rest of you are just to threaten and hold anyone back who tries to fight. You'll smash their wheels so they can't follow or run for help. If everything goes according to plan, no one will get hurt. But if it doesn't . . ."

Arthin waited for more, but the silence swept the room as the men all contemplated what they were about to do.

"Tomorrow night?" his father finally said. The candlelight that flickered among the silhouettes was weakening as it sank to its end.

"Tomorrow night," the gruff voice said, followed by a sharp puff of air and the darkness.

Arthin ran home, chasing the dawn. As he watched the sun cast the world in golden light, he felt a dread gurgling in his chest. How could his father do such a thing? It wasn't like him. They were good people. They had an honest life and took only what was theirs. Had it all been a lie? Was this his father's real self? Had it always been there, this evil, lurking only skin deep? A terrifying thought crept in the depths of his mind. If his father was that kind of person, what did that make him?

All that day and the next, he agonized over what to do. Should he tell his mother? Confront his father? Hide in the grass and pretend like life itself wasn't going the way that it was? Because no matter what crime his father would or wouldn't commit tomorrow, this was all because of rains that never came. Because of the gods. Because of forces other than themselves. And what were people small and powerless as themselves supposed to do?

His father returned in the afternoon, his face solemn but eyes clear. If he noticed Arthin had followed him the previous night, he didn't let on. He squatted under a tree and smoked a bidi until supper was called, their supper of watery stew. He drank it quickly and went back to his bidi under the tree. When dusk came, he called Arthin over.

"Son," he said.

Arthin came to within a few paces away, dreading what his father would say.

"I've heard of . . . a job. I'm walking tonight to the next town to see about it. So I'll be gone for a couple of days."

Arthin held his breath. *Lie.*

"If it's a good job, I might not come back for a while. And you're almost grown, you'll be the man of the house now."

Arthin snorted. He couldn't help himself. Man of their tiny house and scorched plot? But he bit his lip and nodded.

He waited for something more from his father. His father pulled on the bidi and held the smoke, looking up at Arthin. He nodded and let the smoke unfurl from his nostrils. He held the half-finished bidi out to Arthin.

"*Babaji* . . ." Arthin stammered. He'd never tried it before. The stench had never tempted him. But he felt he should take it, like one final covenant between father and son, should this really be the last. He took the bidi, put it to his lips, and inhaled.

■■■

Lodhasuli Forest was a long day's walk from Kharagpur. Arthin heard his father leave in the blue hour of morning, and his mother didn't even stir. But after an hour or so, with a cup full of watery porridge in his belly, he told his mother he was taking a long walk to search the abandoned plots for anything worth salvaging.

"Good idea," she said. "But be careful. Make sure the people are really gone before you steal anything."

After walking for hours, then smuggling himself aboard a passing ox cart, then hopping off and walking some more, he finally made it to the edge of the forest in the late afternoon. As he ducked under the trees, his world suddenly transformed from the dusty brown patina of drought to an oasis of green. It was like the forest was alive and breathing, a layer of leaves underfoot softening his every step. He reached out and touched a coat of moss that covered the trees. The trunks were thin but sturdy, like they had been growing a long time. They wouldn't offer much coverage for someone who wished to hide, so he searched for clusters of overgrown bushes that might conceal an entire group of thieves.

The dying light of day was even weaker in the forest, so Arthin hurried down the main road and listened for voices. There was no one else on the road. Travelers weren't likely to go through these parts in the dark, and Arthin suddenly realized he had nothing to protect himself from the animals that might lurk in the shadows. Panicked, he grabbed the next fallen branch he found and continued.

Suddenly, the sound of voices. Arthin scrambled down the ditch that paralleled the road, and peering over the edge, he caught a glimpse of two men rushing in his direction, coming from the other side of the forest. His heart pounded in his entire body all the way to his toes, and he held his breath for fear even that could give him away. But before reaching him, the men ducked into the trees on the other side of the road. Frantic whispering followed, rustling in the leaves, as they all took position—then silence.

Arthin ducked out of sight and let out his breath. He clutched the branch close to his chest and waited and waited—an eternity or a minute, it all felt the same. He was about to risk being seen to look over the road again when he heard the unmistakable rhythm of hoof falls and the steady sound of wheels rolling in the dirt.

He looked around and spotted a thorny bush growing out of the ditch, large enough to hide behind. He scrambled to it and peeked through the leaves. Sure enough, a covered cart with two men at the front was approaching. He still couldn't see the hidden thieves, and there was no sign of his father, but he knew they couldn't be far from where he hid. The cart continued closer. It was only a matter of minutes now before the attack. How could they be sure this was the tax collection cart? It was getting too dark to properly see the men driving it. He could only hope these farmers-turned-thieves knew what they were doing.

Arthin could feel the sweat tingling on his brow, the adrenaline tightening his muscles, the branch slipping in his shaking hands. What was he even doing here? When his father left that morning, he knew he couldn't just let him go. But what did Arthin actually mean to do now that the time had come? Was he really going to help in the attack? Rush out of the bushes, wielding this half-withered branch that would surely shatter on first contact? Or would he stay hidden the whole time and watch from the ditch like a coward, but return safely home to his mother when it was all over?

There was no more time to think. The cart was coming closer, closer—and passed. For a second, Arthin thought the thieves realized it was the wrong cart and were letting it go, but then he blinked, and before his eyes, five or six men crashed out of the underbrush and swarmed the cart, two climbing on the back while the others flanked the sides and easily caught the reigns of the two exhausted bullocks.

The cart screeched to a halt in the road. Arthin watched as his father jumped aboard the driver's seat and struggled with one of them, and in the gathering darkness, it was hard to tell who had the upper hand. Arthin inched closer, sure that no one would notice him in all the excitement. Finally, the driver stopped struggling and slouched at his father's feet, and Arthin pleaded to himself that his father hadn't just killed a man with his bare hands. A few seconds later, Arthin sighed in relief as the man moved his head, trying to make sense of what had just happened.

The ringleader grabbed the other driver's chin and jerked his face upward. "Where is the money?" he shouted.

The driver cowered with his hands above his head. "None, we have none!" he gasped as the ringleader kicked him in the stomach.

The thieves on the back of the cart had ripped off the cloth covering and were searching the wooden boxes underneath. Arthin's father still held the other driver, but he was looking around as if he were beginning to realize they might have made a mistake.

One of the thieves chucked something onto the ground, where it made a pathetic *splat!* in the dirt. "They're all fucking eggs!" he shouted. Then he dumped the crate over the side of the cart, shattering eggs into a mess of broken yolks and shells on the ground.

For a moment, no one moved. Arthin half believed they would all let the cart go and forget this ever happened. But something was in the air—whether desperation or disappointment or all their collective broken dreams as a result of this forsaken drought weighing over everyone like a cloud that blocked out the entire sky—and the ringleader snapped. The driver didn't see the first punch coming, the one that went straight to his face. Two, three more came, then the ringleader was on him like an animal gone mad. Everyone joined in the chaos: shouts of blame hurled at each other for who had made this mistake, the scout, the ringleader, the drivers for being in the wrong place at the wrong time. Eggs flew every which way, and when the thieves tired of that, they smashed the crates against the cart seemingly just to break things. The bullocks moaned in terror and strained at the yoke, jerking the cart forward and causing some of the men to topple over the sides. And then everyone was upon each other. No time for words, just knuckles and knees and fingernails to scratch and tear and pummel their madness out.

Through it all, Arthin watched paralyzed in the bushes, his mind in agony over what he should do. There was nothing to do, there was no money to steal. But it was like the men didn't care, and they just craved flesh meeting fist in some carnal release. Arthin bit his tongue and glanced down the road, hoping someone might come along and break the hysteria. But of course no one was coming. He fixed his eyes back on the chaos and scanned the scene for his father.

"Oh no," Arthin breathed. And he launched himself out of the bushes, out of the ditch, and plunged into the fight.

On the other side of the cart, his father stood clobbering the driver with a jagged piece of wood broken from one of the egg crates. Blood splattered his chest and arms, but it was nothing compared to the driver's mangled head. Miraculously, the driver looked to still be conscious, but just barely. He had enough faculties to curl his body on the ground to protect himself, but nothing was slowing Arthin's father as he delivered blow after blow.

"*Bandha kara!*" Arthin screamed as he ducked his head and lunged for his father's stomach, avoiding the wooden weapon's swings and catching his father enough by surprise that he fell easily. "*Baba!* Stop it! Stop it!" he shouted as they grappled on the ground, Arthin digging his heels into the dirt to gain purchase and still his father's rage. But with startling alacrity, his father was on his feet again and charging after the driver, Arthin's efforts having done nothing at all. His father was mere steps from the crumpled driver's body when Arthin lunged from behind and grabbed hold of his father's leg from below. In one swift movement, his father swung around and cracked the dented lath across Arthin's head.

In the second it took for Arthin to let go of his father's leg and drop, stunned, to the ground, he felt the peculiar sensation of his mind expanding, reaching back in time and forward at once, as if it were floating around inside his skull. He pictured his father's face in the gloaming, the feral look in his eyes not registering his own son right in front of him. He felt his lips move at the sting of betrayal, trying to form the word that ran across his mind before it went black.

*Baba.*

***

When Arthin came to, he was face down with a mouth full of dirt and his arm numb from laying on top of it. One eye was swollen shut, and the other could barely take in the dawn light that streamed through the wooden spokes of the wheel he had fallen in front of. His head ached as if it had been dragged over rocks all night. He tasted blood on his split lip, and it was all he could do to lift his head and survey the scene. In front of the wagon, two bodies lay on their sides, unmoving. Arthin guessed they were the drivers. No one else remained. He pulled himself up and grasped the edge of the cart, peering over the side. Nothing but debris and splattered blood from the bedlam last night. He was all alone, and he had only a few seconds to muddle over the thought of his father having played a part in this before he heard the *clip clop* of a horse approaching in the distance.

*Shit.* Arthin ducked back behind the cart and tried to get a good view of the rider. A horse almost always meant a British officer, as they'd be the only ones able to afford one in these parts, in these times. Two dead bodies. A British officer as witness. Arthin had no choice but to flee.

The pain in his head exploded as he ran.

"Hey!" the officer shouted behind him. The hoofbeats quickened. And Arthin had the dreaded realization that officers never traveled alone. There was probably a whole company behind him, and they'd all be on his heels in a matter of seconds. With no time to consider where he was going, he veered off the road and broke through the bushes, leaping over rocks and tearing his skin on branches.

He looked over his shoulder the entire way home, and it was like awakening from a dream when he finally crawled over the threshold and collapsed at his mother's feet. The pounding in his head had dulled to a hot numbness, and the thirst in his throat had made his tongue stick to the roof of his mouth. He could barely get out the words to tell his mother what had happened.

The news had preceded him. Gossip spread easily when there was nothing else going on. His mother had heard not two hours ago of an attack to the west, the drivers killed, their cargo spoiled. And that they were looking for a boy who was seen running away.

They decided he must escape. Perhaps the officer had gotten a good look at him. Perhaps they could depend on the *goras'* tendency to see all Indians as the same. But there was nothing to stay for anyway, so the choice was easy. He would cross the river and disappear in the larger city of Midnapore.

She scrambled around their tiny dwelling for things she could give her son, to arm him for what she thought would be a few days, maybe a week alone on the streets of a new city. She stopped, startled, in front of the hook on the wall. It was unadorned.

She didn't have to explain for him to understand. The spare kurta that had always hung there was gone. His father had taken it, and they hadn't even noticed. Arthin was too exhausted to do anything with this information. He felt a numbness on his tongue as words failed to come to him. After everything, this is how his father ended it. He had walked out that door with no intention of ever returning.

It was like the drought had taken even the tears from their eyes. They looked at each other, mother and son, with the kind of emptiness that felt like relief. When there was nothing more to fight for, the pain finally stopped.

He stood in the doorway—nothing but a single anna in his palm with which he would have to beg a boatman to take him across the river—and embraced his mother. He could not know that this would be the last time he would see her, that after all this, fate would bestow him a life of merciful mediocrity. A turbulent first few years on the Midnapore streets would lead him to his friend Neer and eventually give way to promising employment with the Padre Sahib and his young wife, newly arrived on the subcontinent. He could not know that they would christen him Arthur, and that he would feign a belief in Jesus Christ in return for three rupees a month, and that whole decades would pass with barely a thought of the violent night that had set this all in motion. He could not know that his mother would pay penance for her husband's sins by refusing to eat, although one could say the famine played just as much a role in her body's swift and solitary waning. Arthin would learn months later that her body had been found in the barley field.

He could not know all this that would come to pass. In that moment, all he knew was the warmth of his mother's sunken bosom, then the absence of it as she pulled away and pushed him out the door.

"I'll come back, Ma," he said, looking over his shoulder.

"I know you will," she whispered.

And as he turned away from his home for the last time, he felt cold, tiny drops land on his head. The air, stifled for so long by the dust, bloomed fragrant and cool for the first time in what felt like forever. Arthin held a hand out in front of him and watched the sprinkles turn into heavy drops in his upturned palm. It was something he would grow to realize over the course of his life: for him, the rains always seemed to come just a little too late.

# CHAPTER 22

Saturday morning dawned dry and cloudy. The sky, streaked with gray, grew electric as Gene stepped onto the sleeping porch, his limbs tight from slumber. For a few moments, he forgot what had happened the day before, and it was blissful to have nothing but the weather to think about. This was not the usual mildness of early spring in Bengal, but no doubt it was good racing weather. Better than the sweltering, humid heat. He knelt and thrust a hand under his bed for his spikes. He tossed the shoes into a canvas bag, their laces knotted so they would be easy to pick out from his brothers'. He stretched his legs one more time, readying for the crowded ride to Calcutta.

Suddenly, a slammed door down the hall—Ellis's room—and thoughts of yesterday rushed to the fore of his mind. A moment later, his mother appeared at the banister, letting out a heavy sigh. "Come on," she said to Gene, breezing by him and down the stairs.

John appeared in their bedroom doorway, poking his head out of his T-shirt and tucking the hem into the band of his shorts. He ran to the banister. "Uncle Ellis is coming, right?" he called down.

"Says he's not feeling well," Mrs. Hinton said.

Gene shrugged. But John thumped down the stairs after her, already spilling out arguments of how he can't stay back, not again, forget what he said to Dad, this is the *meet*. But the door at the end of the hall remained closed, silent. Lee and Will emerged from the cookhouse bearing leftover naan from last night.

"Can we fit this into the bag?" Will said. Gene opened the zipper and held it out.

"What's the matter?" Lee said.

"Uncle Ellis isn't coming," Will said. "I knew it."

Mr. Hinton already sat at the wheel of the car, waiting. Gene slid in behind him and rested his elbows on the worn leather seatback. "Do we really have to go, Dad? You know, with what's . . . happened and all?"

His father started the car. "We haven't missed it in all the years we've been in India. We're not going to miss it now. What would everyone think?"

Gene closed his eyes and felt the car shift as more bodies crammed in. In no time, they were all packed into the car and rolling past the guards, their clouded faces reflecting the sky.

■■■

They parked the car and walked down to the ghats, a dozen ferrymen clamoring for their business. They took the man who reached them first, his sweaty hand beckoning them down the steps to the water, not resting until a five-rupee coin was tight in his fist. On the other shore, the low brick walls of Fort William rose to greet them, show them the way to the dry grass of the maidan beyond.

To Gene, the maidan was how he imagined America. Its long, orderly fields and wide-open space had room for everything, for families to stretch out on picnic blankets, for children to play games with no boundaries. As they walked the dirt path that led to the center, he breathed in the scent of sulfur from the fort, where soldiers practiced shooting on the leafy grounds. To his right, the rickshaw traffic turned a corner and approached with frenzied bells and honks— whether to warn them to make way or to offer them a ride, Gene could never make out.

He came to a stop at the edge of the path, where his mother waited for a break in the traffic. He turned his head one moment to watch the flow, and in the next, Mrs. Hinton had dashed into the road, paying no mind to the oncoming carts and rickshaws. Gene thought she had lost her mind—the drivers swerved around her, horns blaring as her skirt billowed and swirled with every turn. For a split second, she looked back, the whites of her eyes shining, twinkling, and from somewhere behind him, he could hear his father shouting. "God in Heaven!" Mr. Hinton yelled, running into the road after her, flailing his arms like a sensible person in order to be seen. But before he could reach her, she was on the other side, miraculously unscathed, the tram pulling up slowly yet not quite halting. Mrs. Hinton climbed aboard without so much as a wipe from her brow.

With traffic at a full stop, the boys scooted across after their father and boarded the tram, the conductor making a hasty *namaste* when he saw the Padre Sahib. Gene glanced at Mrs. Hinton as he shuffled past her. She cast her eyes low as though there was something fascinating under her fingernails. Mr. Hinton paused next to her, but when she didn't move over, he sat in the seat behind. Gene made his way to the back, where two Indian men got up to offer him a seat.

"*Dhanyavaad*," Gene said.

"The hell was that?" Will whispered, glancing at their parents as he slid next to Gene.

Gene didn't answer but looked out the window. He couldn't worry about that now; the race had him nervous and jittery all through the night.

Blue, the shade of topaz, the tram dazzled against the verdant life of the maidan. It snaked around cricket fields and park benches on a one-way track that paralleled the roads, where rickshaws raced from corner to corner. From the window, Gene watched the children run, though never very fast, to catch its lazy progress. The tram shifted around turns and creaked from side to side, never quite picking up enough speed to generate a breeze through the open windows.

Occasionally the bell rang to warn the rickshaw pullers of its cross-
ing, and over the treetops Gene could just make out the buzzing traffic of Chowringhee Road.

They disembarked at the royal horse track on the south end of
the maidan, a crowd of Britishers and Indians alike on the central
field, carving out their own spaces for stretches and sprints. Gene
marveled at their pace, some sprinting so fast that the earth seemed
to rumble beneath their powerful strides. He turned every which way
and felt immediately sick at the sight of everyone sweating, pushing
hard, and the races hadn't even begun.

"*Satarka hōna!*" Out of nowhere, a giant mass of glossy skin
blasted into Gene's shoulder and sent him reeling, face meeting grass,
the wind knocked out of him. A few seconds later, he gathered himself just enough to notice a body hovering over him.

"Very sorry, sir," a voice panted.

Gene blinked and looked up at the half-clothed Indian boy, his
hand extended.

"He's all right," Will said, waving the boy off but offering no help
himself. "Watch out for that one," he muttered to Gene once the boy
was gone.

"No kidding," Gene said.

"Can't show 'em you're weak, not today," Will said.

"I'm not," Gene said, though he still hadn't fully recovered his
lungs. They'd only just arrived and already he was out of breath. He
felt a squeeze on his shoulder and looked up to see his father, a reassuring smile on his face. The next second, it was gone, as Mr. Hinton
looked up at the stands where Mrs. Hinton was already headed.

"Think we'll go up in the seats," his father said. "*Saubhāgya.* Good
luck."

◼◼◼

The boys found a spot in the grass and sat down, setting to work untangling the shoes from the bag. Gene extracted his pair and began unlacing them.

"Get mine for me," John said.

But Gene wasn't listening. His ears rang, perhaps from getting knocked down, or was it the bugs in the low grass or the traffic horns on the esplanade? He paused and faced the grandstand, the shadowy depths of the seats still empty save for the odd spectator keen on viewing the warm-ups. Gene spied his mother in the upper corner, leaning forward with her elbow on one knee, chin in hand. She stared straight at the field, and Gene felt the impulse to give a big wave with both hands, the way he used to when he was younger. He tried it, because why not. His mother's expression did not change—no recognition, no startled smile, no "oh!" of excitement, no wave returned. Yet Gene felt sure she looked right at him, seeing him plain as day. He dropped an arm and tilted at the hip, passing it off as a stretch.

"Hello?" John said, eyes wide in exasperation.

"Sorry," Gene mumbled. He tossed the bag at John's feet. John sighed and fished his pair out.

"Think the first race starts soon. I'm going to check the event board," Will said over his shoulder as he jogged away through the crowd.

The rest of them sat in the grass, lacing up. "I don't see anyone else wearing spikes," said Lee.

"Well, they aren't *dis*allowed," said John. "If nobody else has caught on to using them, it's not *my* fault. Though, you'd think the *ingraj* would have enough money to buy real ones."

Gene examined his own, the heel well worn, the hammered nails sticking out of the sole every which way. He stuck his foot into one and tugged the laces tight. The other runners swirled around them, the Britishers clad in sleeveless shirts, Indian boys in too-large kurtas. He recognized some boys from school, though nobody from his year.

"There's Veddie," Lee said. He nodded toward the starting line. Sure enough, a familiar face looked their way.

"Shouldn't we say hello?" Gene said.

But Ved Hari had already come over, a white smile on his sweaty face. "Hello, Hintons! Not like you to be running late, the first race is about to start. Any of you running it? Hundred-meter dash?"

"Will is. I'd expect he'd be at the start already."

"Defending the title, *na*? No doubt been training hard all break. Tough competition though. Indians are out for blood this year."

"Yourself included?" Lee said.

"Ha."

"I'm serious," Lee said. "If you had to pick a side, are you India or Britain?"

"I'm both," Ved answered, hands on hips. "What about you?"

"Neither," Gene said.

"Fair enough. You have God on your side," Ved said. "But they have hundreds on theirs."

"Come on then, let's cheer Will on," Lee said.

■■■

As they bounded over, Gene glanced again at the grandstand. His father was seated next to his mother now, both of them looking uncomfortably close. Mr. Hinton had one of her hands in both of his, as if to hold her there for fear she could float away. They looked straight ahead at the proceedings when Mr. Hinton leaned over to whisper something. She came to life then, her face animated, jerking her head in little movements the way one does when expressing a strong point of view. But Mr. Hinton responded with something short, no more than a word, and the two of them looked straight ahead again. Gene felt he had seen this somewhere before.

Will sprinted in short bursts up and down the track, the other runners following suit. He looked elated, electrified by the crowd itself, downright giddy at getting to race in front of so many people, in such a place as this. This was no ordinary field in some backwater missionary outpost. This was a real course in the old Raj capital, with the shining dome of the Victoria Memorial looming over the treetops to the east, stark white against the glowering sky. Tiny flags waved from the stands as if it were the Olympics, except there was only the Union Jack, like they were all on the same team. But from the looks of the competitors, they couldn't be more different.

"See those two?" Ved said to Gene, indicating two tall boys stretching in the middle of the track. They looked nearly identical, gold, wispy hair and unnecessarily muscular shoulders. "They're twins, just arrived from England last month. Their father is the commissioner general, and one of them is to take over once he keels. Though, don't know how long they'll last in India. Fresh off the boat, looks like. May have yellow fever in no time."

Their faces, gaunt and sweaty, did give Gene the impression that they'd already received the royal welcome of mosquitos and untreated water. They stood with their arms crossed, as though waiting for the race to start just so it could be over and done with.

"Can you imagine?" Lee said. "Won't be much competition for us, from the looks of them."

"Now those fellows over there," Ved said, pointing at the large Indian boys already in their lanes. "They've got the talent. From Howrah, *kushti* wrestlers. Thighs as thick as my stomach. The Hindu Hope, I heard a fellow say. My money's on them."

"What about Will?" Gene said. "This is his forte."

"What about your own?" Lee said. "Any Anglo-Indians in this?"

"Nah. Long distance only, I'm afraid. Except the last relay—I'll be leading off."

"Me too," said Lee.

The runners of the first race, with Will in the middle lane, took their places at the starting line and turned toward the infield, where an officer stood on a platform in front of a microphone. The crowd quieted as the man began to speak in a tinny voice.

"On behalf of his royal highness, the King of the United Kingdom and Emperor of India, it is the esteemed honor of the Organizing Committee to present to you, the people, the eighth Bengal-Orissa Games! Peoples of Britain and India come together on this day in the good faith of the Raj, in enduring friendship, and in celebration of our eternal bond."

The crowd cheered, and Ved leaned toward Gene. "He forgot you Americans again," he said.

From behind the platform came a flurry of trumpets, followed by a shuffle from the crowd as everyone rose to their feet. The first bars of "God Save the King" fluttered over the grounds, and everyone, British or not, took up the words. To his left, John sniggered at the Britishers in the stands, their lips moving with more enthusiasm than necessary. Around them, a few dark-skinned Indians stood stoic and grim, and Gene thought back to the day of the protest in the Midnapore bazaar. It felt strange now to be at something so convivial when weeks ago, people had been rioting in the streets.

In the stands, he could spot Mr. and Mrs. Hinton side by side, pith helmets in hand. Beside them, Mrs. Hari looked spirited in a lilac sari next to her husband, the two of them singing along to the words. Gene took a deep breath and wiped the sweat from his brow. The anthem ended. Another cheer.

"Today and every day, we celebrate unity under one crown, prosperity in competition, and friendship in sport. Let the games begin!"

Will took the lead easily, getting a clean start from the moment the gun went off. Even without the blocks they'd been practicing with—which weren't allowed yet in official races—he sprung from his lead foot practically a whole step before the others, who seemed to startle under the sudden sound. Will hit his stride not a quarter of the way down the stretch, perfection in motion. He was not particularly tall, no taller than the others, but he moved with fluid limbs. Gene gaped at his brother and felt a surge of pride.

The race finished just as soon as it began, Will the clear winner with a bevy of spent runners full steps behind him.

"Will Hinton, ladies and gentlemen!" a British voice announced from somewhere near the finish line. "The American missionary defends his reign over the hundred-meter dash again this year, smoking the rest!" The announcer didn't bother calling out second and third place.

They found Will with his hands on his hips, panting with a sheen of sweat over every visible part of him but otherwise looking fit and ready to go again.

"Bravo!" Ved exclaimed from beside Gene. "Not a bad start at all!"

"Easy," Will said.

"Certainly looked it," said John. "Couldn't have done it better myself."

"Congratulations," Gene said. "They all look more tired than you do."

It was true; the other runners lay spent in the grass as if they had just finished a marathon, not a sprint. They'd clearly given it all they had, but it still wasn't enough to beat Will. Again, Gene felt the pride swell in his chest.

"Only wish Uncle Ellis were here to see it," said Will.

■■■

Neither Gene nor his brothers were in the long-distance races, so they had plenty of time to prepare for the final relay. Ved came a close third in the 1600-meter, losing out to two British boys practically twice his height. As the races continued, Indian runners won in the mid-distance heats and kept a close tally with the Brits. The sun had started to sink by the time the last event finally approached.

"OK," Will said, "we still need to practice handoffs. It goes Lee, Gene, John, then me. Remember, Gene, you run a whole lap—"

"I *know* what the four-hundred-meter relay is," Gene said, scowling.

"Let's just try it," Lee said with a sigh. He grabbed the baton from the grass. "Gene, start right about there, and I'll run up to you. Go when I get about five paces close."

They tested out the pass, Lee yelling "Stick!" practically in Gene's ear before he turned around, the baton passed off so clumsily that he dropped it. As he bent to retrieve it from the grass, he could hear snickering from other racers practicing nearby. He glanced up in time to catch their churlish faces before they feigned away.

"You gotta go way faster, Gene," Will coached. "It's a race, you know?"

"I got it," Gene said, handing the baton back to Lee. "There are just too many people around."

They practiced a few more handoffs, all of them just as shaky for Gene as the first.

"It's just nerves," Lee assured. "Don't think about it so much."

But there would be no more time to think about it. From the starting line, the announcer called for all relay teams to assemble in order. The Indian team took the inside line, although there were no lanes drawn on the grass course. Gene had done well enough in the dirt at home, but he worried he'd slide around the grass turns. He wiggled his toes to be sure his shoes were tied. He prayed they wouldn't fly off.

Some of the boys on the other teams looked familiar, and Gene guessed he'd seen the British boys around town during some state celebration or other. The Anglo-Indian teammates, of course, were Ved and his other classmates home from boarding school. They were Lee's year, tall but skinny, their width not quite caught up to their height.

"Best of luck, Gene," the second-leg Anglo-Indian boy said, a light-skinned arm extended in good sport.

"Same to you," Gene said, regretting that he didn't know the boy's name in return. He gave the boy's hand an extra shake to make up for it.

"Isn't John getting too old for this sort of thing?" the boy said, bouncing on his toes. "He's years above us."

Gene laughed, nervous. "Well, they let us do whatever we want because we're missionaries. All in the name of God, you know?"

"Ha! You're right. Who knows what goes on at that Hinton house?"

Gene's heart lurched into his throat. Had the boy heard something? Gene searched his face for any sign of accusation, judgment. But it gave up nothing, save perhaps race jitters. The boy stopped his bouncing and looked at Gene, raising his brow, waiting for an answer. Or was it rhetorical? Gene managed a weak smile and couldn't help but steal a glance at his parents in the stands. "Just a lot of running."

Everyone but the first-leg runners was ushered off the track. The leads took their starting positions, staggered from inside to out, Lee the farthest ahead. He dropped his head down, clutched the baton in his right hand. The crowd softened, a collective breath held in wait for the starting gun. To his credit, Lee appeared calm as could be, as if he'd been here a million times before. Between the crowd, the fellow racers who looked ten times more fit, his parents' eyes on them, and the jitters of his own body, Gene wasn't sure he himself would even be able to take the first step.

"Set," the starter called.

Lee's head snapped up, his body tensed, baton raised. Then, *bang*. They were off, a flurry of cheers erupting all around, Lee's simple khaki shirt in stark contrast with the pristine white tank the British boy to his left wore, as though outfitting for the Olympics. Lee's strides, confident and even, carried him ahead, while the British boy soon fell behind Ved, who held the second lane. The Indian boy seemed to be keeping pace, but his sweaty grimace betrayed his effort.

They rounded the back stretch, where Gene lost them in the wave of spectators and overly enthusiastic fathers. Mr. Hari chased his son nearly down the whole way before he gave it up, winded from the sprint.

"Seconds! Take your positions," came the starter's voice.

But Gene's feet had seemed to plant roots in the grass, watered by his own sweat and sheer panic. John slapped him on the back with a look that said *Lord help us*. Gene stumbled onto the track with the others, the officials arranging them in order as the lead-off runners barreled around the curve and hit the final straightaway. Lee still clung to first place, several strides ahead of the next runner. All Gene had to do was maintain the lead. He began to bounce on the balls of his feet, shake his arms, roll his shoulders in the masterful way he saw the other racers do. He dropped his head and tightened his laces one last time. When he looked up again, Lee was closer than he'd expected. He could make out his brother's expression, eyes narrowed in determination, hair flying in the wind. The sight of Lee's mouth wide open, like a fish gasping in air, sent a shiver down Gene's spine. If Lee was in this much excruciation, how would it leave him at the end of his leg? But that was it. The faster he ran, the faster he'd finish. Then he could go a whole year more before ever having to race again.

"*Go!*" Lee's voice shattered through his nerves. For a split second, Gene glanced at the runners next to him, one having bolted already. He took a few feeble steps forward, cautious of going too fast, too far for Lee to reach. He turned back to gauge his position, and there was Lee on top of him, spikes skidding in the grass, the baton nearly at his hip. Gene grasped it and clutched it to his chest, turning forward at the open track before him. This was it.

*Be like Will—be Will*, he thought, pumping his legs and arms like a machine. He went all the way around the first curve before he realized he'd kept his eyes on the grass below him. He jerked his head up and made a beeline for the inside track, one smooth and gradual line inward. He could hear Lee's voice in his head. *The shortest distance between two points is a straight line.* He didn't dare look back; it would be a waste of energy. But he could hear the other runners at his heels. He was losing their lead, fast, and all he could do was pray he had enough steam to pass the baton off to John before their lead disappeared entirely.

Indian girls with braided, black tresses lined the track at the second curve. Tan in the Bengal sun, they cheered louder than their modest, fair-skinned counterparts and waved their Union Jacks with so much ardor, and it was in that moment that Gene stopped thinking about running. Everything seemed to slow as his eyes locked on the girls, a fire in their eyes that he recognized was not for him or the flags they waved or the fair-skinned boys in the race. It burned for the Indian boy that passed him, barefoot and all muscle, overtaking him with ease and chugging onto the straightaway, the girls screaming after him, sun in their eyes and on their glistening skin.

Gene's lungs burned as he gulped the air down, propelling his legs to the finish line, where he could see John waiting. His whole body ached from the heat, the relentless sun, the shoes that didn't fit right. It was all wrong, this race. He didn't belong here, among them. Another runner passed him, an English boy. Then another, as he felt his legs turn to lead. But already John took off, far too soon. There was no way Gene could reach him in time.

The runners ahead of him had passed their batons off without error. Their thirds were well onto the next leg. It seemed to only frustrate John, who turned around and bellowed, "Come on!"

Gene thrust the baton out ahead, where it hovered pathetically in the space between them, nowhere near close enough to cover the five or so more paces he had to go. John screeched to a halt, the other runners racing ahead on fresh legs. They were last now. Four more steps, then three, two, and the baton was snatched out of his sweaty fingers. He was finished, finally, yet there came no relief. As he stumbled off the track, he could feel the blisters forming on his swollen feet.

He collapsed in the grass, unable to even lift his head to follow the race. He dimly noticed a hand on his shoulder, and Lee, saying something in some reassuring tone. "We still have Will. He'll make it up in no time."

"Great effort, Gene," Ved said, standing over him with his other arm extended to Gene and not a hint of irony. He was still out of breath and had a light sheen on his face from the run, but otherwise looked lively. Why was it so hard for Gene?

"John and Will are going to kill me," Gene mumbled, gripping Ved's hand and coming to a stand.

"Don't count on it yet. They're just coming to the straight," Ved said, steering him toward the edge of the track for a better view. The feel of his hand still on Gene's shoulder reassured him.

But over the heads of the crowd, he could just make out John in third place, close behind the strawberry blond Brit in second. Will, already waiting on the line, shook his arms and legs out. It would be a tough sprint, but John was making moves. The strawberry blond had lost steam, and John swiftly snuck up on the Anglo-Indian, who'd left a pocket of space inside the second curve. John passed him easily, a whole head taller than the others, so obviously, shamelessly, too old.

The handoff to Will went smoothly, and then Will went to work. He moved down the track, compact and efficient, his arms and legs synchronized in perfect motion. The Indian runner was still a ways ahead, but he was all that remained in front of Will and the finish line. Gene stood alert, but he wasn't watching Will. His eyes searched the crowd for the girls with the braids, to see their faces again. They had moved down the track to follow the runners to the finish line, but Gene could not mistake their faces, red with longing to see an Indian team win.

He thought back to the day of the protest, the day that the Indian boys had beaten and robbed them. It felt so long ago, and today was different, new. These weren't the same boys, and this wasn't the same fight. This was merely meant to be fun, a day of games, where people could forget their color or their accents or their names, even.

As the runners curved into the homestretch, Gene turned away from the finish line. With his gaze upward, he took in the expanse of the sky and the hazy, humid air that hung over the maidan. The hard, marble dome of the Victoria Memorial rose in the east, itself a cloud of white, presiding over the games. He heard the crowd swell as the runners approached the finish, but still he did not turn. Instead, he shut his eyes and breathed deep the smell of the coming storm, the sound of voices cheering together, and the first raindrops falling on his eyelids, and for a moment he forgot everything else, forgot the judge, the leopard, his mother, his father, the riot, the stolen bicycles. He was just there, alone but not alone, in a crowd of people most of whom he'd never met before and yet who'd come here just as he had. One roar went up from the crowd and he knew it was over, and he imagined he could hear the cheers of the girls in the braids.

The noise from the Indian crowd never seemed to die down after that. All around, the air buzzed, a victory at long last through all the frustration. Gene couldn't help but feel relieved and happy for them. He caught the proud eye of one of the winners and nodded congratulations. The Indian boy's face softened. He nodded in return.

"Complete embarrassment." Will spat in the dirt, hands on his hips. His chest still heaved from the race.

"Solid effort, boys," Ved said, shaking Lee's hand. "Finally let someone else win for a change. Suppose that's the end of the Hinton dynasty."

"Terrible way to go out," John said. He collapsed onto the grass. "And no chance to redeem myself next year."

Mrs. Hinton and the padre appeared, hats in their hands. "Right then," Mr. Hinton said. "Can't win them all." He fixed his eyes on the winners, huddled close and still on the track, cracking brilliant smiles as roars of laughter rushed over their brown heads. "Bless them."

"My feet are swelling. Let's get back," said Mrs. Hinton. "Ellis won't believe it."

"Just a second," Gene said. He bounded over to the Indian boys and wiped his hand on his shorts. Extending it to one of them, he said, "Well done."

The boys stared at him, the whites of their eyes in stark contrast with their Bengal skin. For a moment, Gene flashed back to the men at the ruins, their stares, their flat unsmiling lips. But in the next, the boy took his hand and in a heavy accent said, "We finally defeated you!"

The other boys laughed and patted Gene on the back to show it was all in good fun. Suddenly, they fell silent, plain faced, hands withdrawn abruptly behind their backs. A British officer walked past, paused. He leaned in toward Gene. "These boys troubling you?"

"Not at all . . . ," Gene said, but the boys had already dispersed, retreating to the crowd of other Indians, their countrymen, their kind. The officer gave him a stern look and passed on.

"Let's go, Gene!" his father called. "It's a long drive home."

As they left the racing green and headed for the road, Will tossed him the duffle with all their shoes. The raindrops multiplied into a curtained drizzle, so Gene held the duffle over his head, trying to avoid the spikes of the shoes that poked out through the canvas.

"Kindly, sahib," a voice called out from behind him. Even as Gene watched his family move on ahead, Gene stopped and turned. An Indian man stood a few paces behind him, dressed in a clean, white kurta and leather slippers. He looked about middle-aged with graying temples and the bent stature of one who was getting on in life.

Gene didn't know how to address him, so he cleared his throat and nodded at the man.

"Kindly," he said again, "you are the Hinton family? Tell me, is your servant, Arthur, with you?"

"Er, no. He's at home looking after our guest."

The man lowered his eyes. "Ah. Thank you, sahib. Will you please tell him his friend Neer is asking after him. And—and that he's worried for him."

Gene took a closer look at the man's face and tried to remember if he had ever seen him before. In all his years, he couldn't recall meeting any friend of Arthur's.

He nodded again at the man. "I will," he said. As he turned to keep walking, Gene wondered what Arthur must be doing back home at this very instant.

# CHAPTER 23

The ringing floods Arthur's ears as he flings the back door wide. It bangs against the wall, and the force sends something crashing to the floor inside. The shatter of glass pulses new energy through him, and he explodes from the back porch into the grass, skipping the steps altogether. He sprints for his hut. His body hums with adrenaline, his hands vibrate, and he has just enough sense left to hold in his scream.

He leaps over the boys' bicycles idle in the grass, his heart pounding as hard as his feet on the ground. There's no time to look around for the guards. He keeps his eyes straight ahead on the horizon, the lone sliver of sunlight dying against the gathering gray of the storm. His nostrils flare, his throat gulps air. He has started a chain reaction he knows he can't escape. He has only a matter of seconds to try.

The last few steps to his hut, he can hear the frenzied barking and scratching coming from inside. The feeble weight of the door moves aside easily, and Moti wriggles out and is upon him, smelling the house on his clothes, the tobacco smoke, the spilled tea, and his own sweat underneath.

"Let's go!" Arthur turns and skids around the back of the hut, trusting she will follow. As he tears through the brush, he feels her warm breath on his heels. He dares to look back to be sure. The whites of her eyes glow, spit flies from her fangs. She knows as well as he does that they must run.

He has no plan. He has only this moment, only this primal flight. He prays the trees will hide them, the shadows will tell no one. But the shouts of the guards are unmistakable. They sound far back, like something underwater, but all the same, they mean one thing: they have discovered what he has done.

His legs burst with newfound energy. As he scrambles over the terrain, clawing at tree trunks and vines, Moti effortlessly springs ahead, and he swears he can see her float over fallen trees and moss-covered stones like a spirit. She is mesmerizing in her movement. Muscle and sinew ripple underneath her coat, the rhythmic expansion and contraction carrying her body through the forest.

She leads him deeper into the jungle, and he forces his legs to churn faster, faster. Over the sounds of his own steps snapping twigs underfoot, he can hear the guards coming closer. He must keep his eyes forward if he has any hope. Light flashes as lightning roils in the sky. For a fraction of a second, everything around them is outlined in contrast, every leaf vein, every wrinkle in the tree bark, every dust mote in the air.

A memory flares in his mind: rushing through fields as a child, an afternoon spent with friends cut short by a monsoon thunderstorm, the fear of his mother propelling him home down the rows of jute. He remembers the exhilaration of such unbridled movement, the happiness of pushing his body to its highest speed, unbound by walls, perimeters, civility. It feels like a different life, a different person, the boy running free in the fields. It is the taste of rain on his tongue, it is the scent of damp soil, it is the sensation of his arms swinging back and forth with so much force that he almost believes they will fall off, it is all this that brings the past screaming back, the sweetness of his youth, the oblivion of his childhood. But his body is aged now. He feels it slowing. His breaths come heavy and hard. He cannot keep up. The guards come closer, so close he can hear the bandoliers jangling against their chests, their boot buckles rattling. He cannot keep up.

When Arthur feels the first hand close around his waist, he looks ahead at the streak of white as Moti disappears for the last time.

"Run ahead," he chokes out to her. *I'm right behind you.*

# CHAPTER 24

The Hintons drove home in a velvet rain. It was much too early in the season for the monsoons, but it felt like it all the same, the dirt road transformed into a river of mud. The open sides of the car let in the torrent, and everyone was soaked in their own puddles by the time they turned down the drive to the Big House. Through the dripping leaves of the frangipani trees, the light of early evening held strong and illuminated the yard. For a moment, it looked to Gene like a painting, a scene out of a storybook, the house on the edge of the jungle, the soft rainfall, the gleam of moisture sunken in the lane.

Gene's legs ached from the race, and it was only made worse by the long drive. Even the last few yards home seemed to drag on as his father drove carefully through the gloom. He tried shifting his body, getting ready to spring from the seat the moment they stopped. He looked over the car's dashboard and spied something in the road. An animal, small. There in the headlights sat Minnie, dripping and paying no attention to the rain, her monkey eyes blank. She moved out of the way only when the car came right up to her, as though she hadn't been aware of it until the last moment. Then she sauntered off, slow and tired, looking like she'd been stunned.

"That's strange," said John. "Who let her out?" He put his hand out the side of the car and tried to beckon her, but she ignored them. They rolled past as she sat on her haunches, staring into the rain.

The car was halfway down the lane by the time a guard appeared, running toward them with his rifle raised. When he got closer, he lowered it, but kept his pace. Gene felt the car slow, then halt. The guard gave a flustercd salute, started speaking in his language, which none of them understood, and began waving his hands in an attempt to translate. He pointed at the upstairs corner window, but it was much too dark to see anything inside. Then he touched his chest with urgency, pressing into it with his fist, all the while his eyes wide. Before anyone in the car could respond, he ran off, back down the road, his soaked red turban flinging water drops with every step.

For a moment, there was only the pounding sound of the rain on the roof of the car. Gene had caught just one phrase in the Afghan's words: "burra sahib." Mrs. Hinton spoke. "Go," she said, then gave a wet smack to her knee. "Go!"

■■■

From outside the house, everything appeared ordinary. The tire tracks in the dirt from when they left this morning had turned to mud. The mosquito nets trembled on the sleeping porch, caught in the evening breeze. The door to the cookhouse stood ajar, and Gene could imagine Arthur in there right now, whipping up dinner for them on their return. But he could sense something beyond the veil of raindrops that dripped from the roof. He did not need to look inside to know Arthur was not in the cookhouse.

Mrs. Hinton flung open the front door, dashed up the stairs, and disappeared down the hall. The sound of a bedroom door opening. Her screams.

When Gene entered the room, it took his brain a moment to distinguish anything wrong. Uncle Ellis was sat up in bed against a stack of pillows with his head back and turned toward the window, as though he had just spotted a kingfisher outside. On the bed next to him, an overturned tray and empty glass, an orange stain set in the linen. Splattered all over, like ripe fruit dropped from a high branch, the blood from the bullet hole in the judge's chest.

Gene looked away, and tried to latch on to anything else, any sound or sight, that still had the semblance of ordinariness. The door to the wardrobe was open just a little, and from inside he could see the gold letters gleaming from the darkness. It was the judge's suitcase with his initials, G. H. E. Gene realized he had never actually learned what they stood for, only having ever called him Ellis.

His mother had stopped screaming. One of his brothers was muttering swears. Gene looked back at the linen sheets. Not at the stain, but at the part still white and unsoiled, because if he looked at it long enough, he could believe that all was as it used to be before the judge ever set foot in this house.

His father knelt by the bed and put a hand to the judge's heart. The eyes were still open, and they had a hard-set look to them; even in death, the man remained defiant. Mr. Hinton shut the lids and muttered, "Christ."

"Who did this?" Mrs. Hinton choked between her sobs.

"Boys, leave the room," Mr. Hinton said, voice growling in his throat. They left without being asked again. Gene, relieved to be away from the body and the blood, pulled the door shut and glimpsed his mother's face in the stark contrast of the window's light against the rest of the room's darkness. Her eyes flashed to him. *Get out.*

Gene stood with his brothers in the hallway, so dim he could hardly see their faces. Just as well that they couldn't see his. To his surprise, the tears had come. He didn't want to admit that he was crying for that man, but there he stood, wiping his face. Surely the judge hadn't meant that much to him? He heard a sniffle from one of his brothers and knew he wasn't alone.

"Who could have done it?" Will whispered. "No doubt this entire country had it in for him."

"Could have been one of them," John said, nodding toward the yard. They could see the Afghan soldiers still at attention, as though they expected the judge to rise any minute and start barking orders at them again. "Otherwise, why didn't they come and fetch us when it happened? By the looks of it, he's been dead the better part of the day."

"Not his own guards," said Lee. "Why would they still be here?"

"They must know, then. Must've seen something. Shame they don't speak a lick of English or Hindi."

"It was Arthur," Gene said. He couldn't believe he was saying it, but he knew it was true. It remained the only explanation for why he wasn't here. But he couldn't understand why. What had the judge ever done to Arthur?

"He couldn't do such a thing," said Lee. But his voice came out weak with defeat, as though he, too, knew it to be true. No one wanted to believe it.

"Well, where is he then?" said Will.

They heard the door open downstairs, a slam, then boots up the stairs. For the first time, they saw one of the soldiers in their house, dripping water on the rug. He held something in his hand. "Padre Sahib?" the soldier said.

"In there," Gene said. Realizing the guard hadn't understood, he moved down the hall and put his hand on the knob. But before he turned it, he couldn't help eavesdropping on his parents.

"We shouldn't tell anyone yet," his father said.

"Tell anyone! We have to tell someone. We're not safe here. The boys!"

"But don't you see? It would cloud the whole mission. We don't need that kind of attention, that kind of affiliation."

"Ellis has been murdered in his bed, and you're thinking about the mission?"

"Well, what else is there to do? He's already dead. Nothing we can do to save him."

"So that's it."

"That's what?"

"That's how you've always felt about him. 'Nothing we can do to save him.' As if he hasn't saved us countless times before."

"And how have *you* always felt about him?"

Silence.

Gene took his hand off the knob, entranced by their conversation. He was vaguely aware of the expectant guard behind him. His brothers had moved closer, huddled next to the wall like thieves in the night.

Then, a slap. The sound of it cracked through the door and echoed down the hall like thunder. More silence. Gene pushed the door open.

His mother sat on the bed next to the judge, her cheek red, hair ruffled from the rain. Mr. Hinton turned.

"The guard has something," Gene said barely above a whisper.

The Afghan gave a wet salute in the doorway and held out a folded paper. Mr. Hinton snatched it out of his hand and went to the window, where there lingered just enough light to read it.

"Impossible," he said.

Gene knew it was about Arthur; he could sense it. He worried what would happen to their servant. Even if it were true—that Arthur, who had been with them Gene's whole life, could do such a thing—he couldn't help but feel sorry for him.

"What is it?" Lee said.

"They're holding Arthur at the jail. In town. It says he's been there since late this morning. Why didn't anyone tell us?" his father said, crumpling the note. He looked at the guard, as if he could explain.

"You mean they didn't just shoot him?" Will said.

"Some guards," John muttered.

"We should go and see him," Lee said. "See what all this was about. There must be some explanation . . ."

"There isn't. I suppose some people are just born evil and do evil things," Mr. Hinton said, though his gaze rested on Ellis's body. "Let God judge him as he will. I don't want any part of that evil."

"So what do we do?" Gene said.

"Get me a candle. We'll say a prayer. And then we'll send for a coffin to be made, and return the body to England. He would never want to be laid to rest here."

*Why not?* Gene thought. He'd spent quite a lot of time in India for a person who hated it so much. He made for the hallway and dug out a candlestick and a matchbox from the chest—his mother's chest, from some little town in America. The lid snapped as he closed it, echoing in the dim. He felt the presence of the guard standing near him, waiting for whatever order would come. Gene lit the candle and slipped back into the room.

His father grasped the candle. He raised it up, his other palm open to the ceiling. The boys followed suit. Mrs. Hinton bowed her head.

Mr. Hinton went to the judge and placed a hand on his body. Gene thought he saw him hesitate, but it could have been a trick of the light. His father cleared his throat. "God in Heaven, hear our prayer. Behold, I tell you a mystery. We shall not all fall asleep, but we will all be changed, in an instant, in the blink of an eye, at the last trumpet."

"For the trumpet will sound, the dead will be raised incorruptible, and we shall be changed," they responded, their voices braided into one solemn note.

"For that which is incorruptible must clothe itself with incorrupt-ibility, and that which is mortal must clothe itself in immortality. And when this which is corruptible clothes itself with incorruptibility and this which is mortal clothes itself with immortality, then the word that is written shall come about: 'Death is swallowed up in victory.'"

"Where, O death, is your victory? Where, O death, is your sting?" Gene said along with his brothers. He saw that his mother's lips did not move.

"The sting of death is sin, and the power of sin is the law," his father said.

"But thanks be to God, who gives us the victory through our Lord Jesus Christ. Amen."

Their voices faded and seemed to echo off some surface deep in the house. A beat passed, a silence expanded. Gene kept his arms raised and dared to look again at the bullet hole. It gaped like an eye, red iris against the white, watching them. His mother stared at it, too, disbelieving.

"And so it is," said Lee, his voice barely audible over the dripping from the eaves.

"Amen," they all said solemnly. The rain on the roof seemed to murmur in agreement as they dropped their arms. Mr. Hinton gestured at John.

"Send a chit to the club; have one of the guards go. Ask them to find a coffin and bring it here at once. An officer will run it."

"Why don't we drive down ourselves? Would be faster," said Lee.

Mr. Hinton turned away, heading into the darkened hallway. "Time won't save him now," he said.

# CHAPTER 25

The night air was sour on the sleeping porch as Gene tossed in his bed, unable to quiet his mind. They had watched from the upstairs windows as the British officers came in the rain to take the body away. Gene felt he would never forget the image of the tarp in the back of the truck bed, a mound underneath, as if it were nothing but dirt being moved from one place to another. And after they had gone, and the brothers had climbed under their covers, he couldn't stop thinking about a sermon of his father's, one more somber than usual. He couldn't remember the occasion, but he could distinctly hear all these years later the exact way his father had intoned the sobering words: "Remember you are dust, and to dust you will return."

The only sound in the darkness was the wind through the rushes, bringing relief from the monsoon damp. Clouds blocked out the stars. The breeze picked up and sent Gene's mosquito net fluttering, then died as suddenly as it started. There lingered the scent of fruit, like the infused water Arthur used to leave for their visitors in their bedrooms. He breathed deeply, and his stomach gurgled in response. He sighed and threw the covers back, swinging his legs out and over the shadowy floor.

The guards had left, having no one to guard. As Gene crept through the dark hall, the house felt lonely, left behind. Outside, the mango trees loomed over the tennis courts and stood tall and sheltering, their thick trunks like temple pillars, their fruit the heavenly bodies above. Gene, in his nightclothes and bare feet, could feel the monsoon ants crawling over his toes. He stepped over wet roots and reached up to feel the branches. His fingers followed one, over glossy leaves and dead-end twigs, until he found the smooth touch of mango skin. He grasped it firmly, his nails breaking through, and tugged it down. It snapped free and sent the branch flying, and he heard somewhere in the darkness the sound of more fruit dropping from the force. He would remember to pick them up tomorrow in the light, so that they wouldn't rot.

He brought the fruit close and sniffed it. Fresh, mellow, not quite ripe but close. It was too firm, and he'd have to use a knife. He looked in the direction of the cookhouse but of course couldn't see anything. Through the darkness, he could hear a slithering, snakes tangling among the roots of the tennis court. He turned and hurried to the cookhouse, surprisingly sure on his feet without light to see—though maybe it was the darkness that made him see things so clearly. He remembered the knife in the grass the day they had returned from the Old Gope, and the story the judge had told. He said the woman had tried to kill him that day. Could it have been her, and not Arthur, who had shot him? He shivered in the dark. Forgetting the knife, he clutched the mango to his heart and ran back to the house.

When he burst back onto the sleeping porch, he was surprised to see a lantern lit next to John's bed. His brothers were all sitting still in the weak glow.

"I've just thought of something—" he began.

A sharp hiss shushed him.

"We're holding a moment of silence for Uncle Ellis," John said.

"At this hour?" But no one answered. He could only hold his breath while they prayed to themselves. Even Lee had his eyes closed, but he peeked at Gene with one open, raising his brow. Gene stood there, the juice from the mango drying sticky on his fingers.

"Amen," said John.

"It was Jaya," Gene exhaled.

"Who?"

"The woman! The Indian woman who stayed here last and ran away weeks ago. Ellis said she'd pulled a knife on him."

"But it doesn't make sense," said Lee. "She came out of nowhere and left just as soon. Why would she want to kill Uncle Ellis?"

"She seemed awfully friendly with Arthur," said Will. "He'd know something. In fact, I bet you they were cohorts. But a woman couldn't have done that. Now Arthur—never liked the look of Arthur. Always felt strange with him around."

Gene shook his head. He couldn't believe after all these years with their servant, his brother could say such a thing. He felt that Arthur couldn't be guilty, but he didn't know for certain so didn't say anything. Still, he couldn't deny the emptiness he felt in the house now that Arthur was gone. For as long as he'd lived here, Arthur had always been around, always faithful. What could have changed?

"Uncle Ellis was a fool to not go after that woman," Will muttered. "Couldn't he see people are getting more violent in this country?"

"He thought he was impervious," whispered Gene. "That it would never come to this, no matter how things have been building."

"He was a fool," Lee concurred. "But an innocent one."

"What!" Gene cried. "He was a vile, ignorant—"

"Oh, come off it, Gene," said John. "We all know you didn't like him for whatever stupid reason, but the man's dead, for God's sake! Can't you keep your ill thoughts to yourself now?"

"I'm not saying—"

"You never even called him *uncle*," Will whispered.

"That's because he wasn't our uncle!" He hurled the mango at his brother, smacking him in the chest. Will seemed too stunned to know what had hit him, but Gene, fresh off the adrenaline of his sure shot, kept going. "He was just some sad, old man lost on this continent, where everyone who knew him hated him. Except you all, for some reason! Or maybe that's it. Everyone hates us, too, pedaling our

God to people who don't need him. So he decided to tie himself to us, to Dad and Mother, and their thoughtless sons, who think guns and bullish talk are admirable." Gene could sense the air turning, a hardness setting on his brothers' faces. But he couldn't stop. "What are we even doing here? We're just outcasts. Indians hate us, the British look down on us. It's high time we left India."

"Then go," said Will.

"What?" said Gene.

"Sis. Did you ever think that maybe you don't belong in this family?" He picked up the mango from where it lay at his feet and hurled it back at Gene, who dodged it and heard it thump against the door frame. "You never join in on things we do, you always complain, and I for one would gladly take your extra helping at suppertime."

Gene was speechless. He looked to Lee, but his face was cast in shadow.

"And you've got no right, speaking about Uncle Ellis like that," said John, rising from his bed. "Sorry your pea-sized brain can't remember all the great things he's done for our family, but it doesn't mean they never happened. Dad and Mother had no one when they first got here. We've got to stick together now, in times like these with the whole country getting angrier by the day."

"What does sticking together have anything to do with this?" said Gene. He could feel the hairs rising on his neck, like some wild thing, as the wind kicked up through the rafters. "It's sticking together that got us into this mess. We don't have any friends here, and the only so-called ally we had has just been shot in our own house."

"So what are you saying?" said Lee, his calm voice all but lost in the wind.

"I'm saying we should leave. We were all going to America eventually. Why not now? I mean, can you honestly say this place is the same? We don't even have Arthur anymore! How are we going to survive on our own?"

"Gene's right," came a small voice from the doorway. Mrs. Hinton stood in the cold glow of the lantern, her eyes wide and sparkling as though she was seeing them all clearly for the first time. Gene wondered how long she had been standing there and how much she had heard. She bent down and picked up the mango, one side of it smashed and oozing. Taking her little finger, she traced the lesion in its skin and tasted the juice.

She stepped closer, her footsteps making no noise at all, and went to sit on Gene's bed. The covers were still pushed back from when he had left it, and the way she perched among the folds gave her the appearance of a mother bird. The boys, Gene included, awaited with dropped jaws the words she would feed them next.

"We must go," she said, louder this time, as though to convince herself just as much as them. She handed the mango to Gene, who took it and sat beside her. She stroked his hair, then cupped his cheek, making him feel, for a moment, like a child again.

"What about school?" Gene blurted, then realized what a stupid question it was at a time like this. John shot him a look like ice, but Mrs. Hinton gave a faint smile, understanding.

"You'll carry on in America, and I'll write to my cousins to help us get sorted. We'll tie up things here. Your father will speak to the mission about what's happened. They'll no doubt understand. We've stayed on longer than they ever imagined, I think. Besides, there's more work we can do in America. We were going to leave soon anyway. Now is the time."

"But I like it here," Lee said. Gene felt sure it was the first time any of them had ever said that, and he wondered if it were true or if it was just that India was all they'd ever known. "This is home," Lee added.

John shook his head, his dark hair growing frizzy in the humid night air. He looked wild in the flickering shadows of the lantern, illuminating the young wrinkles and sun-worn patches of his skin. "We can't go," he muttered.

"John," Mrs. Hinton began, but he raised a hand to stop her.

"We can't just leave India the second Uncle Ellis drops dead. *Someone killed him.* And how would it look if we fled now? We've got to stand our ground."

Mrs. Hinton rose from the bed and stepped toward the door. "Then you're a fool," she said, turning.

John walked over to the doorway, his left fist clenched. He stopped inches from her, obscuring the light from the lantern. She all but disappeared in his shadow. "And what would that make you?" he said. "You, who have stood by all this time and just let things happen to you. To all of us. Who are you, to have spent so many years building a life here, only to abandon it in an instant? Does that make you a fool too?"

Gene felt sick, like the room was spinning, the Earth upside down. John wasn't wrong, and that was more terrifying. He couldn't see his mother's face, but a noise, like a squeak, escaped from her mouth against her will. When John turned from the doorway, she was gone.

"Well?" John said, staring at the rest of them through the dim light. "Am I right?"

"You shouldn't talk like that," Lee said. And then, in a small voice, "Even if it's true."

No one spoke as they all took in the prospect of actually leaving. Now that it seemed a reality, Gene realized he didn't have anyone to miss or to say goodbye to in any meaningful way. They were well known as that family of Baptists, but over the years, they hadn't ever managed to grow close with anyone. They had relied too much on their apparent need to "stick together," as John had said, instead of making any personal connections. Ved was the closest thing Gene had to a friend, but even then he'd always felt the pressure to appear as the padre's son, never being himself—with anyone. In fact, the only person he'd ever been his real self with, however briefly, was Arthur.

He leaped out of bed and tried to remember where he had left his bike as he pulled on his shorts, which were hanging on the bedpost. "I'm going to see him," he said.

"Who?" said Will.

"Arthur. If we're going to leave India, I want to say goodbye."

"He doesn't deserve a goodbye."

But Gene was already out the door, his shoelaces untied and dragging against the hardwood. He found his bike leaning against the cookhouse. As he pushed off, he looked in the window and thought he saw something. A trick of the darkness, perhaps, or of memory—he could picture so clearly Arthur through the window, surrounded by the earthenware pots and tarnished tins on a hot evening, working away.

# CHAPTER 26

**A**rthur thought he was hallucinating when he saw the blurry blond head through the bars. The guards had knocked him out cold not far past the cookhouse, and he had awoken in the jail with the taste of blood in his mouth and his left eye swollen shut. For all the kicks he'd sustained to his body, he didn't remember being punched in the face. They must have kept beating him after he had lost consciousness.

Blue eyes blinked at him in the dim light. "Arthur," Gene said.

When Arthur didn't answer or so much as move from his slumped position, the boy knelt to the ground and waited. He held his topi in his hands, running the brim through his fingers. Ridiculous. Always wearing their pith helmets, even after sundown. How desperately they clung to their symbols of superiority, even when it no longer made sense. Just the sight of Gene, his shining hair amid the filth of the prison, made Arthur laugh out loud. More like a rasping hiccup, but it was enough to make the boy perk up.

"Arthur?" he said again.

The way Gene said his name seemed to Arthur he wasn't mad about what happened. More curious. Then, he realized it must be past midnight. The bureaucratic bustling of the day had long subsided, and the corridor seemed quiet, except for the metered paces of the night guards.

"How did you even know where the jail is?" he wheezed. Grains of dirt loosened from his teeth and scraped around his tongue as he spoke. He swallowed. "You're the last person I'd expect to see here. And alone? They'll worry about you, *na?*"

"It's not hard to find," Gene said. "We bike past it on the police line every time we ride to the Gope."

Arthur raised a stiff eyebrow. He was surprised the boy even noticed something as mundane and irrelevant to them as the jail.

"I came to see you," Gene added.

*Well, see me*, Arthur thought. *Though it won't do any good.*

He stretched his legs out from under him and heard the pop of his knees echo through the chamber. It would have been a painful movement a day ago. Now, nothing compared to the true hurt of a throbbing head, breaths that came too short, and the heaviness as he felt his life coming to an end.

"Where did the woman go?" Gene said.

Jaya. He could still see her face, that night in his hut. She had seemed so fearful then, after she had told him what she planned to do. So afraid in fact that he had volunteered to do the deed for her. She had probably thought she had convinced him, but in reality, he had done it for himself.

"Long gone, I imagine," Arthur said. "I'm not even sure she knows what happened." He debated whether to tell Gene the story she had told him. But he wasn't certain it was true. She had lied about being pregnant. But what other reason would she have for wanting the judge dead?

"Did she have some part in this?" Gene asked. His voice quickened. "Because we can catch her. Make her confess. And you can go free."

"No. I did it." Arthur hoped there would be some relief in confessing, but there wasn't. It held all the comfort of stating a cold fact. If he felt anything at all, it was fear of himself. Not that he had done it but that he felt nothing as he pulled the trigger. It was as though he had been destined to do it.

"But surely she did something! Ellis said she attacked him. And then suddenly she leaves. She must have come back to finish what she started."

"She never attacked him. He attacked her. The burra sahib tried to rape her."

There was silence through the bars. Arthur wondered if the boy even knew what it meant to rape someone. He sighed and turned his head toward Gene, focusing on his shining face.

"It's me. I'm the one who shot the judge. In the end, she didn't really do anything at all." He said it to convince the boy just as much as himself.

"So she's just—gone. Into the air, like smoke," Gene said. His young face marveled at the prospect, that people disappeared from others' lives as quickly as they entered. "She must know what happened. It must be why she's stayed away."

Arthur breathed in the stale air. It would be easy to be mad, to curse her for her cleverness. She got what she wanted and was still free. And so quickly. She came through their lives like the blink of an eye and left just as soon. It scared Arthur that that's all it took, and it was why he felt certain that he had meant to do this all along.

"Do you remember that day, when I caught you smoking?" Gene said after a while. His juvenile voice was no louder than the dripping sound coming from some far-off corner of the jail. It was so young, his voice. The sweetness of it dulled the ringing in Arthur's ears.

"Mm," he said. "You thought I was a sinner then, *na*?"

"No. I thought you were finally one of us."

"You make no sense, sahib." Arthur allowed the effort of a chuckle to escape his parched lips. "None of you smoke."

"No, but we have secrets, too, that we tell each other and no one else. We show each other who we really are. That day, you showed me your real self."

"And how do you like this real me?"

That seemed to puzzle the boy. "It's not that," he said. "Not about how you were smoking when you shouldn't have. It's that you weren't afraid I'd tell. Like you trusted me. I liked that, anyway."

Arthur's head was swimming, and he couldn't make sense of what Gene was saying. He remembered that day differently. He hadn't *shown* Gene anything; he'd been caught. And he trusted him only because he had no other choice. But if the boy wanted to believe there was something meaningful borne out of that day, Arthur wasn't going to stop it. It didn't matter now. Even if they'd been the very best of friends their whole lives, it wouldn't save him.

He realized the boy hadn't asked, but he felt some sudden urge to explain why he did it. As he searched for the words, he could sense something in him trying to get out, the truth and its fearsome effort to escape his dying body.

"You know, sahib—" The words sputtered out of him as though his mouth were filled with water. He cleared his throat. "When I met your father and mother, you were not even born, and this country had not touched them yet. They told me how they wanted to bring the word of God to the people. My people. And I looked at them, in their plain clothes and little hut back then, and I thought they didn't seem at all like other *goras* I'd heard about. Actually, do you know they were the first foreigners I'd ever met? And I thought they weren't so bad after all. So I was proud to work for them.

"I know the Big House doesn't look like much now, but it actually used to be beautiful, before you were born. Memsahib had all these velvet chairs and great rugs to cover every room. And paintings on the walls! Can you imagine? Money went so far back then. But you know how the house is always open; windows let the animals in. She had me wiping bird shit off the windowsills and dirt off the cushions. One time, we came home to paw prints on the stairs. And I thought, these people have no idea how to live here. Fine foreign things have no place in India. They will be ruined. Or stolen. So over time, and as each one of you boys came, those fine things went away, and I forgot to wipe some specks here and there, and memsahib didn't notice.

"I remember the day that the burra sahib first came to the house. They'd met him at the train station, and they invited him back for tea. And I thought it was strange. What would a judge like him be doing at the little Midnapore rail station? But I'm not allowed to ask such questions. I poured the tea and wiped up the mud stains from his boots. It was monsoon season, you know. But what I remember most about that day was how much your mother *laughed*. I'd never heard her laugh so much. Maybe not even at all, before that. She was so filled with worry about living in India. She didn't have the blind faith your father had. But she was so relaxed around the burra sahib, she seemed like she'd known him her whole life. And all the while I was thinking it was so strange, *na*, that he was even there at all, that he even cared to know people like them. I could tell he was a big person, you know, in spirit. Big power. But your parents, they were just the opposite." Suddenly he was overcome with a fit of coughing.

"So he wasn't always so bad then. Uncle Ellis," the boy interjected amid the coughs. "I thought my brothers were crazy."

"Oh no, sahib," Arthur choked. "He was. You all just didn't see. Because you can't see what isn't done to you. But to me, he was most certainly bad."

He didn't know if he should tell the boy all that the judge had done to him. The slights, the mockery. The orders barked at him like a dog, intentionally cruel in their wording so as to make him feel inhuman. They all seemed to blend together through the years, and as he looked into the wide, blue eyes across from him, he didn't see the point. The burra sahib was dead now.

"So, that's it, then," Gene said. He wound the chin strap of his topi around his finger tightly, then let it go. "You finally just couldn't take it anymore."

"Me? Oh no. Indians are used to that sort of thing from the *goras*."

Suddenly a sharp clang came from down the corridor. A British voice shouted, "Five minutes!"

Gene ignored the officer. "Jaya told you to do it?" he said.

"Yes and no. She only showed me what I already knew."

"What was that?"

"That the burra sahib had ruined you."

Arthur let his voice settle. He had never thought of it in words before, only in the darkness that filled the house every time the judge came to stay. He could see the boy's brain working; he could imagine it running over the last twelve years, the way his parents had changed, darkened. The way that more money was taken from the collection tin on Sundays, but no new works ever came of it. The way his brothers only ever cared about themselves and never, not once, invited an Indian to join them, as friends.

"But he's ruined you, too, now," Gene said. "Killing him. You're no better than him in the end."

Arthur detected the slightest hint of hatred in the boy's words, and it took Arthur aback. It was this that made him move from the wall and lean toward the bars, to get a better look at Gene's face.

"You look very much like your father," Arthur said. Gene looked down and focused again on the topi, inching his fingers along the brim. "So does Lee. And Will. Do you know your father's white hair was that golden color too, once? *Sbarnakesi*, we say. But you know this word." He coughed again; the movement left an ache in his battered lungs. "John—he does not look like the padre. I know you see it."

Gene wouldn't meet his eyes. The boy did not want to know.

"His dark hair. Almost like mine. Or like the burra sahib's." Grabbing the bars, he brought his face right up to the light, to the boy. The cold of the iron shocked Arthur's skin, but he held still, the sudden movement shooting a pain through his whole body. Gene looked at him then, startled. "Ah, suddenly it all makes sense why he would still be around, all these years. Do you see? There are men like me who do terrible things for decent reasons. But there are men like the burra sahib who do terrible things for terrible reasons. The day he killed the leopard. Do you know, I never felt pain in my heart as I did at the sight of that leopard's body in the grass? He has ruined India. He has ruined my India."

He leaned against the wall again, spent from the effort. But his eyes remained on the boy, who looked at him with a kind of numbness, the kind that appears when children are forced to grow up too soon. He'd seen it many times in Indian children but never in a foreigner.

"We are leaving for America," Gene whispered. "With everything that's happened . . . Mother thinks it's time we quit India."

"Yes, you should," Arthur said.

"I know we are different," Gene said. "But don't forget I have only ever known this country. I was born here. It is my India too."

"Sahib." Arthur laughed. "Can you feel India in your blood? Does the dirt stick to your toes like it does mine, or does it merely scuff your shoes? Does the sun warm your skin, like it does mine, or does it burn you? No, no, sahib. Your India is nothing like my India."

He was sorry to see the sting of hurt in the boy, but he knew the truth in his words. The guard appeared then, his fair face dripping with sweat under the lamps of the corridor. "Time's up, boy," he said. From his dismissive tone, he must have never met the Padre Sahib or his sons.

Gene stood up and put his topi on.

"Wait," Arthur said. "Will you look after Moti?"

"Who?"

"Ella. The dog, I mean."

"Oh. I think she's run off," Gene said. "We haven't seen her since we came home from the meet."

Arthur cleared his throat and nodded. "Right."

All their years came down to this, one free to leave and one to die in India. Arthur watched Gene's back disappear down the hall, then listened to his footsteps as they faded out into the night. The guard returned to wrest him up from the ground, only to throw him down again and beat him, every inch, with a lathi. Between the blows, Arthur started to hear a high-pitched tone in his brain. He thought at first it was the ringing in his ears, his hearing dying as the lathi came down on the sides of his head. It kept getting louder, punctured by cries that weren't his own, weren't human. With a last effort, his mind worked out that the whimpering was coming from somewhere outside. And it was a sound he knew, a sound he'd heard his whole life, from the thresholds of butcher shops and corners of the market-place. Out there, beyond the bars on the window, a dog whined for him. He curled his knees to his chest, covered his face, and smiled to himself on the cold stone.

# CHAPTER 27

They had some trouble securing the tickets to America. Gene accompanied his mother to the Midnapore rail office one morning and stood in line for what seemed like hours, even as the clerk recognized them and gestured for them to come forward. But Mrs. Hinton stared straight ahead and didn't seem to hear the clerk over all the bustle of the station, so Gene put up a hand to signal they would wait their turn. The clerk wobbled his head and went back to his work.

It was common for British officers to return to Europe before the monsoons hit, but there seemed to be even more than usual this year. Passages were booked for the next month. Gene knew one of those ships bound for England would carry the judge's body. He realized he had no idea who would be there to receive it.

"Apologies, memsahib," the clerk said.

Mrs. Hinton sighed. "Whatever's next available." When the clerk finally issued a handwritten slip—stamped and signed—it felt real that they were leaving India for good.

Just as they turned from the counter, the clerk spoke. "Condolences, memsahib."

Mrs. Hinton looked stricken, her eyes wide. "What did you say?"

"About the judge. It is in the papers this morning. What a surprise to see it mentioned that he was found at the house of the Padre Sahib."

"Oh. Yes. Thank you." She started toward the door, the next person in line already moving forward.

"Probably right to leave," the clerk said after them. "The Raj will—what is it you say? Make much ado about this."

Mrs. Hinton nodded, then walked away. She had left the slip on the counter. Gene grabbed it, tucked it into his chest pocket, and straightened his topi on. The clerk had already returned to his paperwork, the shining top of his balding head bobbing up and down as he hummed along to his tasks.

As they walked down the front steps, Gene thought he saw a blur of peach out of the corner of his eye. He turned so swiftly that he stumbled on the steps, catching himself on the brass railing.

"Sahib! Are you all right?" an old man said from below him on the steps. He held his arms out to catch Gene should he fall again.

"I'm fine," Gene said, shaking himself. He turned around to look again for the woman in the peach-colored sari, but she had disappeared inside the crowded station, if she had ever been there at all.

■■■

They held one final sermon in the village. The people were unaware that this was the padre's last until the very end, when he rose from his kneeled position and said, in measured Bengali, that they were leaving for America and wouldn't be back. The people gave no reaction at first, as though they had not understood their own language. But then one man rose, and then another, and another, until they had all come to the padre's feet and touched his bare toes in solemn respect. There was no protest, no demand for explanation. It was as though the Savior himself had informed them he was going to Heaven. Then they came to where Gene was sitting, along with his brothers and Mrs. Hinton, and greeted them. It occurred to Gene, as he looked each one in the face, that this was the first time he had truly seen them. They were kind faces, every one, with a smile offered like good luck for their journey ahead. Their hands pressed together firmly, shaking as if to sprinkle the good tidings over them.

Minnie, from her throne on John's shoulders, reached a paw out to a boy as he passed. She clung to the boy's sleeve, and he turned to loosen it. But she only held on stronger, with both paws now, and leaped from John's shoulders to the boy's side. The boy looked to John to see what he should do next. But John waved him on, and Gene guessed that his brother was relieved to have found someone to take care of her. The boy was the same brave one who had approached her at the last sermon. Gene was astonished to think that Minnie could like another human being other than John.

When they left the village that Sunday, Gene found himself reluctant to go. He lingered behind to take one last stroll around the huts, which he hadn't much noticed before but that now fascinated him and held on to him, demanding a place in his memory. Sunlight scattered over the thatched roofs, the shadows of tree branches dancing across them. Village boys played with a hoop and stick on the uneven dirt road, free to run after sitting still through the sermon. Mothers started their cooking preparations, squatting in their doorways with buckets of potatoes and onions to peel. Dogs scavenged for scraps with the laziness of Sundays, side by side with docile cows.

Not far from the edge of the village, Gene came to the remnants of a Hindu shrine. It was only a small alcove with weathered concrete walls barely higher than Gene's head. From the outside, it looked forgotten; Gene felt the crunch of leaves as he approached the unswept entrance. But as he got closer, the dreary hues of the outer stone gave way to an explosion of color inside. Marigolds arranged along the dais lent the impression of sunrays radiating from the center, where stood a carved sandalwood icon of Kali, the goddess of time. He recognized her necklace of severed demon heads strung low to her exaggerated hips, the burnt, black body posed in victorious dance, arms raised in mischievous triumph. He recalled the massive ornate goddess at the Kalighat Kali Temple in Calcutta, her three eyes just barely peeking out from an intricate veil of marigolds. This tiny shrine was hardly that grand, but it looked like it had been cared for with all the same devotion.

"I expect some will convert back now," said Lee behind him. He approached the shrine with his hands behind his back, leaning close to inspect the craftsmanship.

"Won't the mission send someone to replace us?" Gene said.

"Didn't you hear?" Lee said. "We're not the only ones leaving. Nearly half the mission will be going after the monsoons. Not all to America; some are moving to Delhi or Bombay." He reached a closed hand out to the altar and left there a short stack of silver annas. "Won't be needing them anymore," he said with a sideways smile at Gene. "You're all right?"

It was a silly question—none of this felt all right. Their house was no longer their home, their mother seemed a completely changed person, and John wasn't even their full brother.

He almost told Lee. If he were going to tell anyone, it would be him. Lee would know what to do. He always did. But what was there to do about it?

And then Gene had the thought that Lee might have known all along. It was so obvious now, the way John took after the judge. He glanced at Lee, who had already retreated from the shrine and was gazing at the sunny courtyard and the women in lighthearted conversation as they chopped and peeled. It occurred to Gene that he would never hear their lilting language again.

"What's going to happen to us?" Gene said.

"Dad and Mother will pick up work again. John will go to college. And we'll finish our schooling."

"No. I don't mean that," Gene said. "So much has changed. I don't think I shall ever be the same person again."

Lee let out a slow breath and placed his hand on the concrete wall, seeming to steady his thoughts. "You know, I feel like it was bound to happen. Don't you think so?"

Gene assumed he meant their leaving, but in a way, it seemed like everything that had happened in the last few months was indeed destined. "Our whole lives we've been taught to trust in the power of the Lord," he replied, "but I didn't know what that really meant until all this happened. Only God could have planned this. Right?"

"That's the only way to get through life, I think. If you don't believe it's God's work, then it's just madness."

"I suppose people in America have never even heard of Kali. Or Krishna, or anything Hindu. Anything *Indian*, for that matter."

"Mother will have trouble finding the spices in the grocery stores," Lee said with a chuckle.

Gene smiled at that, but then sobered as he thought of Arthur and all the times he'd seen him busy at work in the cookhouse or shopping in the bazaar.

Lee must have seen his face fall. "Arthur," he said.

"He's going to die, I heard."

"Yes," Lee said.

"Do you think he should?"

"I don't know what to think. I don't even believe he really did it."

"He said he did," Gene said.

"What are you talking about? When?"

"When I visited him in the jail, the night it all happened. Do you know what he said? He said that whatever he did, it was nothing compared to what the judge has done. And not just about the leopard or anything in the last few months. What he did to us. Over all these years. He said Ellis ruined us. We're not the same anymore."

"But maybe we were bound to change. We can't live in India our whole lives and come out the same. And I'm not defending Uncle Ellis or saying Arthur's wrong, but it's not so simple as believing that everything that's happened to us is anyone's fault but our own."

"I don't know," Gene said. He reached out to feel the marigolds, but pulled his hand back. "I can't help but think we should never have been in India in the first place."

Lee looked at him hard and straight. "If we are really so evil, as Arthur said, then the people wouldn't have given Dad—and us—such a goodbye. Look at them. Look at the good we've done."

"But what good did we do? We didn't save them from anything. We didn't bring them wealth, or give them power, or any of that sort of thing. Even religion didn't make much of a difference. You said so yourself—they'll probably all convert back after we leave."

"Fine. You're right. They probably did more for us than we did for them. They made us feel like we had a purpose, a reason to be in India. But if there's one thing we did, it's that every Sunday we gave them peace, and welcomed them, and talked about God and kindness and community. For one day a week, everyone gathered together, and it was joyful."

They stood in silence as they gazed at the village, another afternoon, the last for them here. Three boys played tag between the huts, their movements so jumbled Gene couldn't tell which one was "it." The way they giggled in pure happiness made Gene want to smile too.

"But we could have done so much more," he said.

◼◼◼

"It's time to board," Mrs. Hinton said.

Gene barely heard her voice over the buzz of the docks. The ship waited in the murky waters of the Hooghly, a hulking presence amid the small dinghies that zipped by. The gray sky held steady above them, a solid sheet of cloud cover. It was early morning, and their boat was the first headed downriver for the Bay of Bengal. The Hintons stood on the dock, waiting for the gangway to fall. Gene took one last look at Howrah Station across the river and its vibrant redbrick walls, and he thought he could hear the whistle of trains all the way from the docks. He removed his topi and held it to his chest. He squeezed his eyes shut and tried to imagine standing there, the chai stall, the guards and their lathis, the clatter of tiffin boxes. He tried to remember it all, one last time.

"Let's go," Mrs. Hinton said again.

Gene opened his eyes and put his topi back on. They all reached for the handles of their trunks. All except one.

"I'm staying on," Mr. Hinton said.

"You're what?" Mrs. Hinton said.

"I'm staying on," he said again, as if that explained it.

Mrs. Hinton stared hard at her husband, the wind sweeping strands of hair across her face. She did not move a hand to brush them away. She did not say that his trunk was already packed and here on the dock, ready to go. She did not say that he already had the ticket in his pocket, the ticket they'd had to beg the mission to buy for them, as they had barely any money. She did not say that there was no Big House to go back to, no Chevy; everything was given back to the mission. She did not say, through exasperated tears, that his sons were getting on that ship and heading to America, a long, long journey, a place foreign to them, a place where they had their whole lives ahead of them, and wouldn't he like to be there? And she didn't even ask why, because they all knew why.

"I'm sorry I waited until now. But it's the right thing."

They all looked at him, with only the breeze running across the planks and the distant hollering of the ship hands to fill the silence. Gene was not surprised to feel unchanged by his father's words. In a way, it would make no difference where in the world his father was if he was never there when it mattered.

John dropped his satchel and hugged their father tightly, then withdrew and held out his hand as though remembering his age. Lee and Will followed, then Gene, who felt a surprising warmth in his father's hand. Gene looked up into his eyes and saw something new he had never seen before. He looked relaxed, a softness around his face that made him look younger, like the years had turned back and he was starting anew. Gene couldn't help but feel hurt by it. Tears sprang to the surface despite himself, and he dropped his head and stepped back.

"You'll have to take the train back," Mrs. Hinton said. Her face was set hard, but her trembling voice gave her away.

"You'll write, and tell me how you're getting on in America," Mr. Hinton said.

Mrs. Hinton didn't answer. She just stood there, clutching her handbag in one hand, the other free to slap him, shake him, or whatever else she must have wanted to do. But she didn't. She turned and walked up the gangway, her steps thunking hard against the wood.

John, Will, and Lee all followed her, not looking their father in the face. Numb, Gene turned after them.

"Gene," his father said.

He looked down to see his father's hand on his elbow. In the other, his father's reed flute. "I'm sorry I never taught you all to play it." He glanced up at Gene's brothers, who had stopped on the gangway and watched with stoic faces.

Gene took one end of the flute in his hand. It felt heavier than he would have thought. He realized he had never touched it before. The wood was worn a dark brown around the holes where his father's fingertips had played countless melodies. On the underside, toward the tip, the initial *H* had been engraved decades ago.

"What will you do?" he asked, looking up at his father.

"My calling is with the mission. I feel my work isn't done yet."

"What happened here—"

"Never speak of it. To anyone. Nobody in America would understand what it's like here."

There was so much, and yet nothing, left to say.

"Goodbye, then," Gene spoke the words, but it was as if he hadn't said them himself. They sounded strange in his own voice, like hearing himself speak underwater. His father only nodded back, a curt, single dip of his chin.

Gene slipped the flute into his trousers where it stuck out awkwardly, then shuffled up to the viewing deck, where passengers clung to the railings and waved over the edge to the people below. Stacks of luggage were piled everywhere, with shirtless workers hoisting them off to some out-of-the-way place. But Mrs. Hinton sat on their piled trunks, refusing to move. Gene saw something white in her hand, a piece of paper. He watched her examine it for a moment, her eyes squinting in the daylight. Then she crumpled it, not out of rage but as if to hold it closer, and raised it to her chest with her eyes closed.

Something brushed against Gene's backside, and he turned to see a massive trunk and two deckhands waiting for him to get out of the way. He stepped aside and found his brothers at the railing.

"Look," said Lee. He pointed out Mr. Hinton in the crowd, his topi blending in with so many others around him, but Gene could tell it was him.

"Can he see us?" said John.

"Why don't you wave," said Will. But no one did.

Gene wondered if their father could even see them from so far below. He gripped the iron railing and felt all the vessel's voyages ingrained in the metal, staining it, polishing it, leaving marks that could never be erased. He thought about how many times this ship must have sailed around the world. How many more journeys it would make. There must have been a time, years ago, when it first set out to sea, and perhaps there had been a boy aboard, just like him, leaving home for the first time. The blare of the ship's horn signaled their departure, and Gene felt the deck lurch from beneath him as they pulled away from the port. But their father did not stay to see them sail off. Instead, they were the ones who watched him turn his back, make his way through the crowd, and disappear among the people, the winding streets, the stench, the alleys, the men working, and the children playing with the kind of freedom of those whose parents were not watching.

# ACKNOWLEDGMENTS

When I first had the idea to write this book back in 2014 during my undergrad at the University of California, Santa Barbara, Chris Newfield was the one who suggested I take it seriously and pursue an MFA for it. His encouragement set me on the path that would encounter the bright minds at Pacific University, where this novel started as my thesis. From the faculty there, I especially want to thank Pete Fromm, Valerie Laken, Laura Hendrie, Willy Vlautin, and Jack Driscoll for their wisdom and valuable critique.

After the program, I continued to write draft after draft, and it is during this time that I must thank my friend, Tiffany Taing, for her editing prowess and words of encouragement that ultimately got this manuscript cleaned up and ready to publish.

From the team at She Writes Press, thank you to Brooke Warner and Lauren Wise for welcoming me to the publishing world. I want to thank everyone else from the larger team for all the important but unsung tasks that go into bringing a book to market. I would truly be lost without them.

Thank you to Georgina Kamsika for her important role as sensitivity reader. It was crucial to me to write this novel with care and respect, which brings me to a few texts I want to particularly highlight for their influence. First, *The Autobiography of an Unknown Indian* by Nirad C. Chaudhuri, and *Pather Panchali* by Bibhutibhushan Bandyopadhyay, which greatly informed my writing of Arthur. For further reading of the Raj and India's independence, I recommend

*Staying On* by Paul Scott, *The Far Pavilions* by M. M. Kaye, *A Suitable Boy* by Vikram Seth, and *A Fine Balance* by Rohinton Mistry.

While the act of writing a book, word by word, can feel like a solitary pursuit, there are actually quite a lot of people who influenced me in one way or another. If I may be poetic for a second, I sometimes think I am like a galaxy made up of all the stars that have ever shone over me. Some of them may be farther away than others, but they all make up the me I am today. Thank you to my family: my parents, my sister, my grandmothers who always encouraged my writing and who I wish could see this book finished, and my Howard relatives who dusted off our firsthand accounts from India; to my friends Victoria and Madeline who feel like family and who asked all along how my book was coming; to my thoughtful and talented classmates at Pacific University, especially Elizabeth, Anita, Meredith, Teresa, Tina, and Jacqueline; to Cash, who inspired Moti and got me out of my chair every few hours; and lastly, to Kyle, who is the warmth and the light at the center of it all. Thank you for shining your light on me.

# ABOUT THE AUTHOR

photo credit: Kyle Hauser

**J**OANNE HOWARD is an Asian American writer from California. She holds an MFA in writing from Pacific University. Her poetry received an honorable mention from Stanford University's 2019 Paul Kalanithi Writing Award. Her fiction has been published in *The Catalyst by UC Santa Barbara, The Metaworker Literary Magazine* and the *Marin Independent Journal* and her nonfiction has been published in *Another New Calligraphy* and *The Santa Barbara Independent*. She lives in Santa Rosa, CA.

## Looking for your next great read?

We can help!

Visit www.shewritespress.com/next-read
or scan the QR code below for a list
of our recommended titles.

She Writes Press is an award-winning
independent publishing company founded to
serve women writers everywhere.